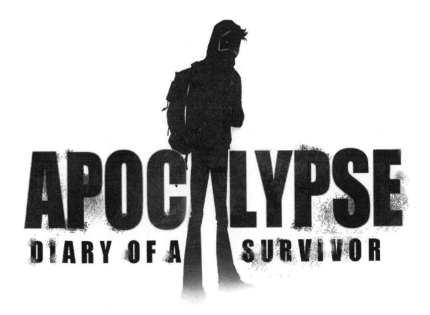

APOCALYPSE
DIARY OF A SURVIVOR

Matt J Pike

****

Published by Zombie RiZing Books

Paperback Edition: November 1, 2016
ISBN: 9781540402233

www.mattpike.co

Cover design: Matt Pike/Steve Grice

****

Also in this series:
Apocalypse: Diary of a Survivor 2
Apocalypse: Diary of a Survivor 3
Apocalypse: Diary of a Survivor 4

The Parade: Apocalypse Survivors
War Parade: Apocalypse Survivors
****

Other books by Matt J Pike

*

SCI-FI COMEDY
Starship Dorsano Trilogy:
Kings of the World
War & Quel
*
Hart & Sol

Zambies! An A.I. Apocalypse for the Ages

*

MIDDLE GRADE FANTASY ADVENTURE

Zombie RiZing:
Deceased High ZR1-3 *(formerly The Beginning)*
CataclysMall ZR4-6 *(formerly Dreeks' Horde)*
Dragon's Wrath ZR7-9
Death's Door ZR10-12

****

For news on promotions, competitions, appearances and future releases,
sign up to Matt's mailing list at www.mattpike.co

Big thanks to Lisa Chant for her editing skills – check out her hilarious novella Shark Ass if you get a chance.

Also thanks to Lisa Smith, Steve Grice, Derek Pedley, Wayne Bosch, Jan Pike, Michael Owen-Brown and my three kids Sophie, Sam and Abby.

****
A big thank you
You have already helped me!
My youngest daughter, Abby, has Rett Syndrome – a neurological condition that affects mostly girls. Abby cannot walk, talk or use her hands in a meaningful way. Part proceeds from the sale of each and every book I sell go to finding a cure.
Your support is appreciated.

****

Crowdfunding

This physical book would not have been possible without those who contributed to the My Out of This World Pozible.com campaign. One thousand thank yous go out to...

BRONZE

Lisa Chant, Rannveig Marie Eide, Bel Giles, Louise Treccasi

SILVER

Brendon McKinley, Morne de Klerk, Trudy Virgo, Raymond Hirst, Leila Auld, Sabrina Ricci, Michael Owen-Brown, Tara Hancock, Sarah Kipling, Bob and Marilyn Pike, Michael Boehm, Lauren Rose, Lisa Hall, Lucinda Munro, Rachel Salisbury, Cheryl Edwards, Dan Lato, Lisa McIlwaine Woolford, Kirsty Grant, Cara Jenkin, Spud and Helen Lovegrove

GOLD

Chris Bowden, Lisa Smith, Christian Trigg, Anthony Keane, Anna Pike, Neroli Hutchinson, Antimo Iannella, Deb White, Jo McDougall, Rod Waters, Elisa Black, Sharna Halls, Darren DeBono

GOLD PLUS

Rod Savage, Cathy and Rodney Ramsey, Bret Fisher, Pam Maxwell, Carolyn Dominic, Anne Kelly, Angelo Iannella

PLATINUM

Lynne & Garry Mechan, John Tugwell, Sam Kramer, Dannielle McBeath, Victoria Bickford-Johnson

DIAMOND

Dan Demaria, Ken Herd

DIAMOND PLUS

John and Jenny Pike, Joyce Pike, Jan Pike

****

Wednesday, April 9, 2014

So it's 5am and I'm not even close to tired, even without the Red Bulls. And I've started a new diary. I tried writing all this in the old one but I was still scribbling this entry over April 27, so I pretty much screwed the whole thing up. Anyways, I've started it all again in this notebook Auntie Sarah gave me for my birthday. It's perfect, because I can start the new entries whenever I want, which could come in handy... if I live through the weekend... if anyone does.

Man, I'm rambling. I've just read everything back and it's crap. LMAO... sip of Red Bull... that's better. Doesn't even make sense to me and I wrote it for me... hence the whole diary concept. Weird, everything's weird. I feel numb, like the last four hours have been some strange out-of-body experience. It's like I know every move I make between now and Friday can, and will, make the difference between living and dying. For some reason I know the rock's not going to kill me... can't explain why, I just know. It's like I feel I'm destined to survive... and to document it. Goddammit, that's what I'm gonna do.

Hahaha... still rambling... Snickers... Red Bull chaser (not the best combo, it has to be said). Deep breath... think, think.

Before I go any further I'd better explain why I'm even writing this.
*

12.14am: Finished the shift a bit late (that plonker newbie, Toby, held us up again). Jen was on tonight... damn! Officially the only person who can make a Drakes uniform look hot. She totally caught me pegging her out, too. And she smiled. At least I think she did. It could have been her 'what are you staring at, freak?' look, but I'm taking it as a smile.

Anyways, when I got home the last thing I could think about was sleep, so I cranked up *FIFA14*... for a change ;) Ended up playing a few games against ProGunner95 – he's some Yank kid I've been playing online for years. All was cruising along pretty well. I was up four games to one (and he pulled the W out of his coight) when he broke the news that would change my life... everyone's life.

He took a call from his bro... in the middle of the sixth game (I was up 2-0, but I digress) and that's when all hell broke loose. He dropped out of the game – so not cool – but then he sent me an invite for a private chat a few minutes later.

He told me his brother worked at some observatory – Near Earth Asteroid Tracking (NEAT) program – and they'd just discovered an asteroid heading towards Earth. Yeah, Earth. And it's a big one, too. Actually, they weren't entirely sure of the size, because they've pretty much only just confirmed its trajectory, but it was epic.

Like I said, I've known ProGunner95 for years and he isn't the sort of guy who would make up something like that up, like ever. But I still didn't believe a word of it. I mean an asteroid? This ain't a bad sci-fi film, this is real life. Asteroid strikes don't happen in the real world, they happen on screen or on dinosaurs, end of story.

I tried the 'yeah, real funny' approach. I tried the 'whatever' approach and the 'get stuffed' approach. But he didn't back down, he was solid. He had either turned into the best BS artist I'd never met (except online) or he believed what he was telling me. Let's just say he convinced me enough to believe he was convinced.

Maybe his brother was stirring him up?

"No way," he said. "My brother's got me phoning half of north America after I stop talking to you. This is his job, there's no way he'd do that. Besides, he's a straight-out nerd, it's just not in his make-up."

At this point I officially started thinking this is, well, at the very least, plausible. Aside from everything else, there was something in the tone of his voice that was pretty convincing - like there was genuine panic and more than a dose of pissed-off-edness at me for not believing him. He also used a few technical expressions that seemed beyond a 16-year-old from New Mexico called Deacon (no wonder he prefers ProGunner).

That was pretty much the extent of our conversation. He was off to contact all his rellies, then buy supplies – a shipload of supplies. He reckoned I should do the same.

Of course there was a parting grenade or three before he left.

Boom#1 - There were just over three days until impact. Three days!

Boom#2 - The NEAT program is supposed to pick things like this up well in advance. Apparently it's not unusual for asteroids to get this close to Earth before they're detected, but it is very unusual with one of this size. They're embarrassed as hell and are still investigating theories as to why. They would normally expect at least several week's heads-up, sometimes months. Not that it would make much difference – his bro reckons we're pretty much screwed. There's just not enough time for any Bruce Willis *Armageddon*-style heroics.

Boom#3 - He wasn't sure when the public would find out but it wouldn't be long. Maybe not so much of a boom just yet... but that little nugget will explode soon enough.

If it's true all hell's gonna break loose.

*

1.30am... ish: That was it then. ProGunner95 dropped offline and I was left sitting there in the FIFA game lobby listening to the crap wannabe anthem music with my headset on, completely stunned. I reckon I sat there for 15 minutes – could've been five, coulda been an hour. I just let the info wash over me.

Plenty of things went through my head...

Three days? Three tiny little days. I had tickets to the Crows match on Sunday, was gonna be my first game for the year. Luckily it was only against the Saints.

The guys at the NEAT program were embarrassed? Fail! You get embarrassed when you put the wrong price tag on the soy milk at Drakes. When you miss an object on a collision course with Earth, and that's your one and only job, that's not embarrassing, that's an epic screw-up. Didn't the Japanese used to jump on their own swords in situations like this? Why did that tradition have to die out? That seemed like a perfectly nice tradition.

Still, embarrassed or not, if it's true we're screwed.

I thought of Mum and Dad, down in Tassie on one of their roam-the-forest fests. So annoying ... worst of all they're completely non-contactable. Not even sure if that part of Tassie is in 4G range or not, and it doesn't matter, because the group they went with *deliberately* left their phones behind. Getting back to nature and all that... dumbasses. Oh no, couldn't even just take their little devices with them and flick them on at night to see if, I don't know, THE WORLD IS COMING TO AN END.

So stupid. I'm tempted to leave a message on Dad's mobile to tell him exactly that, but I resist... for now.

Then it hit me. If this was true – and my gut was starting to tell me it was – then I'd probably be one of the first people in the world to find out. Pure dumb luck, but I'd take anything right now. And there's no question I was definitely one of the first people in Australia to know. In some weird way I'd been given a gift... I'd been given as good a chance as anyone to survive.

*

2.15am: I hit the web, starting with all the major news sites. Nothing mentioned. I checked facebook, twitter – nothing. The NEAT website – still nothing. Not even in their latest news section! Apparently inevitable global catastrophe is not as important as January's open day. FFS. Still, clearly out-of-date and unimportant info in the news section makes me think it's still more than probable this is real.

I did find out NEAT has an Australian branch at Parkes. So now I'm not the only Aussie to know. I wonder if they've told family and friends, and if they're told others in turn. Each second I wait I lose my tactical advantage. If it's true that is... I still have no actual evidence.

I do a quick flick around the interwebs for large asteroid strikes. There's heaps of info on massive asteroid strikes in the past and how much of an impact they've had.

Bottom line: not good for Earth inhabitants.

There was also some CGI video of what damage an epic asteroid would do. Not sure where it was from, some National Geographic series, no doubt, and someone had put the vision to a Pink Floyd song. Haunting is the best way to describe the end result. Now, I'm pretty sure this thing was 10 times bigger than what's heading our way but, basically, it incinerated everything. EV-ER-Y-THING! The Earth became a fiery ball of death. If this happened, nothing would survive.

It's all a bit overwhelming to be honest. I mean, to think something like this might actually happen (not that big hopefully, but still)... in three days. I decide to focus on things I can control for now. I figure the no.1 priority is food. Most shops open any time from 6-9am, depending on what you're looking for. The whole world might know by that time, so my window is now.

It's time for a servo run.

*

4.30am: I've just unloaded my first round of supplies from the car. It's amazing what's open at this time of night – equal only to the variety of freaks who inhabit these venues in the hours before dawn. Particularly in the city... ewww. It's the early hours of Wednesday morning people! WTF?

I guess the amusement at the sad-acts was offset by the need not to make eye contact and then completely undone by the ridiculous prices I was charged. I probably paid the desperate druggie premium of 50% on every long-life food item I bought. Ouch. I'm glad it's not Armageddon every day – I don't have deep enough pockets.

So the bottom line is about $600 down and a whole lot of canned bland in the hand. I kept the receipts, but I don't like my chances of getting a refund if this is a hoax. I'll be sending the bill to ProGunner95, that's for sure.

*

5.30am: Finally finished loading the supplies in the cellar. 'Supplies'. Listen to me, five minutes into this and I'm starting to use army speak. What a try-hard. For the first time tonight I'm starting to get tired. But I can't sleep now, the (proper) shops will be open soon. Plus, I want to check out the morning news.

I did another sweep of the web and didn't find anything on the normal news sources... weird. But there were a couple of posts on news-sharing sites about 'asteroid rumours' – made me feel not totally insane. There was also a Facebook group. It's called I'm gonna survive Asteroid 2014DM3 – geez – now this thing has a name! I join the group and post it as my status saying, 'I heard this is legit... *link*'. I felt guilty not posting anything when I first found out, but since I'm still not 100% convinced now – and definitely wasn't then – I was hardly going to make an ass of myself online. But I'm happy with this contribution; it'll keep my friends informed. 2014DM3 is also starting to trend on Twitter. If this is a prank I'm not the only one falling for it.

I wanna hit the shops again soon, but after that – assuming this thing is real – I'll start making some calls.

I had a few minutes to kill before the 6am run and decided to check out some survival websites. It's amazing what's out there, really. It seems there are a bunch of folks who spend way too much time thinking about situations like the one that's about to happen. Well, maybe just the right amount of time, in reflection. Still, I got some good ideas – things I'd never have thought of myself.

*

8.30am: Another two runs down now. I hit the Cash & Carry store for some buy-in-bulk action. I managed to buy about three times as much as I did on the service-station run and it was cheaper! Still, I did kind of miss the deros.

I dumped it all in the front lounge before I went back out to the local Coles, which opened at 7am. I got there about 7.30am. I got serious this time and took Dad's 4WD. It probably doubled my storage capacity, which meant I was able to plough three trolleys full of stuff in.

I did my best to clean Coles out of anything that was nutritious and had a shelf life of more than a year. I reckon I've managed to bag myself enough food to last at least 12 months. Not bad for a morning's work and 18 months' worth of savings :(

This was the first time I started to get some strange looks. Mostly from the staff, especially when I was on to my third trolley load. Funny, really, because I had been observing people all morning. I was thinking how odd it was that I was on a mission to give myself a chance at survival, yet everyone around me was blissfully unaware anything was wrong. Part of me felt guilty as I looked at them drudging along with their normal lives, knowing things were about to turn upside-down for them. But then, what was I going to do? Say, 'You might want to buy a bit more than that... actually, it might not matter as you've probably only got three days to live anyway, why not do something interesting?'.

I finally got called out by the check-out chick – not one of the cute casuals, one of the bitter old full-timers. She'd obviously seen me go through on my past two loads and was getting carpel-tunnel scanning my bounty. 'What, is the end of the world coming or something?' she said.

I couldn't be bothered lying and didn't have time to go into the details but I said, "Yeah actually, there's an asteroid coming, we've only got three days to live."

The expression on her face changed about seven times as she processed my comment and punched the total into the register.

Eventually she laughed. "Well, you won't be needing all that food then."

I couldn't be bothered progressing things further as I swiped my card and entered my pin. 'Stress makes me hungry,' I said as I left.

I've been monitoring the morning shows as I unloaded the goods. Finally I caught a mention of the asteroid. They cut back after an entertainment update (the usual meaningless tripe) and Karl said something like, 'One out of left field here. A rumour's been circulating the internet about an asteroid that is supposedly on a collision course with Earth. And I thought 2012 was supposed to be the end of the world,' he laughed, with little support from his co-host.

They may not have been taking it seriously, but I was. Before I realised what had happened I dropped the carton of spaghetti in tomato sauce cans on my foot. %*%($@*#&!!! Anyways, he went on as I hopped around swearing. 'Now, I'm sure this is a hoax, but it must be said there is a groundswell of chatter across many social networking and social news sites. We have been trying to get some official word but it appears no one is commenting. Lisa.'

His co-host used her sincerest concerned tone. 'It is unusual, isn't it? More worryingly, the prime minister has called a last-minute press conference for 10am AEST this morning with no indication of the topic.'

Karl continued with something like, 'It's a similar story in the US, with the president due to speak shortly before the prime minister.'

Then Lisa finished with, 'Now, we don't want to be seen as spreading any undue panic, but we are choosing to report these events to keep you informed. It's important to stress at this point the press conferences and the rumour may be unrelated, but in our experience it is unusual.'

'We'll keep you up to date should the situation change in any way.'

Then they went about their regular business, but you could tell they were at least rattled. Something big was definitely up.

That was the first time my heart sank. I don't just mean the expression (which I find a bit naff), it really felt like it sank. It was like in one instant the realisation of the scale of what was happening hit me hard. This was very real.

I had to sit down and let the feeling wash over me for a minute. I started thinking about my mission and, within seconds, a wave of adrenalin seemed to equalise the craziness inside and I was ready to continue. Time to start calling people.

*

9.30am: Well that was pretty useless. Johnno – asleep. Jamie – asleep. Macca – asleep. Hardo – asleep! Only Boof answered his phone... and he thought I was taking the piss. Until I made him turn on the TV and watch a news update – they've now got a countdown to the president's press conference.

The others will get the message soon enough... what a way to wake up. Still – that's probably hours away for them!

President's speech – 9.40am: I was so bloody tired when I watched this I could barely take it all in. But I've got the feeling this will be on high-rotation on TV over the next few days.

There were hundreds of journos at the press conference; clearly, everyone knew this was serious. When the pres walked out the camera flashes went crazy. What he said was a blur for me but I got all of the basics...

- There is an asteroid heading towards Earth!
- It is called 2014DM3... hmmm exciting. 2014DM3? It's got no ring to it at all. Ya kind of expect something, I dunno, epic. But 2014DM3? Really? Can't we give it a proper name like they do with cyclones? Or like call it by the impact date... like a 9/11 kind of thing? It probably seems stupid, given I face a high chance of being pulverised into atoms, but I would've at least liked it to be caused by something with a cool name.

- Well, whatever you call it, it's about 4-5km in diameter – read freaking huge, which means it has the potential to send us the way of the dinosaurs.
- As of this moment there are 65 hours, 11 minutes 'til touchdown! That makes it just after 2am on Saturday morning!
- A bunch of different countries (with space capabilities) are planning to intercept the rock – to either destroy it or divert its path.

Which all sounds good, but the pres was talking about things like planning times and launch windows and... well, to be honest, it sounds like they've all been caught with their pants around their ankles. My best guess is there's stuff-all they can do but they want to make people feel better by thinking they are doing something. There are a few teams having a crack – NASA, the European space agency, Russia, Japan and China. I certainly won't be counting on a last-minute miracle from any of them!

*

3pm: I had intended to sleep, but the fact the news is out in the open changed everything. I figured every man and his dog would be lining up for food. But once the basics were covered they'd move on to survival gear. If Adelaide misses the initial impact and blast concussion and tsunamis and whatever else, there's the potential for complete loss of power, communications... so much I can't even remember it all. Some 'experts' have even predicted an ice age.

Bottom line: Self-sufficiency = survival.

So I've been busy hitting camping stores, hire stores... all sorts of places. I've got, among other things, a portable power generator (Dad's already got a 40 amp one hooked up to the house, which we also take camping, but I thought it couldn't hurt to have back-up), a radio transmitter/receiver (just in case normal communications fail), a bunch of knives, cold weather clothing and three can openers (I'm not getting caught short there).

I also grabbed about 30 water cooler bottles and some resealable lids. I figured I'd better cover my ass in case access to fresh water becomes an issue.

So I was feeling pretty good when I got home and unloaded my new toys, even though my credit card is officially maxed-out. Thank god I have access to Dad's in-case-of-emergency card. I'm pretty sure this situation activates the card into use.

Every TV station has gone to 24-hour asteroid coverage – that didn't take long. I was going to watch while I figured out the radio and generator but it was all too difficult to concentrate. Clearly sleep was the No.1 need.

I have this thing now that I can't be wasting a second, and sleep seemed to be wasting a whole lot of seconds. When you may only have 60 hours to live, eight hours' sleep seems like an indulgent waste. So before I hit the hay I sent a whole bunch of interesting stuff I found on the internet to the printer. That way I didn't feel so guilty.

****

Thursday, April 10, 2014

6.30am: Fourteen hours! I've slept for 14 of my last 60-odd hours and I feel guilty as hell. But I also feel fantastic for it. As I load up on Weetbix for breakfast I flick around the networks to see what's happened. Plenty is the short answer.

They are counting down to the first of the rocket launches. It's China's attempt, due in 45 minutes and they've packed their ship full of kickass explosives. They hope the thing will detonate alongside the asteroid and knock it off course enough to alter its trajectory enough to miss Earth. We'll see.

The other missions are all locked and loaded with launch times across the next 12 or so hours. The last, and I guess the most likely to succeed, is NASA's attempt, which is due for launch around 8pm our time. Basically they're trying everything else they can first and if all fails the Yanks are gonna nuke the hell out of it (something tells me ego has something to do with them having the clutch play in all this).

Back on the home front, it's clear my luck in finding out about this thing early has already paid dividends. There are epic queues for food, drink and other supplies. I do feel slightly guilty looking at the footage of desperate people shuffling along endless lines just to get basic supplies. But then again I'm not giving up what I've got. I mean, I hope it doesn't come to this, but it could get down to survival of the fittest – and he who is well fed is fittest. At least that's how I justify it to myself.

I've got about 30 messages on my phone but I'm struggling to get through to message bank. I'm guessing the system is in overload. Figure I'll try again tonight when the demand is lower.

I hit the internet – man oh man – that was also running slow. I could almost hear the distant sound of a dial-up modem! Anyways, there were so many emails and messages on Facebook for me. I decided to dedicate the next couple of hours to catching up with what was happening in the world and getting in touch with as many friends and family as I could.

*

7.15am: Four words: China. Rocket. Epic. Fail.

Holy explosion, Batman. The first attempt to intercept 2014DM3 ended in catastrophe when the Chinese rocket made it about 2/3rds of its own length into the air before stopping and descending to the ground. It all looked pretty harmless and slow motion until the rocket started to collapse in on itself. Then there was the most almighty of explosions as rocket fuel ignited everything. Wow. They've shown it from several different angles now and, well, nothing else to say but, wow.

I don't think anyone within 20km of the blast has eyebrows anymore.

One down, four to go, I guess.

The boys are meeting up tonight at seven to watch the European space agency launch then have a few drinks until midnight when the NASA rocket blasts off. I think I'll join them. I'm going a little crazy with my own company.

Also, there are a bunch of parties happening on Friday night to count down the final hours.

I've spent so much of my time working out what I need if I'm to survive I hadn't thought about what will probably be the most important part – what I'm actually going to be doing at impact time. I figure spending the moment with people I know and like is as good a way as any. I mean, I could hide in the cellar but I'm not entirely sure how much that will increase my survival chances. If impact is anywhere near Adelaide, I'm screwed anyway. And, as time goes by, the idea of spending the final moments with people you know becomes more attractive.

I've already got nine options on the table through friends and family. I'm leaning towards the party at the Jameson's. Mr Jameson said he thinks my folks would probably prefer I went there anyway, and he's right – they've been good friends for years. A bunch of the usual families will be going, so I'll know a heap of the kids there, too. Plus, the Jameson's place is kickass, it's got awesome views of the city and they always throw sweet parties. Lock.

My bro also sent me a message. We've hooked up a Skype call for 2pm – I think that's before dawn in London! It'll be bloody good to talk to him again.

Still nothing from Mum and Dad though.

*

10.30am: The human race is now one from two as Japan successfully launched their rocket. It's pretty much going with the same tactic as the China one (minus the whole launch fail), hoping to deflect the asteroid from its Earth-bound course. Contact with 2014DM3 is due just after lunchtime tomorrow, about 12 hours before the asteroid hits Earth. Some experts are saying even if the mission delivers, 2014DM3 will be too close to the Earth to affect its trajectory enough to make it miss. The Japanese team think it will work.

It's kind of annoying not really knowing who or what to believe. It's not like I can do the sums myself – they don't teach space maths at school. I choose to go with the 'believe it when I see it' strategy and keep planning for the worst-case scenario. Having said that, the Japanese scientists looked far more credible than the professor speaking out against them – if that's anything to go by. I mean, I back white lab coat over brown cardigan any day.

They've also trained some telescopes on the asteroid and are getting a better picture about why it may have eluded detection. For a start, it's not an asteroid but a comet, and then it's not even a comet but a dark comet. They all sound the same to me, but asteroids basically lurk in the inner solar system and are more predictable, with shorter orbits. Comets can come from way, way out in the solar system and have orbits of tens of thousands of years, maybe more. Trickier to spot, but comets usually carry plenty of ice, and when they get closer to the sun, they heat up and produce a big tail – easy to spot.

But, of course, this bad boy is a dark comet. It's pretty much burnt off all of its ice from a previous orbit (or orbits) of the sun and it's just left with a dark, lifeless nucleus.

So, they reckon this thing would've been spotted a while ago, but – here's the thing, they measure asteroid/comet size by the amount of light they reflect. I thought they just zoomed in on a big telescope or something! This sneaky dark comet hardly reflects any light at all, which would've massively affected how big they thought it was, its orbit – everything.

But it gets better, well worse, really. They've got a couple of potential findings that MAY have been 2014DM3 in their database but none of the trajectories add up. They now think there's a big chance there was something that altered its direction. The main theories are a collision with another object or, as it came closer to the sun, an internal well of ice heated and exploded, causing a reaction and a change of direction.

These theories are both backed-up by the recent visual of the asteroid (erm, comet). It looks almost peanut shaped – penny farthing even. There's a big chunk out of the middle. It's also spinning around on itself, which is unusual.

When they finally identified it and realised how big it was and where it was headed – then it became DEFCON1. Apparently there were a number of days between discovery and the official announcement, which only came as those scientists in the know started telling family and friends and the word got out. So basically, the whole thing is a series of ridiculously unlucky events and political balls-ups. Sounds like another day in life really.

Uncle Mark Facebooked me. He's insisting I join the extended family on crash night. I think he feels responsible for me now that Mum and Dad aren't here. He's contacted me three times already, so I don't think he's gonna take no for an answer. I tell him I'll be there and I don't even feel slightly guilty that I lied.

*

In local news: Apparently people went crazy in the city last night. There were people out partying everywhere – taking their last chance, I guess. Police were struggling to keep control as things got really wild. There were 12 people killed in fights. Twelve! That's three years' worth of violence... in one night. There's also been at least that many murders in the suburbs. Police say they're doing their best to cope and have told everyone to remain calm. What is wrong with people? Are they settling scores or just getting too far out of control? Either way I'm not going into the city between now and Friday night – that's for sure.

I've dropped the security shutters and made sure all the gates are locked – just to be on the safe side.

*

12.30pm: So, I figure I have five meals left between now and impact so I'd better make the most of them. I mean, people who get sent to the electric chair get one last meal... and they've usually killed someone. I figure I've done nothing wrong so I deserve at least five last meals.

My first last meal was a no-brainer. Indian. From the little takeaway place at the Black Forest shops – it's a bit of a hike from Trinity Gardens but it's the best takeaway in town. Plus, the first four places I tried weren't open. They do awesome Indian! We used to live near there and I was a regular. Dad doesn't like it so much as he says he can almost taste the cholesterol, which was kind of a selling point for me. I completely skipped the entree and went straight for double mains. Lamb Vindi and Rogan Josh with a token serving of rice and two cheese and garlic naans. Bliss.

Shops are shutting left, right and centre – but those that are staying open are making a fortune! I realise this could well be the last take-out I get so I'm gonna savour it even more.

God, it was good. It took me half an hour of eating to get three quarters of the way through.

I figured I deserved it as I'd spent the last couple of hours hauling Dad's wine collection out of the cellar to make room for the last of the food cans. I've also converted Dad's study into the water room. I've moved his desk up against the wall and filled up and capped all the water bottles.

Jason's bedroom will be converted into my war room. I've had the printer working overtime pumping out everything and anything that I think might be handy or relevant should I survive impact. I'm using the scattergun approach here as I have absolutely no idea what I could be facing – conditions, communications, anything. So as ideas pop into my head I jump on the net and print out any information I can find.

I'm also torrenting like a mad man. I'm downloading a bunch of survival TV shows in the hope I might get some useful information out of them. *Man v Wild*, *Surviving Disaster*, *Doomsday Preppers* and *Dual Survival* – wow, there's far more out there than I thought.

Fiona J Facebooked me earlier. She wants to give me something so she's coming around at 4pm. Weird, it's not like I talk to her that much at school. I've got no idea what it's about but it's a bit of a pain because I'll have to hide all of the supplies I've acquired – so that means double time on getting everything into the cellar.

On the news front the army have been called in to monitor crowds queuing for food. Apparently, things are getting ugly since they decided to limit the amount of items people can purchase. They've also announced a midnight curfew in the city tonight so there's not a repeat of last night. The army will be patrolling there as well.

Apparently a few trucks carrying food to the shops have been hijacked, so the army are also riding shotgun on all food transport. It's going to slow the distribution process down, they say, but the shops will stay open to the last minute to make sure as much as possible gets out.

It sure doesn't feel like Adelaide any more. Everything's going crazy. People are going crazy. Murders, riots, army intervention – it's like everything that made us civil is starting to unravel, and quick. It doesn't take much to project forward to how things could get after impact, if we make it that far.

Maybe I need a weapon?
*

2.30pm: Finally got to chat with my bro on Skype – awesome meets sad wrapped in weird. Poor bugger has tried to get a flight back from London since the news broke, which has proved pretty much impossible. Time's run out now so he's stuck there. We just chatted about stupid stuff we did as kids – I laughed so hard. Until the end that was. When it came time to say goodbye I couldn't help myself and blubbered like a baby. So did he. I hadn't seen Jason cry since Grandpa died.

When it was over I just sat there with my head in my hands wondering if I was ever gonna see him again. That thought's not easy to deal with... in fact I'm not even sure I can deal with it. It's just too... monumental. And don't even get me started on Mum and Dad. I kinda just sat there and let it all overwhelm me for a few minutes, then I slapped myself in the face a couple of times and got on with things.

I'm not sure whether being in a big city like London is a good thing or a bad thing for Jase. Obviously nowhere's good if it's ground zero! But a massive city like London has so many more people competing for resources. What happens if the food dries up? What happens in winter? London winter... eww.

I think I'll take Adelaide. My figuring is that it's big enough to have ample supplies of everything you need but not too big that it's removed from the environment around it. Even where I live you can be in farm country within 15 minutes. That's gotta be good, doesn't it? Yep, I'll keep telling myself Adelaide is not too big and not too small... it's just Goldilocks right for an epic catastrophe.

There are real doubts emerging about the chances of a successful rocket intervention of 2014DM3. I can't say I'm totally shocked. It's really interesting though, if you watched the mainstream media, you'd think we have an 80% chance of success, but if you do any decent research on the web I reckon you think those chances are more like 10%... at best.

*

2.45pm: So, Russia successfully launched their rocket, making it two of three for humanity. I wonder how many people around the world watched the launch? Probably everyone who has access to a TV. If collective willpower could contribute, these rockets would take off without the need for fuel. You could actually hear cheers from the neighbours when it got airborne. I even gave a fist-pump.

*

19

3.30pm: Just got back from doing a run for paper and ink cartridges. I've been working that printer into the ground, so I'm surprised it hasn't blown up... seriously. I also bought a bunch of folders and dividers and plastic sleeves 'n' stuff. I figure if I actually survive Saturday morning I can sort the reams of stuff into some sort of meaningful order.

At this stage it's just about getting info on paper – in case the net goes down. I've printed everything... everything I can think of. Locations of key storage facilities in the area, survival guides, stores that might have useful bits and pieces. I even found a couple of 'maker' sites... they're hilarious. They're these community sites where people make cool stuff from everyday objects. Well, when I say 'cool' stuff, some of it is actually quite average, but there are some real gems in there – everything from purifying water to making antibiotics. I loaded up the printer queue with about 80 things that have potential value. Like everything, it's a bit of a crap shoot to know what, if anything, I'll be faced with, but better to be over-prepared, I say. I'm not really concerned about the paper wastage right now – any global warming problem we face will be less like a gradual 2°c rise in Earth temp and more like a freaking rapid 2000°c one.

*

4.45pm: Fiona J. OMG. Fiona freakin' Jordon. Just had one of... no, scrub that... *the* hottest... and weirdest... experience of my life. When I answered the door she was wearing one of those sexy little summer dresses. With the light flowing in from behind her you could almost see the outline of her hot, hot body staring back. I'll never forget that vision. Anyways, we kinda just looked at each other for what seemed like 10 minutes. And by the way she was looking at me I knew she didn't want me to sign her yearbook or anything.

Eventually she stepped into me and whispered, "I've always wanted to do this". What, what? She has? She could've maybe just said something about it! Before I knew it we were getting into it right there on the doorstep. She has really soft lips, or soft kisses, or something... it was a real turn on.

To be honest I've always had the hots for Fi to the J. But she was just one of those girls you knew was destined to achieve far more than anyone else in our grade and she pretty much knew it, too. She also had this massive vibe that she'd only date older dudes. Either that or study always took precedence over the social side – none of the guys stood a chance. Until today :D But she's hot – so many degrees of hot. And as I discovered not as straight down the line as I had imagined.

After a few minutes of making out she turned me around and asked to see my room. I led her there but I've gotta say she led everything else. Unbelievable. I've never had sex like that before. It was as if she was on a mission to play out all her fantasies while she still could and for some reason she decided I was the guy to do them with.

I just went with it. Not the hardest thing to do really. She clearly had strong ideas on what she wanted and I just went along with it. I played my part, happily, being the lover she desired. And once we got into it things just clicked. It was pure... in some weird way... just pure desire. Honestly, this stuff does not happen to guys like me. In fact I don't think stuff like this actually ever happens in the real world. Fortunately, at least for this moment, this isn't the real world... this is the end of the world!

It must have been the best part of an hour before it got weird. Not in a bedroom sense (I don't think I'd find too much weird there) but in a totally messed-up sense.

A car horn started beeping out the front, impatient at first, then incessantly. Eventually Fiona swore, got up and put her clothes on. I told her I wanted her to stay a while but she told me she had to leave because her boyfriend was getting annoyed.

Um, boyfriend? As in, waiting out the front of my house in the car while she sleeps with me, boyfriend? Well yes, apparently so. She told me when she found out about the asteroid she wanted to break up with him. But he wouldn't let her go. So this – I mean, I – was their compromise.

I walked her to the door and had one last kiss before this Commodore revved hard then the horn sounded. I certainly didn't stare at the dude in the driver's seat but he definitely looked early twenties at least. I'm sure he sneered at me but I resisted the urge to flip him the bird. No point kicking someone when they're down.

Fiona whispered, "Thank you", and left.

*

6pm: My second 'last meal' was dedicated to the wonderful people of Italy and their magnificent invention, the pizza. It was also dedicated to the wonderful people of Australia, who took this humble Italian cuisine and Aussified it by asking the question, 'what happens when you put on more than two toppings?' We collectively said we shall create such a pizza, and we shall call it 'supreme'. Maybe it's a nod to our convict heritage that the only time you hear the word Supreme is in association with the word 'court' or the word 'pizza'.

Whatever the back story, it was bloody beautiful eating. I just sat and watched the live coverage of the lead up to the US rocket launch. Currently we're two and two for successful launches at the moment after the European effort went the same way as the Chinese one. It looked good early as it cleared the launch pad but it wasn't long before it started leaning to the right, just a bit at first, then a bit more. Before I knew it I was watching the TV on an angle – like a golfer trying to will his wayward drive back on to the fairway. Within seconds the thing was nearly sideways and I think mission control hit the self-destruct button cos for no reason it exploded. Another 1000 space workers on this world without eyebrows methinks. To be fair to them, they were battling strong winds and had it not been an end-of-the-world scenario they would've delayed the launch.

So that leaves us with two chances of hope in the air and the US effort about to set sail. At least that's the official picture. But I'm half watching the coverage and half surfing the web on my iPad and there are so many sources of info saying there is no chance any of these rockets will succeed. Now, I can smell some looney's conspiracy site from a mile away – but there are so many credible sources of info emerging and quotes from some seemingly very creditable sources it's a bit hard to ignore. Not too much coverage on it in TV land, though.

Can't say I'm totally surprised by it all. They're not going to want anarchy in the final days. I mean, people are already going crazy enough without totally losing hope.

Back on the ground in the USofA things aren't looking good for Operation: Final Shield – yeah, I know, they called it that :S

As was the case with the Europeans, the weather is not playing ball. In fact, it was worse. The thing is, the Americans will be carrying a nuclear payload and I don't think anyone wants to press the go button and be responsible for nuking their own soil.

They were trying to move the launch time forward because the weather is deteriorating rapidly – apparently the original midnight (our time) launch time will now face gale force winds. The result was a lot of staring at launch pads, delays and, in the end, Operation: Final Shield becomes Operation: Fail Shield. It will sit on the tarmac collecting rain and rust and not take part in any earth-saving activities. It's pretty deflating, actually. For some reason I just assumed this one would take off. Maybe my mind has been manipulated by too many bad US-centric save-the-day movies, but that just adds to the feeling.

*

7.30pm: Well, the printer is backed up with a bunch of things to print from the net and I'm gearing up for a games sesh with the boys. They're all bringing around their big screens and Xbox and we're gonna system link some serious *Call of Duty* action. I've reconfigured the lounge and dining room so all six TVs can line up along the far wall and, when we start playing three on three, we will switch the setup across to the dining table. It's a bit weird as part of me is feeling really guilty* for not dedicating tonight to preparing for tomorrow but then part of me needs to do it. What if this is my last chance to see all the boys together – or play games? I'd rather go out with one more epic games sesh under my belt than a few more hours of prep. At least the printer will make me feel less guilty.

*Guilty – I seem to be using that word a lot these days!

There's a new star in the night sky tonight. Its name is 2014DM3. It's sitting low in the western sky – you could see it for about an hour after the sun went down. It wasn't as bright as I expected. I assume I was looking at the right one – I was probably looking at Venus or something.

*

2.30am: I rock – that's all that needs to be said of how many ways I powned the boys tonight. I was so good I almost felt sorry for how stupid I made everyone else look. Almost. Great times – and it just made me realise how much a good headshot is like a work of art. Johnno brought a carton of Pale Ale around, Boof had a bottle of bundy and Hardo brought around the VB – but we let him in anyway.

I've just kicked the last of the boys out and the place looks like the asteroid has already struck, but that's OK – it was so worth it. #epicgamessesh

It did get kinda weird towards the end – we actually started talking about meaningful stuff – yeah, I know – about how we felt about the potential end of the world. I mean, we don't talk about things like that – ever. Generally, the fear of dying came up – not the dying itself but missing out on all the living people like us should be looking forward to.

It definitely hit home hearing the boys talk about it. I guess I've pretty much gone into a shell on the subject, I s'pose. It's a coping thing, they'd say – not talking about it and all that. I just break the hours down into what I need to do and, now, what I want to do. Maybe all of which is a cunningly designed thought process by my subconscious to spend no time actually thinking about what's coming at all. And I've heard people talk about it and the potential impacts – but that doesn't count because it's people on TV – experts in this, professors in that – just generally old people. But this was people I know well, who are going through all the same... feelings (grr) I am. Hearing them talk about it all made me realise how nervous and shit-scared I am.

Anyways, when the boys left I jumped back online for a few more games – shooting random newbs made me feel so much better. #ignoranceisbliss

****

Friday, April 11, 2014
9am: D-Day.

I just got up, feeling nasty. Whose stupid idea was it to drink beer anyways? And BBBBs? Well, that was just a really bad idea. Note to self: when your friend's nickname is Boof and he comes up with an invention called Boof's Bundy-Bomb Beers, you don't have to try them. Any 'good ideas' from a guy who accepts being called Boof should be, on the whole, ignored. BBBBs – Just applaud his creativity and move on. It'll keep him happy. And whatever you do don't have one... or another... or another. My tongue feels like it's covered in moss.

There's a really strange feeling hitting me right now. I've done just about everything I needed to do to prepare. At least I think I have – I could always buy another can opener – you can never have enough, right? The thing is, my plans have kept me so busy just preparing this, buying that and whatever else, I really haven't spent too much time dwelling on what it all means; what's potentially coming. It started creeping in last night but today it's hit big time. It's like my mind has found this way of deliberately not letting itself be exposed to the enormity of tonight.

I'm feeling like there's this overwhelming sense of emotion just lurking under the surface and if I allow myself just one second too long thinking about it I might burst out crying or punch the wall or something. I'm toey. I'm so God-dammed toey. Arrrggghghghghghg!!!!!

Need a distraction.

*

10am: Distraction found. I'm now the proud owner of a hydroponics system. All I need is a bit of electricity for light and a bit of water to grow and I'll have myself an inside market garden. All it needs now is my green thumb... ahhh – and there's the chink in the armour.

It was hilarious at the store. I mean, I looked like death-warmed-up this morning and between that and my age, and judging by the people that run the place – there's only one particular plant they thought I'd be growing and it doesn't produce food. But it does make you hungry. Oh did you see what I did there with the jokes? Good irony, me.

PS – I'm putting this purchase in the 'luxury items on Dad's credit card just in case' category.*

PS – my third 'last meal' was Maccas' breakfast. Once again I blame the BBBBs. It's actually getting harder to find takeaway places open. I figure they're running out of people prepared to spend potentially a large chunk of the rest of their lives on minimum wage. But Maccas was flying the drive-thru flag with pride and I obliged.

They say people are splitting into two camps on the whole work issue. The majority have just dropped it and aren't going back until this is over (probably applies for a good result only) and others, particularly those in the service and emergency services industries, are trying to remain on. There's an ad campaign encouraging people to 'do their bit to help keep the world moving'. I heard Maccas are giving their staff crazy bonus money for working, which probably helps.

*I really miss Mum and Dad. I would love just at least a phone call. Just to be able to hear their voices again. To hear Mum tell me she loves me and for Dad to say he was proud of all the things I'd done to plan for survival. God, what's happening to me? Did I just write this? I'm seriously an emotional wreck today.
*

11am: I messaged Fi to the J earlier to say how blown away I was by yesterday's catch-up (I used more eloquent words, by the way). And how much I've always liked her, too. And to wish her all the best and that I was thinking of her. I figured if I was having all these gushy feelings then I may as well focus them on her.

Anyways, she texted back just then with a long post about when we met and the moment she realised she liked me and what I meant to her etc. This really has come out of nowhere, but hell, it makes me feel good. She'll be the first person I call if this thing ends and everything's alright.
*

11.30am: I keep coming across one absolute must basic rule from every survivor website. They all say I need a bug-out bag and a bug-out plan. The bug-out bag is a pack with items you need to survive, just in case your home becomes compromised. You fill it with the sort of items that will get you through a few days so you can grab it and go at a moment's notice. Where do you go? Well, that's supposed to be the bug-out plan – a detailed idea of what to do when things hit the fan, as they say. This is where everything falls down as I have no bug-out plan whatsoever. I don't know where to go if my house is destroyed and I survive.

So I'm going to make a bug-out bag, pack it with a week's worth of food, a knife, a torch, a change of clothes, water and whatever else I can think of. I'm going to take it with me to the Jameson's. I just hope I don't need it.

*

3pm: I was really starting to weird myself out just hanging around the house so I decided to go for a drive. And then it occurred to me I should spend what could be my last few hours driving past all the places that had meant something to me. So I just cranked up the Js on the radio and went a-drivin'.

I started at the first house I remember living in at Cowandilla, then the primary school around the corner where I went until Year 4. After that it was out to our next house at Glandore, then out to Magill, Trinity Gardens Primary, Norwood/Morialta High, then a cruise up The Parade where I worked at Cibo and past the oval where I watched the Redlegs, past Adelaide Oval where I watched the Crows and just a bunch of other random spots where I've hung out with friends, had little moments of love, or some other memorable experience.

It really helped, it did. What do they call it on the talk shows? Closure? Ahh! Closure – I can almost hear the American accent as I write the word. I was giving myself some of this fancy closure stuff, I think. If it does all end tonight … well, then I can consider myself pretty lucky with the life I've lived. I can consider all the openy* bits… closured*.

*These are words because I say they are.

*

4.30pm: Well, it finally happened and I don't know what to think. Mum and Dad phoned. Someone finally alerted the crazy middle-aged hippies hiding in the Tassie forest that they should perhaps pick up a freaking newspaper and find out there have been a few changes since they left the civilised world.

It was such a shock when they did call I balled my eyes out on the spot. It was Dad. Typical Dad – almost zero pleasantries (he's always a bit awkward like that) but a list a mile long of things I needed to do to prepare. I think I impressed the hell out of him when I said I'd done most of them. For the record he didn't say he was proud of me but I could tell it from his tone of voice. If anything he was a bit taken aback by what I'd done, and I think I detected a tone of disappointment (under the pride) – almost as if he felt he was no longer needed. That might just be my spin on it but I'm gonna take it as a huge compliment nonetheless.

Mum more than made up for things in the emotional department. That was hard to cope with. I can't remember much of what was said – apart from a lot of 'I love yous'. But hearing them was as equally fulfilling as it was distant. It was so good to have that moment but it wasn't them in the flesh. There were no over-embracing cuddles, no annoying lipstick marks left on my cheek, no scent of perfume … just the words. The words and the tears.

Dad finished up things by telling me their plan to get back to Adelaide. Approximate itinerary and approximate ETA. When Dad says approximate he usually means within 15 minutes or else it is a fail. He's also got a contingency plan if he can't get in immediate contact, and a list of things for me to do if I haven't heard from them within 48 hours of the event. He made me write a whole bunch of things down. By the end of the call I was feeling pretty good. Good to hear from them and looking forward to seeing them on the other side of all this.

They were also pretty happy I'd chosen to go to the Jamesons' tonight.

There are widely conflicting views about where the comet's impact point will be. The experts are saying the unpredictable spin and the unstable nature of the shape make it difficult to determine. Many are saying the object will break up as it enters our atmosphere. If it doesn't, the opinion is it will strike in the Indian Ocean. It's a good thing in some ways – no direct impact destruction – but the tsunami it is likely to create will be epic. Anything up to 1000m high! That, coupled with the gases ejected into the atmosphere, will cause total chaos.

If it breaks-up, however, that's what the experts find impossible to model. It could explode in the upper atmosphere sending debris across half the world, it could break in the weak point down the middle and create two massive problems instead of one (landing, well, no one knows). Basically, it seems about as certain as a weather forecast!

So, the Russians have lost their rocket. Great. They lost contact about an hour ago and believe it has had a catastrophic failure. They are saying the chances are it was struck by some debris, probably created by the comet, but they're not sure.

****

IMPACT NIGHT:
Goddammit! Holy crap. Swear words – all the swear words, in alphabetical order, then backwards, then random, then finishing with the F one, in a number of variations. I've just got to write now, I've just got to get it all down. Every last second of the last few hours – everything. I'm buzzing, massively buzzing, and the thoughts and memories are already starting to get confused and I need to put them down. I just feel this urge to recall every last detail – it's like if I don't write it here then it will all be completely forgotten.

OK diary – prepare yourself.
*

6.30pm: It was a perfectly clear night – thank god. I would have been pissed off if the end of the world came and I couldn't even see the glorious show that would probably bring about my demise.

The air was thick and sounds seemed to travel forever. It was slightly muggy, too – unusually so for Adelaide – but it kind of added to the eerie anticipation you could sense everywhere. The noise of dogs barking and birds calling penetrated the thick air. I wonder if they knew their fate. More power to them if they didn't, I say. I'm jealous.

I know, I know my words are a bit 'bad romance novel', but I can't think of any other way to convey the 'vibe' of the night. And it's the best I could come up with – so bad romance novel it is. Deal with it, diary.

When I arrived at the Jameson's house there would've been about 60 people milling around. I needed to be busy, distracted – I was immediately glad I came – I just had a sense this was the place I was supposed to be. Mr Jameson – Steve – had set up the big TV on the second floor and he had two smaller TVs on the balcony. It was a great set-up because the house overlooked the city, from the foothills to the sea, so you could see almost endless suburbia, the looming asteroid and get the latest destruction countdown broadcast at the same time.

APOCALYPSE: DIARY OF A SURVIVOR

I knew more than half the people there. There were six families who hung out with the Jamesons and Mum and Dad on a regular basis. Most of the kids were about the same age too – I guess it was the closest I could feel to family. There were a few others I didn't know, but I was happy enough in their collective company. Most importantly, Jamie and Scott were there. They're both my age and, even though they go to private school, they're alright. I've known them for years so I definitely felt comfortable.

The TV was fixed on the Channel 9 broadcast, which had plenty of crosses to NBC in the US and the BBC and Europe. They also managed to get a feed from the International Space Station – either shots of the approaching rock or a birds-eye view of the doomed Earth below. They were the hardest pictures to look at. The Earth looked smaller from that view – smaller and completely vulnerable.

The rest of the broadcast made it feel like an event, like something to watch, not something that would soon impact on us all. In a way it took the edge off the reality we were facing – it was, well normal. Normal like when you see the coverage of an earthquake, or like how they covered the floods in Queensland.

Normal... just too frickin' normal.

So, too, was the gathering – at least in the first couple of hours. Once everyone had been introduced and settled in, the drinks started flowing and if you didn't know any better it could've been any night. Occasionally you'd get a look that said 'this is it', but for the first little while it remained unsaid. Scary.

Mr Mochizuki was hilarious. He'd dressed head to toe in Japanese colours, much to his daughter's embarrassment. He was there to barrack for the Japanese rocket but it also made everyone else smile. He's so funny.

I snuck off with Scott and Jamie, a plate full of BBQ food and a few beers, and we hammered the Xbox in the rumpus room – a bit of *FIFA*. Close games, too – they're both pretty good.

Of course my plan was to stay completely sober. I needed the edge and I knew not being drunk may well be the difference between making it and not. But at some point along the way I thought screw it and helped myself to a Pale Ale or two. The peer pressure may have gotten me over the line but I'm OK with that. I figured a couple of drinks to keep me calm couldn't hurt.

I've got to give the TV stations credit for still broadcasting through this. They are people with lives, too. Apparently they asked for volunteers and they easily had enough responses to go ahead. I think the fact that, apart from maybe Perth (with the tsunami), Australia seems like it will dodge the biggest bullet tonight. I guess they assumed everything would go to plan.

9pm: After a while we joined the masses in the lounge room and on the balcony. There had been a massive shift in atmosphere in the hour or so we were away. The general hubbub of dozens of people talking and laughing at the same time was gone. The TV had been turned up and that was about the only noise to be heard, apart from the odd whisper.

I drifted away from the boys for a while and just watched the coverage. It was full of experts and crosses and infographics and updates and recaps… it was pretty riveting, to be honest, but at the same time completely useless. They were so fast in bouncing from one important bit of information to the next you felt massively informed, but when you stopped and analysed what was being said there was nothing new. I mean, they had an official 'guesstimation' of where the impact would be. But that area was huge – thousands of square kilometres of the Indian Ocean – and that info was old news; nothing we didn't already know. It was the same with everything – stuff we'd already heard, just from a different expert or analyst. The only things that were really new were the numbers on the countdown clock, which was permanently showing on the bottom of the screen. They were new numbers, small numbers. Scary numbers.

Despite the lack of anything substantial or new, it was really hard not to watch. But there was a point with a few hours to go when I just got a little claustrophobic or something and felt the need to get out of there for some Me time (capital 'M' because I'm important). I swiped a couple of Paleys and headed down to the back of the Jameson's garden.

9.30pm: The Jamesons had a nice little spot past the swimming pool where no one ever goes – it used to be an awesome hide-and-seek spot when I was younger. There's this little wooden canopy with grapevines all over it and beyond that was the side of the shed where there's a little bench. I just cleared away a few spiderwebs and sat down.

I really couldn't see too much of the sky from there, but that was OK. I could hear noises from the party, and from other houses in the area. There must've been something pretty wild going on down the street as there was screaming and laughing and doof-doof music cranked to 11. Good on 'em. I was just happy to have a beer and a reflective moment and, in a way, the noise of their partae was all the company I needed.

It lasted about five minutes, but what came next will stay with me as long as I have memories. Alyce, Scott's older sister, came up with two more Pales in her hand. She only said two things to me that night, the first one being, 'There you are'.

Then she sat on the bench and kissed me. I mean this is Alyce – three years older than me Alyce – what? Of course I didn't complain one bit as I've always had a little kid crush on her and I figure it's better to end existence with a moment like this than a little more self-contemplation!

After a while she took me by the hand and lead me around the back of the shed where she pushed me up against the bricks and kissed me harder. I could see what was happening – she was the hunter and I was her prey. I could see it happening and I wanted it more. God it was hot. Her hands wandered and so did mine. Then she kissed my neck, down to my chest, then stomach and then... wow!

OK sorry, this is getting more Mills & Boon than before and it's actually really awkward to write about, but it was such a big part of the night and something I don't want to forget. I'm doing my best to embrace the Mills&Boonedness.

Now, I don't know much about her boyfriends in the past or anything, but I do know she knew exactly what she was doing. I mean it wasn't just good – it was phenomenal! I can remember thinking, in the moments my mind ran off on random tangents in the middle of it all, that maybe it wasn't even us doing this. Maybe we were just characters or actors playing our roles. I guess we kinda were. I s'pose normally we're driven primarily by what people would think of us if we were caught – maybe now it's changed to being driven by what we'd think of ourselves if we did nothing. Other people's judgment may never come. Tomorrow could be nothing – there was nothing to lose.

Eventually she guided me away from the wall and leaned up against it, facing the brickwork. Then she spoke again – the last thing she said to me – "I want you in me".

It was my turn now. I played with her under her short skirt, through her knickers. I could feel how turned on she was just as she had felt me. Then I glided her g-string down and pressed myself up against her – in her.

OK – here's the bit where I admit it was awkward at first trying to... erm... dock... that position ain't easy. But once I could get off my tippy-toes and the docking was complete I was away.

I'm thinking to myself how ridiculous this is all getting – I mean two girls throw themselves at me in two days. I've gone from Mr Average to Ladies' Man in the space of 24 hours. I have doubled the amount of people I've slept with! And not just doubled – had the two hottest encounters of my life. What the hell?

It's the moment, the enormity, the pressure, the infiniteness, the rock – all of which makes you want to explode or do something completely freakin', crazy just to know you did some living on Earth while you had a chance.

And, in these moments, we're just people playing a role in someone else's final screw-it-all moment while they play a role in yours. I don't think I can ever fully explain it. It's just this understanding it was a moment we were drawn towards or destined for. And that it had to be perfect with absolutely nothing left out – no room for blushing, no place for regret, no time for doubt – just a total obsession to make one unforgettable moment.

And it was unforgettable.

I've just got to live long enough to not forget it for as long as I can.

When our moment was over we kissed on the bench a little more before she gave me one last look – a mission sexily completed look, an entirely satisfied look – with a hint of lonely and lost – then she left.

I sat down for a couple more minutes, had some of my beer, toasted the air for the previous 20 minutes and headed back.

10.30pm: When I got back to the party my absence had been noticed – I just told Scott and Jamie I needed a bit of time. Not sure I looked Scott in the eye directly at any point.

Mr Jameson also came over to chat at some point to see how I was feeling. He's a really nice guy. I know it would've been tempting to play a bit of Dad substitute – like Uncle Paul had tried – but Mr Jameson's too smart for that. It was on the level of a peer, I s'pose, which made me feel pretty happy to talk. Not that I had much to say. I just told him about all the things I'd prepared and how the house was set up should we survive the night. He said I could sleep the night if I needed to. I had really intended to go home tonight but it gave me something to think about at least.

The rest of the moments between then and impact were a bit of a blur. I know I had chats with just about everyone I knew. There were a lot of well-wishing adults offering me any help I needed until my parents got back. Some of the younger kids pestered me long enough that I played a few games of table tennis with them. It was alright actually – they needed the distraction and I did too. Of course I didn't let them win, hells no. I did the decent thing and smashed them.

There's not really much else I remember from those couple of hours in the lead-up, apart from joining everyone upstairs and watching the coverage. I remember the groan when the Japanese last-hope rocket went the same way as the Russian one – Mr Mochizuki took it pretty hard (a couple of people gave him a dirty look, which I thought was harsh – it wasn't his rocket). Another thing that stands out to me was not a moment but the general vibe. As minutes passed you could sense the fear growing. The talking all but stopped, the laughter was long gone, families started to migrate together… this was just waiting… there was nothing to do but watch the countdown clock and pray.

I got lost in thought again. I thought about my brother in London and my parents and wondered what they were doing at that moment. I thought about all my preparation and wondered if I'd missed anything. I thought about Alyce and the shed, Fiona J and the visit. I thought about my life. I thought about the rock. I thought about death. I watched the clock.

****

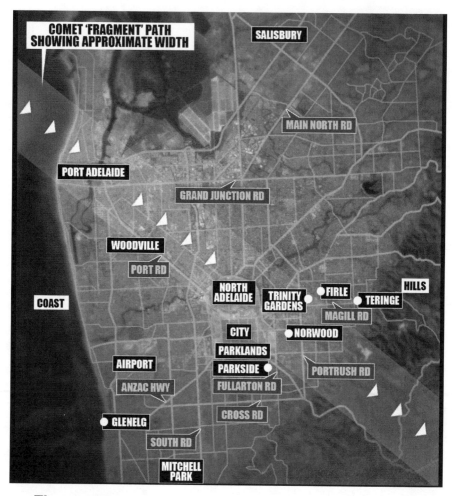

The moment

2am: I'm doing it – I'm gonna write the words down – and it's probably the most predictable quote from any eyewitness to an epic event – 'it was like a scene out of a Hollywood movie'. Sometimes I reckon on-the-ground news crews aren't allowed to go back to the office until they've recorded it. So I feel so dirty for saying it, but the thing is, I can't think of any other way to explain what I witnessed. It was epic.

In fact, I think I'm going to retire the word epic from my vocabulary now. No future event will ever come close to what just happened. Nothing else will ever be truly epic.

The countdown reached zero. There was confusion on the broadcast as they were following the comet's entry with the satellite camera, and when it hit the atmosphere there was an almighty flash of light somewhere above the Indian Ocean. The flare blinded the lens for a few seconds. But we hadn't been pulverised into the Earth's core – we were alive. Everyone cheered and I bellowed so hard tears came to my eyes. I was a-freakin-live!

The commentators were fumbling to relay some meaningful information. Mr Jameson was telling everyone to shut up while he turned the TV up to maximum volume.

But then the night sky lit up bright as day. A ball of glowing fire appeared to our right – it came in from the northwest and just kind of floated past us, right over the city, headed southwest. It looked impossible in so many ways. Night became day. This heavy rock just hanging in the sky. It was spinning end over end, with a large jiggered edge sticking out. It must've been ripping past at incredible speed but everything seemed so slow motion. It almost looked peaceful, gentle, but it was here to bring chaos and pain. For so many reasons it was impossible.

No one spoke. Everyone just stared in silence at the rock and the vapour trail until it disappeared out of sight high over the hills. The whole thing couldn't have lasted more than 5-10 seconds – I think I snapped a few decent pics on my phone, but I wasn't aiming, just firing blind.

A few seconds later an explosion ripped through the Adelaide plains below – then another. I looked out to see two big plumes of debris billowing into the night air – one down near the airport and the other somewhere between Flinders Medical Centre and Marion Shopping Centre – someone reckoned it was Mitchell Park. Then another small rock went sizzling over our heads – very low and very quick. Surely that impacted into the Adelaide hills somewhere? Shit got real at that moment. Things had gone from a news story to an event, to a light show, and now a catastrophe. Underneath those dust clouds there are probably many people dead.

There was panic and whimpering and cuddles and 'I love yous' and nervous breathing and swearing – lots of swearing – then things went quiet. Everything and everyone except the TV broadcast on the balcony went quiet. I realised all eyes were glued to the screen.

The TV guy said something like, 'it seems as if the bulk of the comet has struck the southern-most reaches of the Bay of Bengal. Hopefully those in low-lying areas of India, South-East Asia, Africa and, most importantly for us, the West Australian coast, get to higher ground as a matter of urgency, if they haven't already done so because of the threat of tsunami. We're getting reports of large fragments of debris breaking off from the comet. Reports are sketchy at the moment, but it looks Australia is in the firing line of some of these smaller fragments. We are hoping and praying for the safety of all Australians and will be keeping you up-to-date with everything as it unfolds.'

I couldn't help but think, 'that was a smaller fragment?' How big did the actual thing look when it impacted the Indian Ocean? And the damage... What on Earth is to come?

There wasn't much talking for the next few minutes – just watching for updates on the TV. They seemed painfully slow, but it was difficult, I suppose. Any eyewitnesses to the event were probably fried by the blast impact, or killed by tsunamis, or poisoned by toxins or some such thing. And the camera in space really only showed a mass of blinding light.

Then we started hearing reports about Melbourne – that the massive rock that bulked past us had landed near there. Real close. No one was hearing anything from any Melbourne media outlet – signals had died. And the potential for bad news was high. Just the thought of Australia's second-largest city getting hit was scary.

That's when things got really fricken' real.

That's when some guests start wailing, some were consoling each other, kids clinging on to parents for dear life, others just stood or sat in stunned silence. Some started manically working their phones – presumably trying to contact people in Melbs. I don't think they had much luck – the phones were all but dead most of the night. Some, like me, just watched the TV.

The Melbourne angle was getting some weight behind it. We started hearing some reports about a more specific impact site – near Frankston on the Mornington Peninsula. I'm pretty sure that's an outer suburb of Melbourne – and if it was the rock we saw floating through the sky earlier – then Melbourne looks like it's pretty much screwed. Wow. Melbourne. MCG Melbourne. Footy Melbourne. Wow.

It's hard to recall exact times between events on the night, but it was several minutes before the shockwaves hit – could've been seven, could've been 15 – I'm just not sure. But when it hit, it hit. There was like this subtle little breeze hitting from the Adelaide plains all night, but it started getting stronger and fast. When standing upright became a noticeable challenge that's when the noise began. It started building beyond the hills behind us – louder and louder. Seriously loud. Then louder again – jet engine loud. Then an explosion of wind and debris and rocks and trees came barrelling over the lip of the hills.

This shockwave – presumably from the Melbourne impact – turned into a cocktail of lethal floating objects that just hit the top of Mount Lofty and kept going up and out. It launched objects high in the sky above us – further propelled by the vicious sea breeze that'd swept off the plains. I've got a feeling we got very lucky here – no debris seemed to rain down on us – it pushed over our heads on to the plains below. It was kinda like we were standing at the peak of a giant breaking wind wave (breaking wind wave – that's a bit awkward). Like we were in an air pipeline or something, just in the perfect part of the barrel that held its shape long enough to protect our asses.

It was surreal. The wind hitting us from city side was strong but tolerable, while overhead this crazy blast of energy pushed all sorts of objects well over our heads and on to the city below. I saw a couple of cars go overhead and that was enough for me to head inside. I pushed my face up to the lounge room window and continued watching. I kept an eye on my house as I had a distant view of it from the Jamesons'. It seemed OK, for now.

The shockwave probably unloaded for a few minutes but it slowly subsided after the initial front. The TVs had gone dead – just showing static. But as the winds calmed, panic set in. Mr Jameson called for everyone to calm down and he started getting everyone involved in making a plan of action. It was short-lived though. As soon as he got everyone in a more positive frame of mind there was another big explosion outside. It was distant, but large – the house shook with its force. Again, attention turned to the view of the city below. A huge fireball leapt out from the Parkside area. Then, as everyone was trying to work out what could've caused it, a fiery ball rock or something about the size of a truck came into view from over the hills and buried itself beyond the city in the western suburbs, then another one from the same direction hit Salisbury way out in the north.

A smaller fireball – not sure what to call those things – landed a couple of suburbs away to our left. It took out a couple of houses before something exploded – presumably a gas line or something. I swear I felt a wave of heat. There were more fireballs that could be seen off in the distance. I figured all this was emanating from the Melbourne impact, which didn't bode well for anyone closer than us – 800km!

I got distracted so much by the light show and taking a few pics, I nearly missed the really bad news.

Someone pointed out the sea was receding. Fast. With the conditions that night the water just looked like a black slick, with the moonlight dancing off the distant waves – now all partly obscured by the dust of the shockwave. I hardly noticed ... until there was no moonlight glimmering at all. The water drew out of the area fast – real fast. That could only mean one thing – tsunami.

Now, I know enough about geography to know that lil old Adelaide, hidden as it is up St Vincent's Gulf had no direct line of sight with either Melbourne or the Bay of Bangal – there were hundreds of kilometres of water separating us from the Southern Ocean. So, I'm not sure if there was another impact spot or the world's seas had been distorted so much by the impacts the whole thing was going crazy like a giant washing machine. Either way it wasn't good.

That was the moment I remember thinking there's no chance I would survive. It just seemed every few minutes another disaster played out in front of me. I'd be scared stiff, braced for the worst, watch the horror unfold, survive, start to adjust to what I'd seen, then something else bigger and badder would happen. I mean, what next?

I don't think I was the only one hurting either as no one spoke – we just consoled each other and braced for more pain.

The gulf looked nearly drained from our distant view in the foothills. I felt for those beachside – something big was coming and there was no way to get out of its path now. I'm not sure if this was the case earlier but I noticed the cars backed up on both the Anzac Highway and Port Road – obviously the word was out to GTFO.

Then I saw the wall of water. It came in fast. 'Wall' probably doesn't cut it for a description, but I can't think of any other way to describe it. All I know is when it hit the shoreline I was looking at Glenelg – the only real beachfront buildings of any decent size are at Glenelg. And the wave just swallowed them all. It ate them and kept going.

I'll never forget the screams from the people around me at that moment. I'm not sure if I'll be able to describe them properly either, but there was something in the tone of peoples' wailing that changed from an 'against all hope' scream to a 'there is no hope' scream.

It was horrible to watch but I couldn't look away. The wave rolled through the west from the south, over Marion Shopping Centre, past the airport, up Anzac Highway, across Port Road, further and further in until it hit the parklands. And it didn't stop there – it just kept on rolling straight into the heart of the city. It was only then I started to realise my house was in jeopardy. This was not part of my survival plan, which required my house and all the things I'd collected for survival. If the wave got as far east as Trinity Gardens I was screwed.

I saw a couple of buildings collapse in the CBD, along with the light towers and one of the grandstands at Adelaide Oval – definitely won't be seeing the Crows play this weekend :S When it hit Fullarton Road my heart was out of control. I think I actually held my hands together and started praying. I think I remember saying 'please, no, please, please, no' over and over again.

Most of the people at the party were from the eastside – we were all praying for the same result. The wave's momentum seemed to slow once it hit Fullarton Road. Someone pointed out that the incline increases east of the city as you head towards the foothills. And it was true – no sooner had the water hit the bottom of the Parade at Norwood than it peaked and slowly started withdrawing back towards the beach.

"Here comes another one," someone said. I swore.

The first wave had probably retreated to the airport when the second rolled over the top. It was hard to tell if it was bigger than the first one or not. It reached the Parade again, this time pushing up as far as Osmond Terrace before falling back. I breathed hard and thanked whomever I was praying to, as that was only a few blocks from Portrush Road – and only a few more from my house.

Another random fireball ploughed into the retreating water. Watching the fireballs didn't have the same impact anymore – whoever lived where that thing landed was dead already.

There was a bit of a mixed bag with the rest of the waves – the next few fell well short of the eastern suburbs before a couple more massive ones rolled right up to the foot of the Parade again. Once they retreated, the worst was done – the high watermark was set.

New Adelaide took shape in front of us. The west utterly destroyed; the north plains similar; southern plains gone too – not sure about the fate of those on the other side on the hills down south. But for those in the Adelaide hills behind us, and judging by the force of the blast that sailed over our heads earlier, there'd be little to nothing left. All that remained liveable – at least by the looks of it – was a crescent shaped band of suburbs in the shadows of the hills.

We just happened to be in the right place – far enough from the sea not to be affected by the tsunami, close enough to the hills to be shielded from the blast winds and lucky enough not to be dive-bombed by comet fragments or fireballs or cars or trees or God knows what else.

I looked at the snowy TVs, hoping their signal would come back so I could find out what was going on. Mr Jameson was trying to find a radio signal without luck. I tried my phone – no signal, no internet. Instead I went and grabbed another beer and stared at new Adelaide.

****

Saturday, April 12, 2014
7.15am: I woke up to the first day of the rest of my life. Sure, I could define every day as that, but this one really was. The little moment where I woke up and thought maybe the whole global disaster thing might turn out to be a bizarre dream… it didn't happen. Nothing would ever be the same again. It was pretty quiet at the Jamesons'. Most of the party-goers left last night to find out what had happened to their homes. I was going to do the same but decided to stay. Without any access to a TV signal or internet, the thought of being able to see the devastation from the Jamesons' awesome vantage point would help me get a picture for my next move.

Mrs Jameson, Jodie, cooked up pancakes on the BBQ for the dozen or so people who still remained. They were beautiful (maybe a little fluffy for my tastes) and went down a treat.

I sat out on the balcony with Mr Jameson, Mr Eldridge – who lived with his family in the beautiful but now destroyed suburb of North Adelaide – and a few of the other kids. I was not entirely sure what reaction I was expecting from Mr Eldridge, but I was surprised he was quite upbeat. Turns out they thought long and hard about staying at home last night and the decision to come saved their lives. So losing their house has some serious perspective I s'pose. I can't help but project forward as to what will happen to them. Without a house, without resources and shelter things don't look good.

Maybe the Jamesons would take them in. Maybe. I'm not sure how much food and resources they have for themselves, let alone an entire other family. It's hard to know how far friendship will stretch in a time like this.

But that wasn't really my concern and, judging by the conversation, it wasn't front-of-mind for Mr Eldridge either. We just looked out at the utter chaos that was the Adelaide plains in front of us and tried to work out what it all meant.

There was a fire virtually everywhere you looked. The city centre was alight in various spots – and there was no evidence of anyone fighting the blazes. It looked like most of the tall buildings survived the tsunami, although most of the residential housing areas around Hutt St/South Terrace way looked like they'd been levelled.

The same could be said of anything in line with, or west of, the CBD – totally destroyed. Gone. Same with the north as far as the eye could see. We talked about the possible toll from Adelaide alone and came to the conclusion that possibly four out of every five people no longer had a home (assuming they were still alive) – that's about 800,000 people! It made me want to get back home as soon as possible – despite Mr Jameson insisting I stay.

We started talking about people we knew who lived in the affected areas but it got a bit too much and we stopped. Then we tried to guess global tolls – again, that was too overwhelming to consider.

But from the moment I got the idea in my head about home, nothing was gonna stop me. Again, Mr J tried to talk me out of it, but I declined. I managed to leave under the agreement I would hang something red from the chimney when I got home so he could see I was OK.

*

11.30am: I'm so glad I used my bike to get to the Jamesons' last night as there's no way I would've gotten my car back home. The roads were covered with all sorts of debris and the ones that were clear enough to at least drive a car down (most weren't) had so much junk on them I'd have had four flat tyres before I got out of second gear. It didn't take my bike long to get punctures in both tyres. I resorted to carrying the thing on my back rather than trying to repair the damage very early on – thank God it's light. It was probably only 3km from start to finish but it took me the better part of an hour.

There were plenty of people out and about inspecting property damage. I got a few nods of acknowledgement but no one was saying hi. Maybe they could sense how pissed off I was carrying my bike. I did see a few people up on their roofs too – either checking for damage or getting a better view of the surrounding area. Some of them must have very little idea of the devastation. They didn't get the view I did and all of the TV and radio transmitters got blown away by the Melbourne shockwave. So they'd have no idea about the tsunami here, or even the fireballs (actually that name is starting to sound like a genital disease, I think I'll have to come up with something better).

So I don't know if that makes me lucky or not. I tried my phone again and still nothing – I really hope not working isn't a permanent new feature.

I nearly cried when I got home and saw the place still standing. You kinda just take your house for granted usually – not today though. Today it represented my chance to survive this mess. If my home was gone, so was I.

All-in-all the place was looking pretty good, although it was covered in dirt and small bits of debris. No broken windows or anything like that, so I can't complain. And, to be fair, when some houses lay flattened at the bottom of an impact crater, others are probably 2km from their foundations (thanks to the tsunami) and more are on fire, then complaining about anything I face here seems a little petty.

The one scary site was the hub cap buried into the Jacaranda tree on the median strip out the front. That thing must've been travelling at some speed to find its way 10cm deep into the trunk.

*

1.30pm: Power, I have power! And it's not the generator either. When I opened the door and flicked the lights on, I did a little happy power dance!

Just made myself some toasties for lunch and flicked through the pics I took last night and this morning on my phone. I've uploaded the JPGs to my laptop so I can see them at a larger size. It's unbelievable. There's so much about the scale of what was going on in front of me last night I didn't fully take in. I mean, some of the explosions looked big yet distant, but when you took the time to look at the size of the houses around the explosions you started to realise how big it all was.

I also got a couple of cracking good pics of the Melbourne fragment as it passed overhead. I can't believe it, actually. I mean, I didn't even aim the camera really, just pressed the button a few times in hope. One of the pics was nearly in portrait where you can see the city of Adelaide at the bottom and the comet high in the sky at the top. Looking back on this image makes me realise how big this fragment must've been. I mean it's kinda hard to slap an accurate guess of size as I don't know how high up it was or anything but it certainly dwarfed any planes that usually fly over a similar route. Seriously – that thing could've been a kilometre across, maybe more!

I also did a few separate series of pics I've just stitched into panoramas in Photoshop using a trick Dad showed me. I love creating them and I pretty much slipped into auto-pilot last night and snapped images after each major situation. Thank god I had the forethought to take a picture before anything bad happened – the 'before' shot. It gives me such a great frame of reference for all the other shots. I don't know why I took it really; I think it was just to remember what Adelaide looked like.

I probably sat there for 30 minutes or so just looking at the screen with the panorama of pre-disaster above the panorama of devastation. It's all still sinking in but, wow! I think I'm gonna print out a copy of everything and find a wall to stick them on.

The toasties were a vegemite + cheese win, by the way :)

3.30pm: I've just taken stock of the place. The electricity still works, although that's the solar panels feeding into the grid – not sure how I can find out about the grid. Gas is down, phone lines are down and the majority of the TV signal is still down but I was able to pick-up ABC. Apparently the normal service is completely screwed and they're broadcasting from a local signal on top of their building on North East Rd, which has been damaged by the tsunami but they've tricked something up. They're saying the range is not great but I'm getting a reasonable signal from here.

Most importantly I was able to get some news about what's going on beyond what I have seen and it's scary...

- As the experts feared, the comet split due to its instability and heat and forces in the upper atmosphere. It made the damage close to worst-case scenario.
- The main comet impact – estimated at just over 3km across – ploughed into the Bay of Bengal, causing utter catastrophe in the region. The blast, ensuing tsunamis and 'fireballs' have pretty much wiped life off the map from India to Indonesia and as far away as China.
- The western coast of Australia and the east coast of Africa took the full brunt of tsunami waves estimated at anything up to 500m high. Perth has been utterly destroyed – Darwin is all but gone, too.
- The shock waves/tsunami were so powerful they bowled over (or through) South-East Asia, across the Pacific Ocean and still delivered a 30-40m wall of water to the west coast of north and south America. This surprised the experts, whose modelling didn't predict a big effect that far from the impact site. In fact this all gets a little confusing because another guy just came on the telly and said the tsunami was from the Melbourne impact. I don't think anyone really knows what's going on! It was off the scale.
- Most Pacific islands were completely inundated.
- The east coast of Australia also suffered a 30m+ tsunami – again we had different experts saying different things about what caused this tsunami. Some say the Bengal impact, some say Melbourne impact.
- Melbourne has been obliterated, as has the north coast of Tasmania.

- There are reports of hundreds of minor strikes in the areas surrounding and between the two large impacts. I saw at least two of those hit Adelaide with my own eyes – they were nasty!
- The 'fireballs' I've been referring to were created in both of the large impacts and rained down across the globe. Oh, and they're called ejecta – rocks and stuff that exploded out of the comet's impact points.
- There have been several reports of earthquake activity around the world and it's expected to continue.
- There is a global stop on all aircraft as the dust (kicked up into the atmosphere from the impacts) will seize their engines. This doesn't seem like much compared to everything else but I reckon it is – especially here. It means Australia is all but isolated for the foreseeable future – we are on our own. And it's even worse for Adelaide – we are as isolated as Perth was (probably two of the most isolated one million+ population cities in the world) and now the only way to get here is by car – if the roads are still together. Besides which, the nearest city was Melbourne! I think it's safe to say ain't no one coming to help us out any time soon.
- Electricity, gas and water are out for a large portion of the world's population – some of the damage may take months to fix, that's assuming they have the means and expertise to do so.
- Communications are down in most parts of Australia and across the globe.
- There are widely varying estimates of the number of casualties, but with the two biggest countries by population being heavily affected – India and China – they are 'guestimating' one-third of the world's population. That's well over two billion people dead. Maybe more.
- And that's just from the initial impact and devastation. It's gonna get worse...
- The latest threat is the giant dust/ash clouds, emerging from both impacts – but more concerning is the Bengal cloud. The predictions are frightening, with some experts saying the world could be on the verge of a nuclear winter that could last from several months to several years. Most concerning of all is it may trigger an ice age – whether that is global or limited to the northern hemisphere varies on who you hear talk. Acid rain may also be a nasty bi-product of the ash cloud, which could in turn ruin any crops that survive the nuclear winter.
- The other big threat is starvation, as people in several affected areas will struggle to get anything to eat at all. There is little chance to deliver supplies as most of the rest of the world is suffering in one way, or the

other and looking to sure-up their own communities first. Plus the global no-fly-zone means no airdrops are possible. It basically looks like they're gonna have to fend for themselves.
• Just like us in Adelaide

So, all-in-all, a cheery morning, really.

Oh there was one bit of good news – Canberra survived intact. Yep, that's right, the place that has more politicians than anywhere else in the country survives… unharmed. That's… just… great. One in every 10 people in Australia is probably a politician now!

It just makes me numb. Everything I saw, everything that was reported – the world has changed and it's never going to be what it was again. I have so many questions about how that all affects me and my brother and my parents. And where the world is heading – and Adelaide – what is to become of Adelaide? There's no Melbourne, no Perth and the east coast is dealing with the aftermath of a 30m wall of water. And no one can fly here.
We're on our own.

I think the news is better for my brother. From all reports Europe is one of the least affected areas on Earth – that and the east coast of the Americas. Ironic really. If there's ever a movie about global catastrophe it's usually these areas that cop it big time – it seems they get their revenge in real life. Although I won't be seeing my bro any time soon with the global no-fly zone to last as long as the nuclear winter. And this potential ice age will put Europe/Russia/Canada and the northern US right in the firing line. So that's it – pretty much the last safe havens from this mess will become frozen uninhabitable wastelands. Great.
Of course it might not turn out that bad – but given everything else has been just about worst-case scenario, I'm gonna assume the worst and take the pleasant surprise if it turns out any better.
From what I can work out the only place worth living on Earth right now and into the future is Rio. Well, not just Rio but the east coast of South America – and maybe the west coast of Africa – although I can't say I've heard too many reports from there. They're the places that seem to have missed everything and have the potential to miss the coming ice age. I think I'd choose South America over West Africa (no offense West Africans – if you had the Carnival I would've picked you). Argentina, Brazil, Uruguay and a few other

countries – that's it – that's the sweet spot on Earth right now. Buenos Aires sounds nice, and you can't not want to go to a city named Montevideo, but when it all comes down to it I'll choose Rio. Rio, I wonder how I get to Rio?

It's either that or Canberra and I think I'd rather try to swim to Rio than drive to Canberra!

*

5.30pm: I had all these plans about what I was going to do today, to get the place all set up survivalist-style, but I can't seem to move too far from the TV. It's totally addictive watching. They seem to do this loop. They start with a report on the local disaster here in Adelaide (I must've seen the same report seven or eight times by now), then they talk to an expert, then to one of the politicians who survived, then sum things up. Once they've done their little loop they update you nationally and repeat the same pattern – report, expert, politician (or famous person), then they pick a different part of the international scene and repeat the same process again. It's just the same disaster loop pattern over and over again, like chaos clockwork.

But I keep watching because I want to see that footage of Adelaide just one more time... again. I'm still in this weird semi-denial phase where part of my mind is refusing to accept any of this has happened. That everything I witnessed last night was some shared delusion on a mass scale. But each time I watch the helicopter shots from above the city, or the dozens of angles of amateur footage, or even the professional shots, a little bit more of me begins to believe – maybe not *believe*, maybe *accept* – what is happening and has happened.

I just find myself staring at it. I don't even know if I'm really processing it at all. Just looking. It's like I've been lobotomised and some mad scientist is running experiments on my fragmented brain to see if there's any response. Just flashing up horrible image after horrible image. I have visions of some bad '80s heavy metal video clip with me sitting in an electric chair with this crazy wired helmet strapped to my head. Wooooo! I'm on the chair baby!

But do I look away from the images? Hell no.

I have my chance to break away when they switch to the national scene but I can't quit there either. I need to know what happened in Perth, in Melbourne – see the utter carnage there. They've had helicopter shots over both cities now and the vision is devastating. Melbourne... well, I think it's best summed-up as there is no Melbourne. They can't even get the chopper in close enough to see anything other than ash, and fires, smoke and dust. It looks like a total wasteland.

46

Perth is not too much better off. The only real difference is the weather is fine and relatively clear around Perth (although the ash cloud is getting close apparently) and the helicopters can go in real close. Again it's total devastation. The difference is the killer in Perth was water. They're saying the tsunami that swept through was maybe 200-300m high – there wouldn't be too many buildings taller than that in Perth*!

They just mentioned Perth had three buildings 200m+.

Anyways, the water hasn't fully receded yet, so it makes judging the full extent of the damage impossible. But, given the destruction to what is visible, there is little hope for what has yet to be revealed.

The CBD is now a series of building skeletons – and there's not that many of those. The force of that water has pounded everything but the most solid structural elements to another part of Western Australia – or perhaps further. Some of the buildings had no remains whatsoever – nothing – total obliteration.

Some of suburbia (on the higher vantage points around the city) had revealed itself again as the water receded. The signs were no better there either. Homes were either shredded to their foundations (if they still had foundations) or buried several times over their own height in debris from the Indian Ocean or the rest of Perth.

Every now and then you'd see bodies floating by. Occasionally you'd get one or two in a certain spot but they'd often appear in large groups. Sometimes the TV crew would comment on them, sometimes they'd ignore them – maybe they didn't see them.

They gave the 'viewer discretion advised' warning a couple of times after some of the more graphic shots. In a weird way I felt like if I looked away I would be doing an injustice to those who died there. I made myself watch every second. It feels as if the 'viewer discretion' warning was for a different time. That was for the era that ended yesterday. That was for the place where you had the choice of whether or not to protect yourself or those around you from the horrors of the world, or face them.

We don't have that luxury anymore. Disaster is not random bad luck from the edges. It's not some earthquake in Turkey that killed 6000, or the plane crash in Sierra Leone that killed all on board or the terrorist attack in Iraq – none of which would make the top of our news reports. Disaster has changed. Disaster is now life. Life is disaster. Pretending anything else is just plain denial and looking away just seemed wrong… even rude.

In my past life, I liked to bag the TV coverage a bit – it's a habit I picked up from Dad. But I've got to give them a shout-out actually. I mean, what they did last night, and today, was huge. And who knows what personal losses these people are going through and what family are missing them; they are just devoting themselves to keeping us informed. I'll probably continue to bag them – it's in my DNA – but the information was and is priceless.

*

7.30pm: At some point I realised I've missed almost the entire daylight segment of the day. Given the circumstances that was mostly acceptable – I mean, there's still so much to learn about what happened – and understanding what's going on out there may help me deal with life here.

And then there's Tasmania. My parents spent last night in the highlands. I need all the news on Tasmania so I can't afford to miss any updates there. And London.

But I soon realised daylight might not be a luxury I would be afforded much longer, so I've set the small TV up in the courtyard down the side of the house so I can switch between blue sky and broadcast.

The news seems pretty good from the family front. Well, in truth, I'm not actually getting much information about central Tasmania or London, but I figure no news is good news. I mean the Tasmanian coastal regions are as battered as anywhere - particularly in the north where they copped the direct fury of the Melbourne blast, but there is little mention of any damage inland, which should've been protected from harm by the rugged terrain. As for London – I've only seen two reports and they seem to confirm London is unharmed – bracing for what the possible nuclear winter might bring and food shortages, but unharmed.

So I'm pretty sure my family are still alive. In fact, I know it. I can't really express this belief into words but I'm sure they're alive – utterly convinced. It's just… I know. And it makes me feel a whole lot stronger for everything I'm facing (and about to face) knowing they are.

*

8.40pm: Well, the sun has all but gone from the sky but I've decided to stay out here for a while. It's still pretty warm for autumn and I'm set up with the TV, a stack of unhealthy things to eat and a few beers, and I think I well and truly deserve it.

There's a stink out here though – a burning stink. Although the evening's clear, you can see plumes of smoke rising from all around. I don't think the smell is from anything close or a particular fire, it's just a general apocalyptic scent. It's just enough to remind me that, even though I got lost in the TV coverage, I am still in the middle of this disaster.

The moon tonight is freaky as all hell. Close to full and blood red. Seriously blood red. Usually the moon looks white and light as it passes by, but this thing – this red moon – looks like a hulking, metallic marble that will fall from the sky at any minute. And that red colour staring back me – it looks ominous. To me, it looks like some giant warning sign. It's like it's just sliding through the sky, looking at all the damage big brother Earth has taken, and it is saying, you think you're screwed now, just wait 'til you see what's next!

*

9.45pm: There's so much information to get my head around I'm struggling to keep up. I've decided to get the giant atlas pin-up board from the shed and fill it with a bunch of sticky notes so I don't forget anything. As soon as I hear a new piece of info about anywhere in the world, I write up a sticky note and add it to that region of the board. Who knows, it might all add up to nothing, but I just feel that cataloguing info now will be worth the time at some point in the future. I mean, if we're without internet or other communications for the long haul, then good ole TV + sticky notes might be the limits of my research options. My *Encyclopaedia of New Earth*. My Bible.

The Australian updates are still as useful as before. It looks like the eastern seaboard took an Adelaide-sized hammering from the tsunami gods. As reported, it looks like the entire coast is affected – Sydney and Brisbane both took massive hits. The damage patterns were slightly different though. In Adelaide the tsunami just started beach side and bludgeoned its way inland across the vast plain as far as it could go, In Sydney the damage was dictated by the waterways – the harbour and low-lying areas were inundated before the water took to the smaller waterways and rivers. Pretty much anyone who lived near water didn't make it – those up on the hills may have got lucky. Brisbane was about halfway between the Adelaide and Sydney experiences.

It's funny, I've never really had an appreciation for local geography when I've travelled through a city or looked across the Adelaide plains. But geography – the literal 'lay of the land' as the old people like to say – has been just about the biggest determinate of survival for everyone.

Anyways, in some strange way, my mind has started to see Brisbane and Sydney as the competition. I really don't know why that is. I'm not sure if I want to be able to say we in Adelaide have had it tougher than them, or whether I want to rebuild better, or faster – I just don't know. Why is it that I feel the need to be competitive about this? Even my whole survival plan was really a competition to out-do everyone. What the hell is that? Is it weird? Am I weird?

Or is it some crazy primal survivalist thing kicking back in? Nah, it's probably coz I'm wired (weird) like that.

*

10.50pm: I'm really starting to hit the wall. I'm attributing it to a combination of pure exhaustion, info overload and post epic event burn-out. Bed beckons – I'm accepting the beckonising (that's a word)!

Oh, there was one last thing I forgot to mention from today. They're putting together a survivors register to get an idea of numbers and where everyone is etc. So I'm heading there to name myself as an official survivor.

Survivor. That word has some connotations – 'lucky' springs to mind. I realise I'm lucky, big time. All the planning and preparation I did pre-rock didn't make a lick of difference to getting through impact night. This thing didn't care that I was prepared. I don't know what I'm saying here really. I guess I feel guilty when I hear the word survivor because I know I earned the tag through dumb luck. Dumb luck kept me alive but it could've killed me just as easily.

****

Sunday, April 13, 2014

Noon: Massive sleep in. Comaesque. Just about 13 hours of sleep. Wow. That's gotta be some sort of personal record (oh wait, I just remembered my 14-hour comathon pre-rock). I can't believe it. Mum always did say sleeping was one of my strengths. I guess the last few days are catching up with me. The funny thing is I've woken up feeling more dozy than when I went to bed. I assume that will change at some point after something to eat.

I've got the TV running 24-7 at the moment – and there's still plenty happening. I've decided to take my documentation of unfolding events to the next level, so along with my world map pin-up board I have a map of Australia and an Adelaide map. I'm gonna set them all up permanently somewhere at some point – in brother's room... or HQ.

They keep plugging the survivors register – it's a nationwide thing and it's gonna be a bigger deal than I thought. I don't have to go far to register because they're doing it at the primary school, which is only a few minutes' walk.

It's actually inspired me to do my good deed for the day – I'm gonna go up and down the street and let everyone know about the register. I mean I have the luxury of solar power so I can still get TV, but I wonder how many others are getting the info I am. Besides which, it'll give me a good chance to nosey in on everyone and see how they're doing now and how prepared they are for what's to come.

*

1pm: Just had breakfast – erm – lunch. Food conservation starts as of now. My first aim is to not let anything perishable go to waste. So basically I'm deciding what to eat based on used-by dates. Oh well, that means plenty of fresh fruit and veggies over the next week. I could probably use it too – the closest I've come to eating vegetables in the last week was a bag of potato chips (oh, and the veggies on the pizza).

*

4pm: Well, that took longer than I thought. I probably got to about 60 houses and most of them had at least someone home. I've been living in the area for over a year now and didn't realise how many neighbours I actually knew. Either I'd talked to them in the past or just waved when they walked by. That all seemed to come in pretty handy because there were a lot of very suspicious answers at the door. I don't know what people were expecting to find when they saw me, but I was getting a very distrusting and protective vibe almost everywhere I went. I wonder what they were hiding from, or protecting.

Anyways, the info on the survivor's register was news to most of the people I spoke to, and they seemed pretty happy to hear about it. So I think I earned myself some neighbourly kudos that might come in handy one day.

It was really interesting seeing inside some of the houses, too. Some had electricity but most didn't. That's a big win for the solar panels. Of the other houses some people had loaded up on candles, others were using torches and some had just moved all their living activities close to the windows so they could see what was going on.

Apart from that there were no really noticeable changes to most homes. That shocked me I've got to say. I mean, as of right now those places are barely coping without electricity. What's it going to be like if this nuclear winter hits? If what's coming is half as bad as they're saying, then I can't see half these people surviving a month. And what about extra food, water, supplies? What about the kids and the elderly – they're not gonna cope.

I've got a feeling this situation is going to get a whole lot worse before it gets better. If it gets better.

*

5.30pm: I've been robbed! I can't believe it – robbed! FFS. Worst of all it must've happened when I was out letting all the neighbours know about the survivors register. Wow – that's bloody low – so much for helping out your fellow man and all that! I'm mightily pissed off right now and feel massively violated. Dirty almost. My heart's racing like anything and I've been pacing back and forward not knowing what to do. Grrr.

OK, the good news and perspective first – the only thing that's missing is food from my fridge and pantry. But in this day and age that's serious theft. Forget cash or electronics – food and water, they're the blue-chip commodities of 2014. That food was mine – it was important to extend my survival – and some douchebag nicked it! I'm not overreacting on this. And to think it could have been one of the neighbours who knew I was out of the place talking to everyone else. I'm dirty about that – massively dirty.

They got into the house through the sliding door in the side courtyard. I'd locked it but hadn't bothered locking the main door. Rookie error – won't be happening again. They came over the fence, forced a hole in the flyscreen then made their way in.

There are no real clues as to what went on while they were here but it doesn't look like they hung around for long. I'm guessing they just fridge/pantry raided then left. Lucky for me – as none of my main supplies are kept in the kitchen. My secret stash remains secret.

I wonder what they would have made of it all if they'd seen it – the water, food, maps, notes, plans, print-outs, generators, the war room – all of it. Would they have been intimidated? Jealous? Would they have laughed? Would they want to come back, kill me and move in here?

God, what if they did want to take over my set-up? What if it's a family with a big strong dad and a couple of teenage boys bigger than me? How could I stop that? This all makes me feel very vulnerable.

I'd never really thought too much about personal security. I never really thought it'd be that big of an issue. But I see now it really could be. It'd be so easy to get into a house if you wanted to – even if it was occupied. And who's gonna stop you? Most of the neighbours are too busy protecting their own property – they're not gonna look out for others. Police? Forget it. I haven't seen one and, even if my phone worked to get in touch with them, why would they come? Are they even still operating?

The other thing that's really opened my eyes to this all today is seeing how the other people are living. To be brutally honest, they've got no freakin' chance of surviving without help. And I don't think many of them realise how entirely dire their future looks. But they will. Soon. When the clouds obscure the sun for good, when the food runs low, when it gets cold and there's no electricity. They'll get desperate. Desperate people are dangerous.

Whatever the case, I really need to beef-up security. I can't believe I all but overlooked one of the most important aspects of survival. That's my new mission.

I can't believe I was so dumb today. Sure, my intentions were good, but I've basically drawn way too much attention to myself already. And it's already cost me in a small way. At least I had the smarts to avoid any questions about food and water supplies – if anyone asked I'd just tell them that I had enough for a couple of weeks. I didn't get the vibe anyone was scoping me out – just being friendly – but I know enough about poker to know you don't tell everyone you're holding the best hand at the table.

It still bugs me. I'm almost convinced it was someone I visited today who took my stuff. It had to be. They realised I'd be out of the house for a while, they knew where I lived and they took advantage. When they broke in they either started feeling really guilty, or were paranoid that I'd come back, so grabbed all they could carry and did a runner.

I'm fuming. If I ever catch the prick who did this I'm gonna go ballistic!
*

6.30pm: I've finally raided the remains of the pantry for dinner. I'm still angry, but now I'm starting to realise how lucky I am. Things could've been so much worse. I could've lost everything I've worked towards. But the thing that sticks with me most is that this will happen again. That is a guarantee.

It's got me thinking about every aspect of the house and how I spend my time here. I definitely want to live low-profile. But how many things am I doing that are going to give off signs to others? Electricity for example – I have it, so does anyone with solar. For now. But should I be advertising that? Should I make sure the volume on the TV is down so people can't hear it walking by? Should I use the family room rather than the front lounge at night so I'm not showing my lights to the world?

And what happens when solar goes down? When I have the generator and few others have electricity? I've got to be extra careful then. I'm gonna be surrounded by very desperate and curious people. Must lay low then. The stakes will be higher then. Much higher.

What about tomorrow? I should really make an appearance at the registry. But how do I know no one is watching me when I leave the house? Do I sneak out over the back fence?

Or am I just being super paranoid now? Just out-clevering myself by trying to see too far down the track? Wow, it's getting ridiculously intense inside my brain already! I think I'm gonna hit some games and chill for a while.

11.30pm: Well that was a completely far less satisfactory experience than expected. I'm so used to online multiplayer that playing against console AI is a waste of time. It's not nearly as fun. I started a tournament in *FIFA* and got three games in before I was bored. Three games! That's usually a warm-up, not a session.

I ended up going all retro and firing up one of the old *Call of Duty's* on the Xbox360. I played the campaign mode, which I haven't done before. It was pretty damn good actually so I might be able to stretch out some more gaming love like that if I'm desperate again. Better than playing multiplayer against the computer.

The funny thing is I couldn't really concentrate on the gaming at any point – I know something's really not right when that happens! I couldn't let the break-in go. I was stewing on it. I still am, to be honest.

Anyways, I'm really getting this drive at the moment, or inclination or something, that whenever I've got a problem with something I need to deal with it straight away. It might be that I'm trying to set up good habits in this new world as it evolves in front of me – I've got to stay fresh and be prepared for anything at short notice. It's partly that, but I have this feeling it's mostly driven by the fact I feel like a completely useless sitting duck waiting for whatever disaster to unfold next. I feel like if I keep moving and stay busy that... I dunno... I'm a harder target to hit.

Whatever the reason, that thought process lead me on my evening security set-up mission.

- I found a couple of small combo locks, which I've used on the side gates either side of the house. It's hardly gonna stop anyone who really wants to get in, but if it deters 'curious' people from becoming trespassers then great.
- I've used a bunch of the extra-thick black garbage bags and gaffer tape to completely block-out the front window. With that, the exterior blinds down and the curtains closed you can't tell if there is a light on in the front

lounge, even if you're standing right outside the window! The only light visible from the front of the house now is around the entry door frame. Still, that gives me something to work on for tomorrow.

- I've set up a little webcam in the courtyard that can run straight into Dad's laptop. Next time someone comes to visit when I'm not around I'll be able to get a good look at them. Maybe I'll put up a few warning signs to keep people out too.
- It's times like this I wish I had a dog. I've never been much of a pet person but a dog would be a perfect deterrent right now.
- I'm also armed too! It's amazing how many weapons the shed offered up. First of all – and I cannot believe I hadn't remembered this until tonight – was Jason's archery gear. Yes, feeling slightly stupid right now. But in my defence I was mentally playing the 'keep myself alive as long as possible' game and it's only now I'm starting to think 'survive as long as possible'. Big difference. It's like survival of the fittest – with adequate firepower. I really hope the world doesn't degenerate to that, but just in case, I've dusted off a crossbow and sweet looking camo-designed standard bow, plus 15 arrows… and I killed a big-ass redback spider that was guarding it all (not with the crossbow, that would've been overkill). #ihateredbacks
- I can also add a bunch of filleting knives, a hammer, a nail-gun, a cricket bat and a baseball bat to the collection. I'm thinking of going all Mad Max on the baseball bat and hammering some massive nails through the head of it. Badass!

I've got my weapons cache spread out in front of me on the kitchen table. Looking at it now I'm actually starting to feel a little too weaponed-up. It made me feel safer while I was getting it all out of the shed but now that it's here in the house I'm feeling a little daunted by it all. I certainly couldn't imagine actually ever using any of it in anger. In fact I think it's gonna make me even more paranoid having weapons lying around everywhere. I'm not sure what to do with it all now. I think I'll spread it around the house and out of sight for the time being, until I can figure out a use for it all. #rambowannabefail

Anyways, I'm probably blowing all of this out of proportion – and the weapons are just a reflection of my paranoid state from today's break-in. Or maybe it's the first sign of me going crazy. Here I go again with the thinking – time to stop it with the thinking already.

Random thought for the day:

Just realised I'd have been at the football today if there hadn't been this whole end-of-the-world thing happening – Crows v Saints at Adelaide Oval. Footy's been so off my radar the last week, obviously, but jeez I miss it. Worse still, I doubt it will ever be back again. It definitely won't be back like it was before. There won't be 50,000 people packing Adelaide Oval again.

Aussie Rules. Damn, I love that game. It's the whole reason winter is tolerable. Not having it any more – that's a pretty empty thought. I mean – that's like a chunk of me... gone. It's not even worth thinking about really.

I wonder how many AFL players even survived this thing? I mean Melbourne and Perth are destroyed – Geelong, too no doubt – so there's 12 teams wiped from existence. Adelaide's two teams are based in the west, which is annihilated. And of the east coast teams, Gold Coast, Brisbane and Sydney were all in the tsunami firing line. In fact the only team based in an area that could possibly be safe is Greater Western Sydney, which may have been inland enough to miss the tsunami damage.

Thinking about information like that makes you feel numb. I've got to change my thought process because nothing good's gonna come of this one.

I love football.

****

Monday, April 14, 2014

1pm: Just got back from the survivors register (no one broke into the place while I was gone, by the way). It was really good. Really busy too. The army was in charge and it was more organised than I expected. I probably lined up for about half an hour before I could register myself. The guy I spoke to – Sgt Barker – was great. He tried to answer all my questions. Not that he appeared to know anything substantially more than me, but he tried.

It seems everyone was talking about the weather. It was a strange day out – the dust and vapour cloud finally made an appearance over Adelaide. It was in the upper atmosphere, kind of blurring and dimming the sun but not obscuring it altogether. At 'normal' cloud level it was just like any other autumn day with some thin, wispy clouds rolling in and out. At least that's the sense I got, but it's hard to tell as there was smoke rising from a number of fires; they seem to be everywhere. But the junk in the upper atmosphere gave everything a sickly yellow look. If this is as bad as things get I think the solar panels might be able to cope with my electricity usage. That would be a massive win – might be deluded thinking though.

I didn't speak at length with Sgt Barker, but long enough to get a sense there was a plan being hatched to keep everyone safe. He dropped a few hints indicating the register was designed to get enough info from the community to work out how best to plan for the future. On the surface that all sounds really good and encouraging, but is it wrong that the cynical side of me senses it's to keep the 'general public' calm? Weird. Despite all the formality today there were only a handful of army people there. I certainly don't get the sense of limitless resources behind this. Regardless, I did get a sense of trust and relief from it all.

They also had a heap of supplies to give out, which was awesome. Everyone got a pack with a couple of boxes in it. The first box contained flour, long-life milk, pickled onions, biscuits, water and preserved fruit. The second contained a bunch of different canned foods, a can opener, torch and a stack of batteries. It was heavy as anything but I was able to pop home and grab the car to take it all back.

The second box also contained an info pack on where to go for services and information. The plan is to keep parts of all the regional shopping centres open as distribution networks so people can get food and other supplies. If you needed other help – like medicine etc – you could get in touch through these centres (assuming the phone network has recovered). They're also going to try to keep ABC TV and radio broadcasting news and information. It all sounds very handy and there was a sense of community out there, which was more than I've felt since this thing started. There was definitely a positive energy and a sense this thing can be beaten.

They're coming back in a fortnight and they hope to have a more substantial plan in place by then. I look forward to it. I really do. I could not feel a more polar opposite to yesterday's paranoid low.

To top off the good vibes, I bumped into Hardo and Boof when I was packing up the car ready to go. They seemed, well, normal... for them. I'm even heading around to Hardo's this arvo for a bit of a FIFA session. His folks' place is set up with solar panels as well and they were having a few people around anyway.

*

3pm: My phone just burst into life for the first time since the strike night – someone must've pressed all the right buttons to get the network up and running again. Stoked! It then started having a spack attack while it tried to spit out texts and messages and push notifications and what-not. I don't think the coverage was too great and every time I tried to do something on the phone something else would beep or download or alert. I think I'll let it sort itself out while I go to Hardo's.

*

7pm: Well, back from my first post-apocalyptic BBQ – it was quite the afternoon actually. Good people, plenty of food, a sneaky beer or two and *FIFA* and *Call of Duty* for the boys. The adults just left us alone really, which suited everyone.

It was great – just to sit down, have a few beers with your buddies, then shoot their newb arses over and over again. It was fun – it was so normal. It's probably the first normal moment I've had since this whole thing began. Man, I needed it.

I did get the aside conversations with Hardo's mum and dad at different points. Clearly my 'going solo' approach to all this is a talking point amongst the oldies at the very least. Hardo's parents are both pretty cool I have to say – they were clearly checking up but were very relaxed about it all. They come across completely unparenty about the situation, which made it OK to talk to them. I feel like they trust what I'm doing.

On another note, my inappropriate thoughts per minute count towards Hardo's mum was still at near record level, despite her post-apocalyptic attire not being as revealing as earlier this summer. #imabadbadfriend

*

9pm: I'm shaking, I can barely write. I am gutted. I got home and started trawling through the phone messages and found one from Dad. Couldn't have been too long after I spoke to them for the last time. He was in a good mood because he'd found some transport out of Tassie quicker than expected and they were leaving that night for Launceston. From there they had a chance of getting on a boat to Melbourne that night. They hoped to be back in Adelaide by Saturday night.

That puts Mum and Dad around the heart of ground zero at the moment of the Melbourne impact. Shit, shit, shit. I'm trying to think of some logical way they would have been somewhere else, somewhere safe. But nothing I can come up with makes any sense. And if their plans had changed Dad would have let me know – he's obsessive like that.

They were there. They were in the wrong place at the absolute wrong time. They are dead. My parents. Dead.

There are no words for this.

I… I don't know what to do. I don't know where to go. I don't know what to say. I am just numb. Shaking, sick, alone and numb.

****

Tuesday, April 15, 2014
7pm: I don't feel like writing today. I don't feel like anything.

****

Wednesday, April 16, 2014
5pm: See yesterday's post. Add a ditto.
Oh, and just to add to my perfect mood, the weather has closed in. It was windy and dusty and freaking dark all day. The sort of dark that it's hard to tell whether it's day or night. And it got nasty cold all of a sudden. The winter has hit. This is depressing. I'm not in a good place. I am a long, long way from a good place.

****

Thursday, April 17, 2014
11am: This is crazy. I'm paralysed with bitterness. I can't move. I'm just eating, going to the toilet and sleeping. I'm completely detached. I'm a zombie – a human zombie.
It's disgusting outside. It's been storming for three days straight. It's dark and dusty and windy. There's a layer of debris and ash in the yard that has caked everything. It's already higher than the step into the house. The next time I open that door I'll let that gunk in and if I don't go out soon I could be sealed in. But I'm not moving today. Zombie not moving.
The house is dark - the solar panels aren't getting anything. Nothing. The phone is dead – all the ash in the air is screwing the signal.
Is this what the end of the world is like? Is this what I've survived for?

****

Friday, April 18, 2014
4.45pm: Another day of zombiness.
I've gotta stop this. I can feel it sucking me under. I've gotta deal with this before it gets too crazy. Before I get too crazy.

****

Saturday, April 19, 2014

9.15am: OK. Today's gonna be tough, but I've got to do it. It may sound weird but I'm giving my parents a funeral tomorrow. I'm gonna spend the rest of the day planning it – writing speeches, displaying pictures, having food, sorting out the right music. I'm going all out. But I'm gonna need to get the generator sorted first.

*

10.30am: The house is now electrified again – the generator was all hooked up – it just needed switching on. Too easy, really. I was the one who turned it off in the first place; I just didn't want it running unless I was ready. The only difficult bit was dealing with the environment outside. The ash has been falling like turd-coloured snow for days. And it's everywhere. As soon as I managed to jimmy open the sliding door a whole pile of the filth splattered down on to the cream carpet. Pretty sure that stain ain't coming out any time soon. So I changed tactics. I decided to go out through the laundry door – that way the damage is only to the tiles. I also donned all of my footy wet weather gear and tucked everything into my welly boots. I threw on my diving goggles and wrapped a scarf around my mouth so I didn't have to breathe too much ash in. I looked like a joke but at least it kept most of the dirt out of the house. When I got back in I threw everything in the laundry trough, rinsed it and hung it out on the shower rail to dry. So what was probably a two-minute job took the better part of an hour from start to finish! Am I gonna have to do that every time I leave the house? That's a pain in the arse.

*

1pm: This is harder than I thought. Looking though the pictures of Mum, Dad, Jase and I growing up. All those memories... each one a beautiful, utterly sad reminder it's all completely gone. Every family moment I will ever experience has already happened. Those pics used to be things we did – now they're things we'll never do again.

*

8pm: It's done. Everything is prepared for tomorrow. I feel like I have given everything I have from the depths of me. I've run an emotional marathon today. Given how emotionally unprepared I am, I got the emotional stitch at the 200m mark, emotional cramp at 5km and pretty much hobbled home. I seriously have nothing more to give. Nothing. Tomorrow my parents will get a send-off that no one else will see. Will it be befitting? Probably not. Will it do them justice? Definitely not. But I've put everything I've got into it... I'm just going to have to be content with that.

Tonight I drink! And it's not a beer drinking night. This is raid the liquor cabinet worthy... top shelf... at the back... if the proof is over 50 then drink type of night. I'm not sure my folks would've approved, but I think they would've understood.

*

11pm: Stupid house with stupid reminders of family everywhere I look. Stupid.

Stupid whiskey. Stupid weather. Stupid apocalypse. Stupid 2014DM3. Stupid rock. Stupid other cosmic event that probably bumped into it millions of year ago that sent the comet into a stupid collision course with the stupid vulnerable Earth that screwed up my whole damn life. Stupid comet is stupid.

****

Sunday, April 20, 2014
12.30am: Well it's done. Mum and Dad have had a send-off. My send-off. I made a speech for each of them. I talked about what they achieved in life, how they met each other and what they meant to their kids and friends. And I talked about how they died trying to get back to protect their kids. I used the overhead projector to slideshow through images of each of them as I spoke. Then I finished each ceremony with a song. Mum got Wonderwall by Oasis – without doubt her favourite – and for Dad I played Don't Dream it's Over by Crowded House. Dad was much harder to choose for as his taste was so much more eclectic and mood-driven. I hope I got it right. I think I did. I cried. So that's got to be a good sign.

As each of their songs played I put some of their favourite possessions in a box and covered it with a blanket. Shortly after I donned my outside gear, took the boxes and buried them in the ash-filled garden. I erected a cross to mark where each of their boxes lies.

And it is done.

****

Monday, April 21, 2014
10.30am: It's really cold today; seriously cold. It's still pitch-black, windy and ash-laden outside, too. I'm not sure what's worse really: darkness blocks the sun – meaning the solar panels are completely useless, and the wind fills the air with that putrid-smelling ash, which gets everywhere. Disgusting. I can smell it throughout the house. Even though I've only opened the door once

since it started, it's building up inside. There's a thin film of it on just about every surface. Worse still, it blocks the TV signal so I'm not getting any news. Outside it keeps building up and up. It's now becoming a problem because it's sitting about 20cm above the base of the sliding doors at the side of the house. I can only assume the situation is the same at the front door and back door, although I can't see what's going on out there.

I'm going to go on a mission today and clear access to the sliding door and laundry door. I'm still debating whether I do the same out the front – I'm not entirely sure I should advertise any sign of life to the world yet.

I think I'm gonna head out for a while. The house is starting to drive me crazy. As much as I tried to get closure from my parents' funerals – and it did help – I'm constantly looking at, and living with, reminders and memories of them. Everything in this place is a reminder of some part of their lives. I think I just need a different perspective on the world. There's also this sense I'm carrying the burden of what happened to them all on my own. I'm not sure I have what it takes to cope with that at the moment; I need to tell someone. I figure I'll head to the Hardigans – they knew my folks pretty well and the walk won't be too far. Plus, I'll be able to catch up with Hardo himself as I think a dose of peer company is exactly what I need.

It's a tactical move at some level, too, I guess, as I'm paranoid someone will discover how well I'm set up, and the most likely people to rock up at my door are the Hardigans. I'd rather go there and avoid that scenario. Plus, if I clean the ash and then go to the Hardigans I'll avoid the rigmarole of putting the stupid outdoor gear on at least one time. #multitasking

****

Tuesday, April 22, 2014
2pm: Where to start? That was so hard. For a start, the paths around the house were buried deeper than I thought. Probably as much as half a metre in some parts – thank God the door opens inwards; I could've been stuck inside! Before I even started sweeping I had to get the tools from the shed – the wind had piled the ash there over a metre high. I was on my knees, digging with my hands for what felt like forever before I could jimmy the door open. I decided to get out every tool I thought could ever be handy out while I had the chance.

The digging itself was disgusting. Besides the smell, the texture of the ash was just gross. The top layer was somewhat dusty and gritty and not too bad to cope with, but as you got lower it got wetter and turned into this heavy brown sludge. And it smelled like a mixture of over-cooked food and rotting corpse (I'm guessing there, though, as I don't really know what rotting corpse smells like). Most of all, it was bloody hard work to move. Anyways, I ended up clearing enough room in front of the shed to allow the door to open, as well as a path to the back door (about a foot wide) and a path to the side courtyard, where I also cleared in front of the door. Not sure how much ash I moved but it was a fair bit. It took far longer than I thought – probably three hours in total.

Worse still, I think I'm gonna have to do that every few days, otherwise the ash will get out of control. And even if I do keep up that level of maintenance I'm soon gonna run out of places to move the ash, as the two piles I created already look rather large. Surely the ash will stop raining down at some point. I hope so; otherwise my efforts today are a bit like bucketing water from the top deck of the Titanic.

The walk to the Hardos was just plain nasty. I've made that walk dozens of times pre-rock – it used to take 15 minutes. Yesterday it took over an hour – and about the same on the way back today.

For starters it was black. Pitch black. There was literally no light to gauge where I was or where I was going. I was smart enough to bring a torch with me but it was less help than I'd imagined. The ash was so thick in the air that when the light was on it mostly picked up all the bits flying in front of my face. It was very hard to focus on any object more than a couple of metres away and overall visibility couldn't have been more than ten metres.

Then there was the ash on the ground. It was probably an average of 40cm deep – pretty much knee-high. Each step was an effort. I'd have to lift my feet high just to break clear of the top of the ash then stride out as far as I could before sinking it down to get a grip on the ground for the next step. The sludgy lower ash would then cling to my wellies, making lifting off for my next step difficult. Complicating each step was the fact the soles of my boots and the sludge seemed to combine for almost zero traction. Sometimes the only thing keeping me from falling over was the depth of the ash.

That's not to mention the debris hidden under the ash and other obstacles that made me backtrack a few times. A couple of times I bumped into cars not even realising they were right in front of my face. It was insane. As for knowing the way I was going, well, that didn't seem to help one bit. In the complete darkness everything was new, or looked different. It was a slog.

Plus the dark can make you paranoid... if you let it. I was cocooned in my wet-weather gear with a visibility of next to nothing, bumping into objects left, right and centre. When you start to get the thought into your head someone else could be outside, near you, next to you, watching you, it's hard to let go. I felt totally vulnerable.

Ultimately, what I thought would be about an hour's worth of tasks – clearing access to the doors and walking a few blocks to my mate's place – turned out to be a four hour, 20-minute epic. Lesson learnt.

I must've looked like death warmed up when I got to the Hardigan's doorstep because his dad said 'Jesus Christ' in a very pitying way and his mum took one look at me and burst into tears. Then I don't know what came over me. I think it was the emotion of the last few days, the exhaustion of the trip over and knowing I was about to tell someone else about Mum and Dad, because that made it real. I just burst into tears and blurted it out.

Mrs Hardigan – Karen – burst out crying again and swooped in and hugged me hard, despite the fact I was covered in an inch-thick film of ash. It felt good. Not in a MILF way, but in an I-needed-human-touch way.

Mr Hardigan – David – kinda rubbed my head and asked a few questions about how I knew that. I somewhat remember blurting out an answer between sobs and sniffs.

My buddy, Hardo – Jonah – well I think he was a little overwhelmed by it all and he kinda hung back for a while but the look on his face told me the news had hit him hard and that was enough for me.

Anyways, they fixed me a bath and I got tidied up and got myself together before joining them for dinner. They had one of those outdoor gas bottle heaters, which had been moved inside near the dining table to provide heat and light. It was kind of strange but kind of nice. We ate minestrone soup and damper bread then shared a massive bowl of FruChocs for dessert. So many things were out of place from what would have happened if I'd come over for dinner two months ago. For a start we wouldn't have sat down with the adults at all, we would've eaten something totally different, under proper lighting conditions and not freezing our butts off. Then we would've played Xbox all night – but none of that mattered. In fact, we had a bit of a laugh at our own expense.

The thing is, though, it wasn't necessarily that funny, our circumstances. I found it quite nice. Just to mash up all the things at your disposal and come up with some shabby version of the 'old' normal. It was just nice.

They're a great family, the Hardigans – I felt totally welcome. It was strange table conversation – there were plenty of stories about my folks; I really needed that. I was ready for it. Then we went on to chat about things we'd picked up in terms of news from the TV (when it was working) etc. I can't say I learned too much from them, but they were almost as well informed as I was. Karen and David are both pretty cluey and so is Hardo – mostly – when he puts his mind to it. There was also a lot of talk about what we'd been doing to survive – what changes we'd made to cope with the lack of utilities.

The conversation kicked on after tea, too. David pulled out a nice bottle of scotch from his collection and we sat around under gaslight, drank, chatted and played euchre. Apparently, concerns about under-age drinking were also victims of the impact on Melbourne! There wasn't even a mention of not being the right thing to do. I liked it too – felt like I totally fit in. And after everything I've been through I deserve a drink as much as the next man. Besides, I'm 18 in nearly a year, so close enough, right?

The Hardigans plan was pretty similar to mine – just survive until next Monday and see what happened when the survivor registry people came back. They had plenty of resources to get through to then, according to David.

I couldn't help but wonder what life was really like for them on a day-to-day basis. I mean, we were having a surreal moment at this dinner – a break from the mundane. But what would it actually be like to be cooped up with your family inside the same eight rooms, 24 hours a day, every day, for the foreseeable future, with no electricity for entertainment?

I hadn't imagined spending the night there when I'd left the house yesterday but after eating I couldn't imagine leaving that night. I'm glad they insisted I stay. I slept on the pump-up mattress on the floor in Hardo's room and we chatted for a few hours more. Mostly about the girls we felt this cruel apocalypse had denied us the chance to nail. Bad, life – very, very bad.

The next morning they tried to insist I stay and it took me a long time to convince them I was leaving. But having reassured them I had the supplies and the desire to go it alone until next Monday's survivor registry meeting, I went with their blessing. Karen farewelled me with a care pack of supplies – just some cookies she'd made and some chocolate – it was really sweet. A part of me felt very guilty taking it, as I know I already have more supplies than the three of them combined, but I couldn't really tell them that. We've also agreed to meet at the survivor registry at 10am next Monday, so it's good to know I've got another organised chance to meet people I know.

    *

4pm: I've just cleaned up from the walk home. God I hate this ash. Filthy, stinking, gets-everywhere goop! Hate, hate, hate.

At least the wind has died down today for the first time in days. It meant the visibility on the walk home was far better than the way there. When I shined the torch I could probably see up to 20-30m away.

Everything is caked in dark brown/grey ash. There is no colour on the streets at all, just poorly defined brown shapes – cars, houses, trees. It was kinda like that old Cadbury's ad when I was a kid, the one where the world was made of chocolate. However, I'm willing to bet this world wouldn't taste as good. It's interesting walking along and spotting all the houses where there are signs of human activity. You can see them from a mile away (OK then, 20-30m away), the tell-tale giveaway is a cleared front door. I'm not sure if it's a good thing or not that I've decided not to clean the front door at home. Do I want people to know my place is occupied or not?

*

6.30pm: Just spent the last 20 minutes coughing my guts up. Disgusting. Kinda hoping I don't get sick right now because the timing would be far from awesome. I've got a feeling the coughing is more to do with the ash I've ingested during my time outside over the last two days than any kind of illness.

*

8pm: Just had a much-needed shower. Something I noticed with the Hardigan's bath, and again with the shower here, is the water quality ain't what it used to be. There's a definite colour change and maybe it was my imagination, but I did detect a subtle 'off' smell. I'm not sure what that all means apart from that it isn't good news. I do know I won't be drinking tap water anytime soon.

I gave myself a mental high five for thinking about getting water containers and filling them up pre-rock.

****

Wednesday, April 23, 2014
5pm: Totally unmotivated today. I have done sweet FA. The closest I've come to an actual achievement of any note is opening and devouring my first canned meal. Spaghetti bolognese for those playing at home. The result: Highly average – only a short step from meh. Thank heavens for my friend parmesan cheese is all I'll say. But it's short-term gain for long-term pain, I'm afraid - I've probably only got enough for one fleck per can. #tastefail

****

Thursday, April 24, 2014

11am: Felt a strange thing called motivation today. I decided to deal with the issue of light emanating from the front door. I was pretty happy with my solution – I stripped bare the wardrobe from Jase's room (AKA HQ, The War Room, Command Centre) and knocked out its back wall. I then positioned it in front of the entry door – far enough so the door can fully open. I've then used the remaining wood from the back of the wardrobe to extend a 'tunnel' from the cupboard to the doorframe, nailed it into place, then blacked-out the remaining gaps with a combination of gaffer tape and black garbage bags.

OK, it does look slightly weird in the middle of the entry hall – this giant *The Lion, The Witch and the Wardrobe* homage, daring me to climb inside and face some strange fantasy world, Bad Cadbury World, maybe. I'm gonna get some odd looks if anyone comes to visit, that's for sure.

*

1.30pm: I'm trying my best not to project forward at the moment, but it's proving difficult. I'm spending so much time cooped up in the house with so little to keep me distracted for long that my mind inevitably wanders back to where everything is going. But it's not a good place to go to. I mean, if I'm honest, really honest, about where things are at in Adelaide and where they are headed, well... it's not good. Everything so far has pretty much been a worst-case scenario result, and all the experts' (pre-impact) worst-case predictions pointed to decades-long ice age and humans on the verge of extinction. I don't want to think about it because when I do I come to the conclusion that's where we're heading.

I spend most of my waking hours keeping busy looking for distractions really. The problem is the distractions fall into two categories…

1 – Distractions involving my survival. These are things I can keep busy with that I believe will help prolong my life. Things like continuing to adapt the house to deal with the conditions, sorting out all the things I printed off the 'net pre-rock, and clearing the ash from the house.

2 – Distractions from all things apocalypse. Things like playing Xbox, watching DVDs, reading, playing cards and playing darts.

All of these are great, but the Type 1 distractions are so closely tied to my fate I can't help but project forward to where this is all going. And the Type 2 distractions are so meaningless I feel guilty I'm not doing Type 1 distractions, then I start to think of why I'm not doing Type 1 distractions and think of why I need to do Type 1 distractions, which reminds me of how dire things are.

Screwed, isn't it? It basically means whatever I'm doing I'm thinking, at least at some level, about how futile anything and everything I'm doing is. And that I'm probably gonna die in this stupid house, in the dark, with very few people left to give a toss that I came and went.

This is why I need distractions. I'm telling myself not to plan too far ahead, at least until I know what the survivor register people say next Monday.

*

3pm: Ohhh. Exciting (but frustrating)! I'm getting a hint of the ABC TV signal again. This is the first time in days and I'm sure it's no coincidence it's timed with the better weather. The problem is the signal is so bad I'll only see a few frames of picture and a snippet of audio before the signal will freeze and make that irritating electronic 'crunching' sound.

It was like trying to watch TV from my auntie and uncle's shack at Normanville when the weather's bad. The only difference is here I need to know what's going on. Goddamn you, dodgy digital signal! Why did they cut off the analogue signal a few years back? At least with analogue you'd still have an uninterrupted signal, even if it was 'snowy'. I would've been able to pick-up so much more than I did.

Anyways, I reckon I had this semi-decipherable signal for about four hours. I soon gave up on trying to understand the audio – just too inconsistent. Instead I just concentrated on those moments the screen froze with a headline and wrote down everything I could.

Here's the best of what I got (paraphrased, to get as much down as possible)…

• The cloud that has engulfed Adelaide now stretches around the globe. It looks like everyone is facing the same conditions.
• Once again experts disagree on what the effect on global temperatures will be, but the general consensus is a whole lot colder (that's technical I know). Some are saying a 5-10 degree drop, some are saying far, far more.
• If you believe the 'far, far more' experts that means an imminent global ice age. Wow.
• Europe and the US are in crisis. They survived the initial impact but the ash and darkness have brought panic and instability to their populations. The power is not the problem over there, but it soon will be as temperatures start to fall. Food is in short supply already, particularly in the cities.
• Looks like it's been getting particularly crazy in the US. There were riots on the streets in a number of cities for days as people wanted food. Things were getting out of hand with violence and guns etc and they've brought

in martial law. Apparently you cannot gather on the streets in groups larger than five, otherwise the army will open fire on you! Wow!

- Things aren't too much better in Europe, where martial law has also been declared in a number of countries.
- Basically, people living in the big cities are being encouraged to leave. The population density is too high to be sustainable. God knows where they think they'll go.
- The ash cloud is causing issues well beyond the darkness and impending temperature changes. Obviously the global no-fly zone is still in place and will be for months, maybe years (probably years), but coupled with that is the almost complete breakdown of the transport system. Road systems are in complete chaos as the ash sludge keeps dumping inches on the roadways. It can't be cleaned up as quickly as it falls. And it's not like snow, which melts, the ash just keeps accumulating, so finding places to store what's already been dumped is also a problem.
- Rail system are down, too, as it is proving impossible to keeps tracks safe and ash-free.
- Right now the only viable mode of transport on Earth is the boating system. Sure, it sounds like a glimmer of good news, but then you have to take into account at least 80% of the world's sea ports have been utterly destroyed by tsunami and miles of debris now stand between the nearest surviving human and the coast. Well it's not that much hope really, is it?
- The Atlantic Ocean got the easiest ride and sea transport may be an option along the east coast of the Americas and the west coast of Europe/Africa.
- In addition to blocking roads, the sludge is getting into everything. Everything! It's getting into the engines of the vehicles designed to clear the streets of the sludge. Engines seize/clog/die. Nothing is designed to survive operating in these conditions.
- The sludge is getting indoors, too. Nowhere or nothing is immune. Computers are dying, electronic circuits are frying, food is getting corrupted and clean drinking water tainted. Every single element of life is becoming harder. The ash is unstoppable at the moment and there's no slowdown in sight.
- Not one system of life anywhere in the world is coping. It's simply spiralling out of control, rapidly. Even in the 'lucky countries' like those in North America and Europe, where there is still electricity and little in terms of property and population loss. It now looks like they stand in line for an equally cruel fate as the rest of us. People there are going to be

competing against each other for the simplest of resources like food.
- There weren't any local updates in the time I watched. That doesn't exactly fill me with confidence! Something – anything – would've been good but I'm no wiser now than when I started watching.
- There was a report out of Sydney recommending people stay off the streets. They should either bunker down at home or find their way to one of the 'survivor hubs' – large shopping centres or hospitals – if they need supplies or medical attention.
- Worst of all, they didn't even finish their news segment with a cute animal story! They're supposed to do that to make us feel better – it's their rule and they're not sticking to it! What happened to the good old days – news intro, murder in the suburbs, triple fatality car-crash, boring politics, earthquake in foreign land, actor so-and-so died aged blah blah, your footy team lost again on the weekend, some report on some other sport no-one cares about, it's gonna be cold tomorrow... but here's some footage of a panda falling over so everything's OK? I miss the panda.

6pm: I've just been pouring through everything I transcribed from the news reports and trying to work out what it all means. My first thoughts are of Jason. London sounds like one of the last places where you'd want to try and survive this thing. In fact, the UK would have to be one of the most overcrowded countries on Earth – I just hope he finds a way to get out. Even then, where would he go? I've spent way too much time worrying about what might happen to him and it's not doing me any good. There's no way I could cope with losing him, too. The fact is, circumstances don't look good, but he's a resourceful guy in a place unharmed from the initial damage... with electricity. I think it's best for me to leave my thoughts at – just thoughts. He has a far better chance of survival than me, and I'm gonna make it, so he'll be fine.

It's amazing how quick the unaffected parts of the world have plunged into crisis. It's amazing – and scary. In some really weird way I think I'm pretty lucky. I'm not competing with a super-large population for the rapidly-disappearing resources. I've got enough to see me through for some time and when the time comes that I run out, I might be able to scavenge more from parts of the city that didn't make it.

Overseas though, they are going to burn through resources at a rate they won't be able to maintain. How long will electricity last? And food? Even though their crops probably survived the initial impact, surely they're not going to produce this season. Will they survive to the next? How many days' worth of food does the US have in storage, for example? They've got to feed nearly 300 million people. What happens when the stocks run low? And what happens when they're empty? And what happens a week after that? A month? A year?

One thing I do know about Americans is they like guns, lots and lots of guns. They're gonna be hungry, desperate and armed. The chaos reported now is probably as good as it's gonna get for some time. I mean, how many people can actually survive in America when little food can be produced – sustainably? Ten million? Five million? One million? Any?

To me, unless something radically changes with our luck then there's going to be a massive population shift in a short amount of time – a few months maybe? And with life at stake it's not going to be a pretty transition.

To be honest, I think I'd choose my dire, crap-hole of a situation over that one any day. It's gonna turn nasty over there. Dog-eat-dog nasty. Survival of the most heavily armed.

Before I sign off here's my random thought of the day:
It just occurred to me that if I take the word DEAD and the word ALIVE and smash them together I'm left with the word ADELAIDE and a V for victory. Just sayin'.

****

Friday, April 25, 2014
8pm: The weather picked up again today. To be honest I couldn't be bothered doing anything constructive at all, so I spent the entire day playing games, watching movies and reading. It was awesome. I finished the *Call of Duty: Black Ops* campaign I started the other day on the old 360. It was really good, and the good news is my brother has all the *CoD* games in his collection so I've got a few more days' entertainment lined up. Movies wise I watched Reality Bites. It was pretty funny! I'm not entirely sure why I picked it but I think it says something about where I'm at mentally. Normally, if I had the pick of our movie collection, I'd go straight for the sci-fi options, but today, I just wanted the fantasy of seeing the world as it used to be. I'm not sure if it did me any good though. I found it hard to fully concentrate on the film, because I kept fixating on things that used to be normal. Just daily lives, really, nothing special. Even blue sky was confronting – it's been 10 days since I've seen blue sky, or even natural light.

71

As for my book choice, well I decided that the movie was too much reality for one day so I started reading Dad's first Red Dwarf book – *Infinity Welcomes Careful Drivers*. Very funny and a great distraction.

****

Saturday, April 26, 2014

11am: Yesterday was just what I needed, so much so I'm doing it all again today… and tomorrow. That's right; I'm giving myself a long weekend. Hell, I deserve it :D

I did finish one minor task for the house before I indulged – I turned off the fridge. There was no point having it on really; I've used everything but a few of the sauces and the freezer will be empty after I use the last of the puff pastry tonight. All it's doing is draining power from the generator, so I figure I should store the last odds and ends in the esky and leave it in the laundry. It's pretty cold in there anyways.

Speaking of cold, it's currently 7 degrees. Judging by how the temperature tends to peak just after lunch, but doesn't really stray too far in any day, I'd be surprised if it hit 10 today. That'll be the first time it hasn't reached double figures since this thing began. I've never been much of a weather person, but I can't remember a day pre-rock that we didn't hit double figures, not even in the heart of July. Given we're still in autumn that doesn't bode well for what we're heading towards.

But today it's all about forgetting such pesky things as the death of a planet and probably my demise with it. Instead, the focus is on hard-core slobbery. I'll report back in tomorrow night when I've recharged batteries and am ready to face the survivor register people once more.

****

Sunday, April 27, 2014

10pm: Wow… I indulged so much I ended up on the verge of getting bored… now that's saying something! BioShock campaign completed, halfway though *Borderlands* – both top-shelf – Red Dwarf novel one finished, now reading the sequel *Better Than Life*, and I went on a Monty Python marathon last night and this morning, watching all three movies. I'm gonna give the points to *Life of Brian* in a close win over *The Holy Grail*, although the Mr Cresote scene in *The Meaning of Life* was absolute gold!

Nine degrees today... again. I reckon we were still getting 40+ about six weeks ago. I'd hate to think what the middle of winter is going to bring... or if it gets better on the other side... if there is another side :S

Random though of the day:

I sometimes wonder if I'm like one of the last dinosaurs. Sixty-five million years ago a massive asteroid buried itself in the Yucatan Peninsula. It left an impact crater 180km wide and showered the earth with fiery debris. After the fire came the dust cloud and the years of cold. Dinosaurs didn't survive. Sounds familiar.

But some would've survived the initial impact. There would've been pockets of bliss – little oasis from the initial catastrophic chaos. But eventually the change in weather, the loss of food – it was too much for them. The little mammals survived though – it was the start of the human age, I guess.

So maybe this is the end of our age. Maybe I'm like one of those dinosaurs stuck in an oasis that is doomed to be my downfall. Maybe I'm delaying the inevitable. Maybe it's the little guys I share this house with – the millipedes, cockroaches, spiders and ants – that are the future of the Earth. Maybe one day my preserved bones will be discovered by the descendants of these millipedes and I'll be put in a museum for all to see. I wonder what they will imagine about our lifestyle. They will probably be fascinated, pitying, but mostly it'll be a sideshow to their cosmopolitan millipedian existence.

Don't snigger too much millipedes, the next rock has your name on it.

****

Monday, April 28, 2014

9am: Down to business today. Time to find out what is going on at the survivor register. I'm gonna head off in about half an hour, which will give me plenty of time to get there and meet the Hardigans.

Dad's got this little hand-held audio recorder; I might take it with me to record my conversation with any official I speak to. I'm kinda feeling out of the loop on information – especially locally – with the TV all but useless, so making sure I digest every bit of information available seems like the right thing to do.

I might give the backyard a bit of a sweep while I'm in the outside gear too. #feelingpumpedtoday

*

2pm: Wow. Talk about not what I expected.... at all. It was pretty crowded when I finally trudged my way to the school. I'm guessing there were at least 400 people hanging around but it was hard to tell without being able to see too far – I'm basing the number mostly on the noise and general hubbub.

I couldn't see the Hardigans anywhere. It was really hard to negotiate my way through the crowd to really check everyone out, and shining my torch in everyone's face was coming off as pretty rude. So in the end I just kind of laid low.

More importantly, there were no one officials there at all. No army, no guidance, no one to tell us what was happening. It was a complete non-event. Everyone waited pretty patiently, given how cold and miserable it was. Within an hour though, people began to act up. Some were getting pretty emotional too. There was crying – real crying, wailing crying – and shouting and swearing. I could see I was not the only one emotionally invested in this. I know the conditions are tough right now. I mean the ash is well over knee deep and it's pitch black and cold and horrible. I know the logistics (that's what they call it, right?) of getting to the school would've been hard to organise, but to not show up, that's a hope killer.

I remember looking around and thinking exactly that – hope killer. I mean, it's hard to make out people's emotions by sight, with the lack of light and covered faces, but you could hear it in their voices. Hope killer. This day was going to tell them what to do with the next stage of their life now the food is low and the power's gone. The people out there today needed that.

I stayed around for about four hours, waiting for the authorities, long after the first of the people drifted back into the darkness of the streets. It was a really weird moment... a group realisation... we were alone. No government, no police, no army, no help. Unless something changes the brave new world started today.

There was a group of adults trying to organise some sort of action. They were trying to come up with a plan of attack to find out what was going on and let everyone know. I just hung around the fringes of the conversation and listened. It was decided that the next day two groups would set out on expeditions – one to the Firle shopping centre, the other to Norwood – to what had been labelled survivor hubs. They would speak to whatever authorities were there and gather as much information as they could. Then we would meet here again on Wednesday morning and share the information.

I thought the Norwood shops would've been destroyed in the tsunami but according to a couple of the guys there they only suffered minor damage.

I found that weird seeing as though I saw the tsunami get as far inland as Portrush Road.

I loved they came up with that plan. It was just us locals saying we wouldn't give up this community without a fight. I mean, if we lose that – the community – what are we gonna be left with? I consider myself in as good a spot as anyone. I probably have more food to out-live anyone here (unless there's some crazy nuclear bunker types in the area I don't know about) and even I need this. I need the thought there's some bigger level of organisation out there. I need to know things are not going to descend into total, lawless chaos and I need to know someone's looking out for me on the streets.

I'm going it alone but I can't do it by myself – does that even make sense?

By the time I waded back to my place I had mixed emotions about the day. Part of me was totally gutted and disillusioned by the army no-show, but another part of me had hope the community had enough spirit and desire to overcome what was thrown at us and survive together.

Looking back, as I write this, I feel very torn. Deep down I know everyone else is more desperate to make this work than me because I'm set for food and electricity and they're probably not. But am I being selfish? Am I using them? Should I share what I have with the greater community? Am I doing the right thing?

I've been really struggling with this in the background of my mind and it comes up every time I have an interaction with someone else, because I know I've got all I need to live longer than they do. If no help comes or the weather doesn't get better soon there are going to be a lot of people starving to death. I think of all of that and tell myself I need to help – to share my resources. Then I start to think about how that would even be practical. Who gets my help? Where does it stop? I mean, if I were to share my supplies with everyone there today – say 400 people – I'd probably be able to give them each about two days of food, maybe a bit more. My practical (or maybe selfish) side says two days of food for the larger group doesn't help in the bigger scheme of things. It helps those people for those two days but after that they'll be in the same boat they were going to be in anyway… and I'd be right there with them.

So in the end I reach the same conclusion. The only way my resources are going to make a meaningful difference (assuming things aren't getting better anytime soon) is if I keep them all for myself. That's my thought process, that's my decision. Is it right? I don't know. But it is what it is and that means I have to play a careful game.

I can be involved in this community that seems to be developing, but I can't draw too much attention to myself. I can't be obviously well fed, or too sharp and alert. I can't say too much when I speak. It's going to be tough, because I seem to be the sort of person people want to take under their wing in the circumstances. I understand it too, as I'm young and seemingly vulnerable. But it does make answering questions difficult. I have to make it seem like I have enough to get by for now, but not too much. At some point people will get suspicious, I suppose, but I'm in no hurry to bring that on any sooner than it has to come.

Then it comes to things like tomorrow's recon to the shopping centres. Do I go? I've been swaying between yes and no on that one since they first mentioned it. If I don't go, I don't risk accidentally saying something to incriminate myself as a food-hoarder, which is the safe option. But at this stage I'm being drawn towards going. For a start, as much as I want to lay low, it can't hurt to know as many of these people as possible. Who knows when I might need their help or what other unforeseeable benefits there might be to being a contributing member of this posse. Secondly, I'm keen to test myself on a longer walk, and to do it in the safety of a larger group is ideal. Finally, and most importantly, getting out of this place and speaking to other people would be about the highlight of my week right now. I need this mentally as much as anything else.

It's hard to describe the darkness outside these days. It's total light block-out. Even back pre-rock there was nothing like it. Even during the days of the darkest clouds you had decent quality visibility. But here, the clouds aren't water vapour, they're ash – bits of pulverised rock and metal and who knows what else. And the ash doesn't sit nicely at one even level in the sky; it's everywhere, constantly floating around your head and probably floating at every level of the atmosphere from the ground to orbit. The sun doesn't stand a chance of getting through. I wonder when it will.

Even nighttime pre-rock was never like this. There were always lights – street lights, the stars, the moon. Even on cloudy nights the sky would reflect back the city lights to give you some vision. Not anymore. This is worse than anything I've ever known; this is pure dark.

9pm: This afternoon's been quite productive. I started preparing for tomorrow by cleaning up my outside gear, which was disgusting. As for the state of my wellies... words cannot even begin to describe what had become of them. But I scrubbed them up into something semi-reasonable. I also found a pair of steel-cap boots in Dad's cupboard. They fit perfectly, and they're waterproof – I think I might substitute the boots for tomorrow's expedition. Surely they have more grip.

While I was doing all this I came up with a neat little idea. I've copied and enlarged pages from the street directory and stuck them on the wall in the war room. I basically have a 2m by 2m map of the surrounding streets, from Firle shopping hub to Norwood shopping hub and everything in between. My house is just about smack-bang in the middle.

Now I have the perfect accompaniment to my larger Adelaide map, Australia map and world map. I cover every level! I figure observations and discoveries made tomorrow can go on here, which could come in very handy. Also, for the streets closest to my house I've drawn rough property boundaries. I might start keeping a note of which houses show signs of activity and which don't. Again, might not be much, but it could really come in handy one day.

But that's not the brilliant part. The brilliant part was cross-referencing the map with Dad's topographical map of the city. I was able to draw in all the altitude lines right over my street map. Immediately I started gaining a better perspective of the situation around me. For example, I couldn't comprehend the fact people were saying the Norwood Shopping Centre survived the tsunami. That totally contradicted what I thought I saw on impact night. But as soon as I drew the contours on the map it made perfect sense. See, I saw the tsunami hit Portrush Rd just north of my place and assumed the Parade at Norwood was all underwater as it's only a few hundred metres south of here and closer to the beach. But the contour – 75m above sea level – runs at virtually 45 degrees through this area, meaning the tsunami may well have only got to Osmond Terrace at Norwood. I would've never guessed that, even having travelled the terrain often.

So I've given myself a bonus mission tomorrow. I need to work out exactly how far the waters came up the Parade at Norwood then, when I return home, I can work out exactly where the tsunami reached all through my local area. I have these thoughts of one day needing food again and thinking the best place to top up supplies will be houses left on the devastated side of the tsunami.

****

Tuesday, April 29, 2014

10am: I'm starting to get pretty good with daily routines – cleaning, eating, planning etc. I'm actually impressing myself because they are a long, long way from my strong suit. I think it's because life is now so devoid of day-to-day distractions (compared to pre-rock) I'm kinda evolving to just embrace anything that even slightly resembles something interesting to do. Anything that takes me away from the banality of the daily grind helps keep me sane.

Breakfast used to be something I ate to stop me getting hungry until lunch.

Now, breakfast is a myriad of rituals and routines. Breakfast is – what to eat (pancakes, cereal with long-life milk, or make a loaf of bread, which presents a whole new world of options) what mood I think I'm in and what music I should play to either change or enhance that mood. Once I'm happy with the music I make a note of my meal choice... in my little scorecard! Yes, I have a scorecard – to keep track of supplies and the rate I'm going through them. But I don't just mark down what I've had, oh no, I also commentate on what I'm doing, like I'm a TV presenter and it's the last quarter of a close footy match! Then comes the food presentation. I now go to the extra effort of plating up something nice, which I also commentate on like I'm doing the voiceover for a contestant on a cooking show. Then there's the eating. Here, I morph into one of three separate reality cooking show judges, who in turn make comment on the food they're sampling. Once I've finished I become the reality show cook again who is informed of the judges' results. I know, I know, I'm a little sad.

After breakfast I like to get myself a cup of coffee and either jot down things in my diary – like now – or read when I have nothing meaningful to say. Once that is done I crank the music up and do the dishes.

So the whole breakfast process has gone from a 15-minute necessity to an hour-plus extravaganza. It's all about the routine, about feeling like I'm engaged and doing something with purpose the entire time.

That said, I think all this time on my own is starting to drive me slightly mad. If everything I've revealed above isn't enough of a sign, I also talk to myself a hell of a lot. I think it helps keep me engaged and distracted but I also realise it's making me act in ways that are slightly, well, mental. I mean, if a version of me from a few weeks ago was a fly on the wall watching me make breakfast – impersonating sports commentators and reality show judges, and laughing at some of my own jokes – I think he'd have me committed. God, and this is after two and a bit weeks. What am I going to be like after a year or more?

And the irony isn't lost on me – I'm acting this way to stay sane and all it's doing is making me another kind of crazy!

Another little routine I have is one I'm preparing for shortly – cleaning the door entries and paths. I do it every time I leave the house. There's no point getting the outside gear on just to do chores; I'd rather multitask with another outside activity. It makes doing one of the world's dirtiest chores at least semi-bearable knowing you're doing something outside afterwards.

Whatever happens on the expedition, outside days are good days.
*

7pm: What a day. There were as many as 50 people gathered for the expeditions. I was really surprised by the number – it was probably a sign everyone wanted to help keep as much of their destiny in their own hands as possible. I certainly did; that's why I went.

It wasn't too hard to tag along with the group heading to Norwood because when they divided everyone up according to where they wanted to go, there was a pretty even split. There ended up being 19 going to Norwood and 30 (I think) heading to Firle.

A woman called Mia Martin pretty much assumed the alpha-type leadership role and everyone was reasonably happy to fall in line behind her. It's amazing how much a first impression can influence, I s'pose, and Mia, along with her partner, Craig, made the best one of all. They stood out – or over – everyone. Literally. They'd somehow cut the heads off tennis racquets and strapped them to their boots. Then they'd wound some fabric around the racquet head to form a kind of snow shoe. All of which meant their feet had a far greater surface area and didn't sink through the ash. They walked on top of it. Brilliant. I remember thinking at that moment if I didn't learn another thing from today it was already worth my while.

It was a bit hard not to be impressed – the pair of them looked like giants compared to everyone else as the ash was probably 60cm deep! Plus, they each had one of those miner's hardhats with the lights, some really serious looking hiking clothes, drink canteens and a number of containers you imagine would hold anything you'd ever need. I felt like a survivalist amateur in their presence. I knew I had to stay close to see if I could learn any new tricks as the day went on.

The trek to the shopping centre on the Parade took just over two hours. That's a pace of about 1km per hour! So slow. If anything, though, it was slightly quicker than my solo trips. We operated somewhat like a Tour de France peloton, each person taking turns at the front, pushing through the thick ash and sludge, doing the heavy lifting for the one behind, who made each step easier for the person behind them, etc, etc. Once your stint at the front was done you'd just shuffle to the side, wait for the pack to filter past, then join in again at the back where the steps were easy but the pace was super slow.

Mia and Craig skated alongside and over us, pointing out obstacles ahead and generally encouraging us.

I don't think I'll ever forget that experience; it was completely surreal. We had decent conditions weather-wise, and with most people carrying torches it made for the best vision (distance-wise) since the ash closed in on Adelaide.

We travelled along the main roads too, straight up the middle of Portrush until we hit the Parade. It's the first time that 'outside' nearly felt like actually being outside and not like some dodgy movie studio set. With the wide-open spaces of the main roads, the quietness and stillness of it all, it felt so liberating. And then there was us, ploughing through the middle of the wide brown, bad, Cadburyness like we were a bunch of hobbits and dwarves, ferried along by Craig the Human and Mia the Elf in some crazy fellowship on an adventure to Mount Doom.

I couldn't keep the smile off my face for some reason. It was such a release being part of a crowd with a shared goal, tackling the outside conditions without fear. These were our streets.

As we neared the Parade, evidence of other paths in the ash became obvious – it was the first sign of the activities of other humans. When we turned on to the Parade, someone had kindly left their path in the ash, heading in the same direction we were going. We jumped into their trench and picked up speed. It was scary to see what had happened to Norwood since the rock. The first thing that hit me was the smell. I was breathing with a scarf over my mouth and nose to avoid inhaling ash but it was still overpowering. Just about every shop-front had been damaged – windows damaged, goods ransacked (it must've been a looters' frenzy around here), verandas collapsed from the weight of the ash… it was a disaster area.

There was a front-end loader in the middle of the Parade, covered in ash. Obviously, at some point, someone was trying to fight the inevitable torrent of ash, without luck. The loader was now entombed in the very substance it was trying to defeat.

The Parade used to be one of the best shopping strips in Adelaide and to see it reduced to ruin made the enormity of everything we were facing all the more real. As we headed down the street – downhill and towards the city – the smell intensified. I wasn't keen on knowing why it smelt that bad. Was it water damage, rotting food from the stores, rotting sea creatures stranded miles from the beach or, worse, rotting corpses of another kind? I re-tightened my mouth and nose covering and tried not to think too hard about it. One thing I hadn't banked on was how hard it was going to be to work out how high the waters reached – I hadn't taken into account the ash obscuring most of the visual evidence.

I'm not entirely sure what I was expecting to find at the survivor hub. I'm not sure anyone was, but it was safe to say we were all a little underwhelmed by what we found. I guess when I imagined it in my head the night before,

I pictured being ushered through a processing station then into the shopping centre, which would reveal a hive of activity including food and drink disposal, medical check-ups and information. We'd be informed, fed and hydrated, and leave with a plan for the future. That wasn't too much to ask, right? If I'd imagined the champagne version of the hub the reality presented the shit-sandwich version.

I'd like to describe the people we encountered as officials, but they presented as anything but. There were eight of them all up – set up behind a few coffee tables under the shopping centre entrance canopy right next to Cibo. The first thing that hit me was the attitude – we copped plenty of it. Nothing overt, it has to be said, but there was no doubt we were being looked at as outsiders on their turf. For starters they first asked where we were from and when our response came back as Trinity Gardens, the fat old guy, who seemed to be running the show, suggested that we'd come to the wrong place and that we should consider Firle our survival hub. As for the attitude he emitted when he gave that response, well, let's just say we were destined from that moment to leave Norwood disappointed.

Fats also gestured to a couple of other people standing behind him who disappeared into the shopping centre. He then went on to tell us it was closed due to safety fears, any word of a survivor hub had been over-stated, and they were volunteering their time to inform people that was the case. It all sounded like a bunch of BS to me but it was quite clear we were getting stonewalled.

Mia asked where the army was and Fats told her that word was a gas pipe explosion had destroyed the temporary facility they were using and he doubted there would be any other army officials around in the foreseeable future. After all his attitude earlier he did seem genuinely upset when he relayed that piece of information and, for some reason, I believed it was genuine.

For the rest of it, though, we were just brushed off. We were told it was a case of fending for ourselves now and our best bet was to find out what was going on at Firle. We were told there were limited supplies of food remaining, which had already been divided amongst the local community.

A few people from our group fired questions at the fat man. I even got my question in about how far up the Parade the tsunami came – about a block east of Osmand Terrace apparently. Generally, though, the fat man made what he obviously thought seemed like a genuine attempt to answer things, but to me it looked like he was hiding something. Before long, the two people who'd left earlier came back with another dozen or so guys – they were trying to intimidate us into leaving. Or maybe they felt intimidated and, being out-numbered, were trying to even up the game a little. Either way, once that happened there was massive tension in the air. It didn't take long for me to feel totally exposed – if it turned nasty I was the youngest and skinniest person there and I don't think I've been in a fight since I was 12! And I lost (she was bigger than me).

Mia played it well though. She appeased the fat man and just asked for as much information as possible to take back to the people of Trinity Gardens. The fat man obliged and reeled out a bunch of info to keep us happy.

With that, we, the fellowship of the ash, left to trudge back to Trinity Gardens. The way back was much quicker as we retraced our own trail, using the trench we'd carved out of the ash to save time and effort. It was a humbling return though – especially after feeling so invincible on the way down. It seems to me that yet again, geography and dumb luck will be the keys to survival. On the night of the impacts those factors decided peoples' fate and, yet again, they hold the tickets to survival. This time, however, proximity to supplies is your friend. The fat man and his friends had it and we didn't. They sure as hell aren't telling us what they've got but you can bet it's more than we do.

It's difficult to project forward with the world changing on almost a daily basis, but it's not hard to see how things could get very tribal, very quickly. That'd be a pretty sad way for all this to go down, in my opinion, but maybe it's inevitable. Maybe it just has to be that way.

That's not good news for the people of Trinity Gardens. Not that it changes things for me, but for everyone else… it's seriously not good.

I wonder how much could possibly be stored at the shopping centre anyways. Surely supplies would be running fairly thin as it is? I mean, there were queues around the block to buy food for the last 48 hours pre-rock. What could possibly be left? But then again, I know they were having problems distributing the extra supplies that came in and people were still getting supplies on impact night. Maybe there is a goldmine in there after all, enough for the fat man to lie about it.

I hoped the Firle party had more luck but I wasn't holding my breath.

…and with good reason as it turned out. The Firle expedition was waiting for us when we returned. They had heard a similar story about the gas explosion, so we figured two separate sources made it fairly reliable. There is no army in Adelaide any more, or not enough to matter. Apparently the Firle hub experience was a far friendlier affair, but the bottom line was they were almost entirely out of food, with all-but-zero hope of resupply. Again, this gets me suspicious – they're hardly going to say, 'yep, we're loaded, help yourself new people'.

The next hour or so was spent working out our community's next move. Some people wanted to pool food resources at the school so the remaining supplies could be dolled out evenly. Some people were completely against that idea. I'm guessing they were the ones who thought they had more food than they'd get from the collective sharing.

In the end it was agreed the next step was to sweep the streets, determine which houses were unoccupied and swipe all their food. The resultant bounty would then be shared amongst the group. I thought it was a pretty good and fair plan actually, and with any luck we could gather enough food to keep us going for a couple of weeks more.

Some people wanted to head back to Norwood in greater numbers and find out exactly what was going on but it was decided, for now, we would use what we potentially had at our disposal before heading further afield.

It was interesting to see all the politicking going on during the meeting. It seems like a few people were pumping up their own tires to take leadership roles. God there are some real posers out there – it's amazing how many people think watching a couple of episodes of Bear Grylls makes them an expert in post-apocalyptic survival. I, for one, was happy just to observe – I don't think they'd listen to a teenager anyway. Plus, I still want to lay low. I also get the feeling everyone is playing poker with what resources they actually have left. No one was in a hurry to reveal their 'hand' unless it was those who were virtually down to nothing.

So the end result is a group of people who perhaps need each other more than they trust each other.

Tomorrow I'm heading out with an early 30s couple – Mark and Jemma (I think). They live just up the street from me and I met them the other day when I went around to all the houses on the street. They're nice enough so I'm happy to team up with them. We've been assigned three streets to go down, including mine. It'll be interesting to see what we can come up with. The bigger group meeting has been pushed back from 10am to 5pm so everyone has time to get to all the houses they need to get to.

*

9pm: I'm exhausted from today's journey. Even with the help of the fellowship, pushing your way through that much ash takes its toll. It's funny, when I was slogging my way back from Norwood all I could think about was coming home, kicking my feet up and hammering the Xbox. However, when I did finally fire the console up, I felt guilty – I should've been preparing for tomorrow. The guilt won the battle over lazy, I guess, and I spent most of my time in the war room where I finished the street map of the area. The other day I'd started putting in the property boundaries – mostly from memory. Tonight I remembered I'd printed out the Google maps view of the area with the actual property boundaries on it. So I overlaid them on the local map, going out four blocks in every direction from home. I also printed out a couple of copies of the street map view of the local area to take with me tomorrow – one for me and one for Mark and Jemma. It should help us document everything.

Paranoia seems to surround everything I do, even to the point of coming up with a story as to why I have the street view printouts. I'm not sure I want people knowing I have electricity just yet but I think I can justify it all as something I did pre-rock.

So that was my night. I'm getting pretty tired and I might hit the hay pretty soon. In fact I've noticed how I'm getting up earlier and going to sleep earlier these days. Not really sure what that's all about.

****

Wednesday, April 30, 2014

8.30pm: Another day of memories that will stay with me forever. In fact, looking back on today, I feel like I went out this morning somewhat innocent still, but I write in my diary now anything but.

I met up with Mark and Jemma right after breakfast and we began our sweep of the area. They seemed like a pretty nice couple actually. There were recently married and had just bought a house up the street. He worked for the bank and she was a graphic designer; interesting combo, I thought. But they were really nice to me and didn't treat me like a kid. I guess the fact I came prepared with maps, food and drink, a large backpack, tools (a crowbar to open doors and a shovel and broom to clear them) and a knife (just in case) meant I earned a little 'adult cred'.

I think we hit over 150 houses all up and it could best be described as a mixed bag. The general plan of attack was to approach each house, knock at the door and wait for a response. If we got one we'd tell the residents we were taking details from everyone in the area and finding out if they needed anything. It must be said the responses varied greatly. Similar to when I went out by myself the other week there were a lot of non-trusting people. I can't say I blame them really, I wouldn't trust a bunch of people I didn't know if they came to my door – no matter how harmless they looked. So, we got a lot of very short answers from some. Others, however, were very pleased to see us and more than happy to tell us how they were going and what supplies they had. Maybe they were desperate, or lonely, or whatever, but they were the good ones.

Things got tricky when no one answered the door. We'd wait a few moments then knock again, then knock a third time saying who we were, who we were representing and that if no one answered we would enter the property to see if everyone was OK. We got a few responses after that. Clearly there are a lot of people who don't want to be bothered. Most of the time these people answered with a two-word suggestion as to where we should go and how we should get there!

Things got really nerve-racking when we had no response after the third knock. We'd pause again, then Mark would say something like, 'If we don't hear from you in the next three seconds we'll assume you are either not home or injured and we'll be forced to enter the property to see if you're OK'. We did get a couple of replies at this late stage – again of the two-word variety – but mostly we heard nothing. That meant the coast was clear and it was time to go into action.

I was surprised how nervous I got doing it, breaking in, especially the first time. My heart was beating like I'd just run the 100m – Mark and Jemma were the same. Mark would jimmy open the door, Jemma would commentate on what we were doing in a soothing voice, in case there were people inside I guess, and I had my knife at the ready in case there were any unexpected situations.

Fortunately, we didn't come across any shotgun-wielding psychos on the other side of any door. But that didn't stop me getting the feeling there could be one at each house we went to. From there we'd do a quick check of the house to make sure all was clear. When we were satisfied the coast was clear, we'd split up searching the house for anything useful – most importantly, food and water.

If that was the pattern of how the day went all would've been fine but, of course, nothing's ever that easy! I'd chatted with Mark and Jemma about the possibility of seeing a dead body on our travels. I mean, we realised it would be a possibility, but what we didn't realise was how many we'd see. Seven. Seven dead bodies. I'd never even seen a corpse first-hand before today. Even with all the things going on around me in recent days, I'd never actually laid eyes on a real dead body. They're creepy too. Doubly creepy seeing them stone cold and stuck in the spot they'd died in. I mean, if we'd never come, would they've been like that forever?

And the stink. It was indescribably horrid. It seared the hairs from my nostrils I'm sure, even through the scarf over my face.

I'll remember them all, but three stood out to me as sights that'll be burnt into my memory forever. The first was an old lady, she must've been in her '70s or early '80s maybe. She was laying on her bed, cuddling a family photo in a frame – it was her from years ago with, I'm assuming, her husband and three kids. God, it was hard to look at. In a way it summed up how tragic this whole apocalypse situation is. Despite how many people this lady had who cared for her in this world, she died sad and alone... broken. It nearly broke me looking at her.

There were a few other deceased oldies discovered... is it insensitive that it got a bit easier with each one? It did. None of them hit me like the first one. There was even one old guy who looked like he'd topped himself. He was sitting dead on his couch with an empty bottle of pills and a suicide note laying next to him.

The second body that was hard to deal with was the young Asian guy who had hung himself in the bathroom of his flat near Portrush Rd. Judging by the decorations, pictures and posters he had up we reckoned he was a foreign student. Poor guy. I wonder if he'd had a chance to get in touch with his family before he... did what he did. Another sad, lonely, and maybe pointless end. I wondered how many other silent victims there were in this disaster. How many stories will never be told, or never have a proper or dignified end.

The final body I'll never forget is that of the woman up the street. She had been stabbed, a lot. It was a horrible scene. I'm not entirely sure I can bring myself to write down exactly what I saw but there was blood, lots of it. Again you can't help but play out in your mind what might've happened to her. Mark, Jemma and I tried to figure out the lady's final moments from the scene in front of us. Although part of me wanted to leave straight away, the other part found trying to make some sense of it therapeutic. She had cuts on her hands and arms as well as her chest so we guessed she was trying to defend herself from her attacker. We wondered why somebody would do this – vendetta, jealousy, random attack maybe? Mark checked the cupboard and fridge. They were pretty bare and whatever remained in the fridge made opening the door give off a smell almost comparable with the rest of the living area. The sad truth appeared to be she was murdered for her food. If that was the case, things just got a lot creepier. And on this very street where we live! Was it a local who did it? Very likely given how hard it is to get around. Who would do something like this? Probably someone who knew her, or knew enough about her to know she was alone and they could overpower her.

That seemed like a pretty likely outcome to the three of us, and it was a very scary one for me. Wow. Murder near home. If that really was the case, all of my paranoid thoughts have been justified. I mean, if whoever did this knew I lived alone they might see me as a target. I felt very vulnerable. Maybe this was a timely reminder to keep my head down. The community has brought me out of my shell in the last few days, but I can't let that relax me. If someone gets to me at home… well, my survival prospects may be very short lived.

I don't think Mark, Jemma or I could get the visions of the dead out of our heads. It made the task of cataloguing and collecting food a very sombre one. It put a massive dampener on what was a successful trip, because in the end we found more food than we could possibly carry. Most of the vacant houses had a bunch of decent stuff in the pantry – cans, pasta, cereal, jam, biscuits, flour etc. It would take two or three trips to gather our supplies and carry them to the school. And then there was booty house (as we dubbed it), which was abandoned and completely stocked with long-life products. We discovered it pretty late in the day so it made the find all the more special, to the point where we were almost crying with joy (in my defence, I think I was pretty emotionally drained at the time). The find was so big we were wondering who the hell would stockpile so much stuff and not be there to eat it. Maybe they spent rock night somewhere else and never made it back or maybe it was just some crazy pensioner who liked to make sure there was plenty of stock around just in case. Either way, this was the score of the day.

But that was where things took another interesting turn. I knew something was up with Jemma and Mark – they started acting weird. Then they made their move. Jemma was the one who spoke. She talked about how the three of us had gone over and above the call of duty for the community and the rest of the booty was more than enough to come back with, so no one needed to know about the big score. They basically suggested we keep it for ourselves, splitting it three ways. At first I was shocked. I really hadn't expected that from them. I mean, they seemed so genuine and kind. But I guess it goes to show when it all boils down to it this is just a game of survival and even supplying the greater group is not as important as looking after yourself.

They appealed to me to consider their idea, saying if I really thought about how much food I had left it made sense to take more to survive. They told me this booty find was so large and rare we were meant to find it. Of course this all brought back thoughts of how large my own stash already was. The guilt burned.

But, the way I saw it, there was no other choice but to agree. I mean, they made some logical arguments (in terms of appealing to my need for survival) and if I declined it would raise eyebrows at the least and create some massive distrust at most. By agreeing I figured I'd have two people I could trust as we had a shared secret. So it was decided.

It was probably 4.30pm when we headed back to the school – physically exhausted, emotionally drained and secretly pleased. We took as much as our backpacks could carry. We agreed to meet up again the next morning to bury the bodies, take the rest of the food to the school (probably two loads) and then collect our secret booty. So another full day coming up – and maybe burying the bodies will take away some of the guilt from stealing the stash.

Back at the school there were mixed emotions. It seemed the sort of stories we had to tell were echoed across most groups. Small finds, medium finds, suspicious people, dead bodies, even other murders. But despite some of the gore and horror that was coming out, there was a definite feeling of triumph in the air. I mean, yesterday we were low on food and hope, feeling very isolated from the world, but today we were sitting on a bounty of food, with more to come, and a feeling we could make it. However long 'make-it' would go for.

As the food was being sorted the stories kept flowing. So did the newly found alcohol. It was hard to concentrate as I already had so much going through my head. But the things that interested me most were the other murders and the fact no one else had made a large food discovery.

Do we have a rogue killer running around? Or many killers? Actually, I'm not sure I want to know – is one really better than the other? And was our large haul really the only significant find of the day? From what must have been 2000 houses, maybe more. What are the odds of that? I think the chances are better that other people are keeping things for themselves too. So it feels to me that under the surface of all this community happiness, and everything we've achieved today, there's this sickening feeling that I'm surrounded by liars and killers.

****

Thursday, May 1, 2014

6.15pm: Another day, another slog on the road, made a whole lot worse by the weather. The wind was up, which made the already freezing conditions even freezinger (that's definitely a word). My fingers are still half numb as I write this. The wind also meant the ash was falling again, which partially covered the tracks we'd made yesterday. I'm not sure if it was new ash falling from the black sky or just stuff that had been whipped up from the ground, but either way, it was highly annoying.

First up was getting the other goods to the school. We managed the bulk of it in two trips and decided to leave the dregs due to time restraints (plus, it's good knowing we have a little something leftover, just in case).

Then came the hard part – burying the bodies. It was time consuming and hard work but, most of all, it meant dealing with everything we saw yesterday again. At least this time I was mentally prepared but in truth I'm not sure that made it too much easier.

We buried them in the ash out the back of their places. We didn't dig down six feet, but certainly far enough for some dignity. We then placed a simple cross – made by Mark last night – on each of the gravesite. We then gave each person a minute's silence before moving on to the next burial.

We'd been on the move for eight hours before we had to deal with the secret stash. To be honest, it was weird, going from doing something good and honest in memory of some poor soul to doing something quite devious and sneaky for selfish reasons. There wasn't much talking from any of us, apart from establishing how the split would work.

It was decided we would each fill our backpacks once then return in the morning to take another load. We agreed trust was important so none of us were allowed to tell anyone what we'd done, nor return to the property before 9am the next day. With that we left.

*

10pm: I'm absolutely stuffed. My legs ache like I've run a marathon (this is a guess as I have never even thought of running a marathon and, given it is now all but impossible to run 2m, let alone 42km, it's pretty safe to say I never will), my stomach aches, my arms ache, even my butt aches! I don't even know how I'll muster the energy to go out again tomorrow.

I should be sound asleep by now; my body is pleading with me to go to the land of nod, but my mind is sabotaging everything. There are so many thoughts running through my head and I can't get them to stop. The thought of the dead bodies is haunting me. Just imagining potential last moments –

over and over again. And it's not doing me any good. Then I start thinking of Mum and Dad (yes, I cried), then I wonder what they'd think of what I've done – stealing supplies from the group. Would they be disappointed in me? Most likely. Then I start thinking of my brother and if he's safe or not, and if I'll ever see him again.

It's all driving me insane. And when I try to take my mind off it all, the only thing I can think about is my life right now and this house. Which then leads me to think about how safe I actually am, given there's at least one killer on the loose around here.

Wow, talk about messed up.

I think I'd boxed it all up – everything from the last few days – and tonight it's all coming out. Bleak – that's the word. My current situation, the future, who I've become – it all just feels so bleak.

I don't know what to do about it either. I really don't. The best I can come up with is to get all business-like tomorrow, meet Mark and Jenna, collect the stash, then come home and distract myself. I can feel a games day coming on. I don't even know if that's gonna be enough, but it's all I can think of right now to try and take my mind off of things.

****

Friday, May 2, 2014
2.30pm: Done. It's all done. I'm now officially putting the last three days out of my memory. Gone. Did you hear that stupid mind? All thoughts on the last three days are G O N E – GONE!!!!
*

9pm: Well, I did manage to get a couple of hours of gaming in before the whole pointlessness of it, all overwhelmed me. In the end I just felt compelled to put on the most depressing music I could find and draw random pictures. I ended up drawing this A3-sized cartoon art of the comet and death and destruction and darkness and ash. I started to feel somewhat better after that. I should do more artwork actually, it turned out pretty well.

In fact I'm gonna continue my drawing therapy now… with a beer… or two… I deserve it.

****

91

Sunday, May 4, 2014

4.20pm: I'm slowly getting my mojo back after some serious slob therapy. I can put a line through another *Red Dwarf* book, another game campaign (*Mass Effect* – been at that one for a few sessions now) and the first two seasons of *Peep Show* (an awesome comedy discovery on my brother's hard drive).

It hasn't been all fun and games, though. When I've been bored of slobbing I've been working on my own pair of sled boots so I don't have to wade through the sludgy ash any more. At first I set myself to replicate what I'd seen Mia and Craig wear on the Norwood run, but something (my ego) made me want to invent something better.

That's when I remembered Dad's cross-country skis. I figured they'd be perfect for the job as the walking motion in them would be similar to what I need. Because they had no heel clip I was hoping I'd get a result with an easier walk action.

It was totally worth the 90 minutes it took to get into the shed (damn ash) and find them. I cut the heads off two tennis racquets then cut grooves into each ski so the racquet heads locked in. I then trimmed the skis an inch either side of the grooves, put the racquet heads in place and secured them with a couple of strips of metal and some screws. Once the basics were done I gaffer-taped the hell out of it all then cut and stitched the racquet cases so they could act as a giant sole for my new sled-shoes. I've got to say I'm stoked with the results – they're sturdy as all hell and when I gave them a test run on the ash I zipped across the surface.

Now I've just got to find an excuse to test them out in the real world. I might head out tomorrow. I can sweep the paths, head to the school to find out what's been going on or if they need me, then head to the Hardos to see why they've dropped off the radar. Am I concerned? Well, yeah, I am. I try not to think about it too much, but with them just dropping out of existence, coupled with the fact there have been more than a couple of murders recently, well… I just try not to think about it.

*

9.15pm: I've actually enjoyed my time away from the community. I really needed it. It'll be interesting to see what happens when I plug back in though. It's a funny contradiction really. I mean, I need them for the company to keep me sane and to find out what's going on, and maybe other things in the future, but they, the community, bring about more than their fair share of stress.

****

Monday, May 5, 2014

8.15pm: I really think this world is doing its best to strip me of everything I give a stuff about. I think it's conspiring to leave me alone and isolated. Today was just another perfect example of shit-storm city.

I'm shaking right now. Just absolutely shaking, edgy, cold and numb. I'll try and remember as much as I can coz I feel I need to get all this down.

If I recall everything in chronological order then I can get the good news out of the way first. The boots – my new ash boots as I call them – worked a treat. What a difference it makes with travel times and the physical energy required when I can just skim across the surface of the ash. Massive win me.

Here endeth the good news.

I got to the school about 10am (I didn't want to get there too early in case no one was around). Some lady in her fifties was on the gate and gave me a goodie bag of long-life food stuff. I told her I didn't really need it yet but she looked me up and down and insisted I take it. I'm gonna assume that's a comment on how stick skinny I am. In the gym the community have set up some sort of operations area. They had a bunch of people busily working away. The food supplies took up a large chunk of the space (I can't believe how much was gathered the other day) and there were several people stocktaking, I think.

By the far wall I could see Mia and Craig and a few others in deep conversation so I decided to get a bit closer (eavesdropping distance) while I looked through my food gift. I could see on the floor in front of them they'd set up a huge map of the area – much like my war room – and they had a bunch of markers in different colours on the map.

They were talking about supplies, logistics and the number of people we had to feed. I'm not sure I got all the details, but they were saying they'd probably collected enough food for 10-11 days and that we'd have to revisit Norwood. I've got the feeling our Norwood 'revisit' might not be as friendly as the last one – and that was far from friendly.

I found myself inching closer to the conversation to the point where there was no denying my eavesdropping. Not that anyone asked straight away. The whole operation is pretty casual really. I studied the various markers on the map and that's when I started to get that sinking feeling once more. It didn't take long to decipher enough of the code to know what was going on. I just had to recall the street I'd been though on my reconnaissance with Mark and Jemma and match what happened at specific addresses with the icons these addresses displayed. Monopoly hotels marked where the community members lived and Monopoly houses indicated other known occupied properties. Green poker chips indicated where we'd cleaned out food, red chips were the places where people had passed away and the black chips… the goddam black chips… that's where people had been murdered. There were also other coloured chips scattered around whose meaning didn't immediately seem obvious.

I couldn't help myself. As soon as I decoded that black marker I scanned the rest of the map to see where they were. I counted 17 in total – that's not good. I was relieved as hell to see there were none on the Hardigan's property. They did have a white chip marker so I was very curious to know what that meant. I approached Mia for help and she directed me to some guy – mid-40s, I reckon – who was in charge of the search of the Hardigan's area. His name was Malcolm. I asked him what he knew.

He told me the white chip meant a vacant property that had recent signs of life so it wasn't raided for food in case the occupants were out. Mark, Jemma and I hadn't come across too many houses like that in our search, but they did stand out when we did. The true vacant houses (the green chips) had a layer of ash and dust over everything – most places had at least a centimetre's worth accumulated whereas the white chips were weirdly clean – it was an obvious sign of activity. It's amazing how obvious the footprints of our presence are these days.

I pressed Malcolm for more info on the Hardigans but he was frustratingly vague on details. To his credit though, he tried his best to think of something as he knew I knew the family who lived there but he just drew a blank. I do understand the vagueness – most of the houses from my search blur into one now. It didn't make it any less frustrating but I understood. But what he lacked in detail he definitely made up for in his certainty he hadn't made any mistakes. He told me he had a three-check system to mark everything down, so if the place was marked as white chip it was definitely white chip.

I decided to let both Malcolm and Mia know I was going to head over to the Hardigans to see what was up. Mia asked that I touch base back at the school when I was done, which I was happy to do.

She also checked out my ash boots (which I had slung over my shoulder) and was more than impressed with my handiwork. I know it wasn't much, but I was pretty happy to get a compliment from her, given she had set the boots trend in the first place. She also told me about a big community meeting on Thursday morning, which sounded like a must-attend. It was to plan our next move in terms of securing food and drink supplies. She was saying despite everything we had gathered so far, we probably only had enough for another

10 days to two weeks. I have a feeling things are going to get very interesting after that.

As I walked to the Hardigans, my thoughts were divided between why they weren't at the property, what might have happened to them and how impressed I was with the organisation of the community. There was a real buzz at the school today and it felt pretty cool to be a part of it, even though I was on the periphery. I still constantly debate whether or not I should be spending more time there. I think it would be good for my sanity to be in touch with people more often but, at the same time, I can't help but think I'll somehow let slip how much stuff I have. I mean, maybe not now, but when times get desperate – and they will – I might go soft and donate my stash to the cause.

Is it cruel I'm avoiding getting too close so I won't get too sympathetic when things get tough? I mean, if I really get to know these people, surely I won't be able to keep my food to myself? I'll get all guilty and stuff. Therefore I'm avoiding that outcome by keeping myself at a distance. Do I feel bad about? Yes. But that's the choice I'm making.

Anyways, I'm gabbing on right now, just jotting down any old thought that helps me avoid writing what came next.

It took about 20 minutes to get to the Hardigans – a far cry from the hour-long epic a week ago. As I got closer I had a sense of dread, which kept rising. For some reason I knew something was up. The door was closed but not locked. I did knock a couple of times, then called out for Hardo, but there was no response so I just headed in.

I yelled out a few more times as I got to the lounge-dining room – still no response. The place was almost exactly as I saw it last… kinda creepy with no one around.

I did see a note on the table – from Malcolm – saying he'd been in to see if everyone was OK and since there were signs of recent life he'd come back next week.

Then I checked the house from top to bottom. Garage, cupboards, wardrobes – everywhere. Still nothing. I did notice almost all of the food was gone, which either meant they'd done a runner to somewhere else or something bad had happened. Then it occurred to me to check outside – I wish it hadn't. I used the back sliding door to get on to the patio – it was undercover but the ash had still managed to pile up somewhat. There was nothing there and nothing in the shed. It was only when I rounded the side of the house that I saw them – well when I say 'them' I mean suspicious piles in the ash. They were by the laundry door, literally right outside. Dead. I saw Mrs Hardigan first. I got a good grip on her hand and managed to pull her clear of the ash. She was stiff as hell. She'd been shot in the chest.

The other two took more work to pull up as they were both bigger than me. It was gruesome. The blood; coagulated and curdled, covered in ash. The looks on their faces; stuck there forevermore. The smell – it was all so horrible. I just went into block-out mode. I gave myself the job of burying them and didn't think about all the disgusting things I was doing to make that happen. It took about an hour. Just like I did with Mum and Dad's funerals, I found some personal items inside to bury with them.

I didn't cry. Not once. It was almost too much to take in – so much to cry about I wasn't even capable of it. I feel more alone than ever before. Each day something seems to be taken away from me, whether it's someone I care about, my belief I can get through this, or a piece of my hope. Screw this place.

The rest of the day has been a blur. The only thing I really remember with any clarity was walking back into the school, making a bee-line for the map on the gym floor, removing the white poker chip and replacing it with a black one. I then just marched my ass straight out the door. Someone tried to stop me to find out what had happened but the look on my face must've told them I wasn't in the mood for polite conversation so they left me alone.

****

Wednesday, May 7, 2014
2.15pm: Feeling a little guilty for my slackness on diary entries, but I seriously haven't been in the mood. Today I left the house for the first time since Monday. Thank God for the big community meeting, otherwise I think I'd still be moping around. Not that I'm much better mind you, just fresher and slightly more human from the walk.

Things got pretty heated at the meeting today. There are a bunch of people in the community who want to march down to Norwood and start World War III. I thought those in charge did a pretty good job of calming everyone down because it did threaten to get out of control a few times.

The mood has definitely changed from Monday. The food stocks are noticeably reduced – I think that's acting as a constant reminder to people we've got to think of something fast or else it's all going to hell.

The meeting probably went for a couple of hours. In the end it was decided the best approach was to send two representatives down to Norwood to try to get some straight answers out of them. Mia and a guy called Anthony Rossi –

a lawyer in his late 50s – drew the short straw. It was decided they were both smart enough to get to the truth of what was going on yet they didn't appear physically intimidating.

They're going to head down on Saturday morning and there's another meeting at the school later that afternoon to spread the word. If Mia and Anthony don't get support, help or satisfactory answers we're going to send down a posse to open a can of whoopass down there. After tonight's meeting I'm pretty sure there'll be no shortage of volunteers to be part of that group. I'm still deciding whether or not I'll go if it comes to that. I think I'll just play it by ear until Mia and Anthony report back.

I find myself obsessing over the murders when I'm in larger groups at the community. I spend a lot of time trying to suss everyone out to see if they have certain mannerisms or a look in their eye that could mean they are a killer. Probably not a good day to do that with everyone so fired up... almost all of them could be!

*

9.45pm: Feeling pretty lonely at the moment. With everything that's gone on over the last few weeks, and after what happened on Monday, I'm in a bit of a rut. I'm not really sure how to deal with it either; all the usual things I do to take my mind off life aren't quite cutting it. I really need to break things up and do something new, but the options are somewhat limited, to say the least. So I'm at a bit of a dead-end; I just know moping about it all ain't doing me any favours.

The other thing I can't get out of my head is the murders. I try not to let it get into my head because I feel very exposed on my own – especially when a family of three can be beaten. What if someone walks up to the door with a gun? There's no one to protect me, no one to hear me scream, nowhere on the streets to go for help. I'm pretty much screwed. I have faith in the security I've set up, just no faith in the people around here.

****

Thursday, May 8, 2014
2.20pm: There was a knock at the door this morning – scared the crap out of me. At first I froze, hoping they'd go away. There was another knock after a few seconds. I yelled out 'who is it?' but I knew they couldn't hear me through the driving wind outside. I scurried about trying to find one of the weapons I have scattered around the house – thank God for the crossbow!

My heart was racing like crazy when I went through the wardrobe to the front door entrance. I left the safety latch attached and opened the door about 5cm. I was paranoid there'd be a gun pointed at me from the other end so I didn't stick my head in the gap, just yelled out 'who is it?' again. My hands were shaking, with one on the door handle and one on the crossbow. I can't believe I didn't launch an arrow into my foot or something. Anyways, it was all for nothing as it was Mr Nichols from next door. Relief is an understatement – I dropped the crossbow, opened the door and invited him in.

I can't believe I'd forgotten all about him – I felt very guilty. I was at his door the other day with Mark and Jemma when he told us to 'go away' (he can get like that), but it was only seeing him today that reminded me of that. Maybe my subconscious blocked him out or put him in the too-hard basket. Some neighbour I am!

He's got to be in his mid-70s and he looked very frail, tired and dirty. He said he didn't want to come in but needed my help with a few things at his house so I agreed to head over.

Before I left I made sure to turn all the lights off and got mad at myself for not thinking about doing that before I opened the door. What if it had been a stranger? Then I'd be showing off my access to power. That's real smart – they'd be like a moth to the flame until they got into my place. Dumb, dumb, dumb. Rookie error. Won't happen again.

Mr Nichols is a pretty nice guy, I guess. My parents would pop around once every couple of weeks or invite him over for a cup of tea. To be honest though, I've never 100% liked him. I dunno why, maybe it's because he's always given me this look that says, 'you're a kid and I don't like kids'. But either way my parents would've wanted me to help him, whatever the problem.

When I got there the smell hit me straight away – it was like your typical old person's smell but on steroids. I'm not sure what was more toxic – the ash outside or old man reek. I didn't notice how slow Mr Nichols was moving until I followed him through the house; he was favouring his left side and every step looked painful. And the coughing – he had two fits of it when I first got there and pretty much coughed on and off the entire time. The place was in a state of total squalor. It was hard not to feel sorry for him and what his life had been reduced to.

Then he told me he was dying. I really didn't know what to say... I just stuttered and stammered until he told me he has lung cancer. He couldn't get any of his drugs anymore and he wasn't sure how long he had left. God, he'd kept that one from my parents… I think.

Then he cut to the chase – he wanted me to write a letter for him. He spoke between laboured breaths and heavy coughs and I wrote down what he said, as neatly as I could. It was a message to his two daughters and his grandkids, his goodbye. He spoke about how much he loved them and the memories he had raising them and the good times they shared. He then bequeathed (I guess that's how you spell it) each of them a gift.

It was really sad, but at the same time I think I was really helping him. I was helping him come to terms with what he faced. He must've known he'd never see any of them again and that the chances of the letter getting to them were low, but it didn't change the meaning.

I was probably transcribing his words for 20 minutes. Once it was all over I went to get him a drink of water, but realised his only source was the tap – and what came out of there was anything but water. So I quickly nipped back home and got him a drink and a can of soup. He didn't want anything to eat but had a few sips of the water to wet his whistle.

I asked him if there was anything else I could do and, once he'd settled from the drink, he said there was. He asked me to bury him when he was gone. He said he didn't know how long he had left but felt like his time was running out. So I agreed to check on him once a day, and bring some water with me.

I asked where his family lived in the hope I could deliver their gifts. He told me they were at Port Adelaide and Plympton. I'm not sure if he realised both of those suburbs had been overrun with the tsunami, but I offered to take them their gifts. He told me not to be ridiculous and he expected nothing like that from me – he just expected me to 'keep everything safe'. That was the bit that brought tears to my eyes, but I tried not to show it.

After that he all but shooed me out of the house saying he had dying to do. He also thanked me on the way out and told me that when he was gone I was welcome to take anything I wanted.

I sat on the lounge after I got home and thought about this new death experience. After everything I'd seen recently this was so different. Just seeing the state of him and his place and hearing how sick he was – there was nothing in this world anymore for Mr Nichols. I don't usually pray – it's not my thing – but I did then. I prayed he would have a quick and pain-free death.

It's really hard learning to cope with knock after knock after knock. It just goes to show the state of mind that I'm thinking an early end is the best thing for Mr Nichols. I guess that's the thing I need to get my head around most. Death is gonna be regular. It's the new normal and the sooner I get my head around that fact the sooner I might have a chance of coping.

I've just spent a few hours going back through the start of this diary. It was a real eye-opener too. Just reading my thoughts on everything that was happening then, my naive optimism, my plan, what little I knew. I mean, it probably has really helped me (my plan), but back then I would've never thought things would end up like this.

I also really noticed how many details I remembered from events I'd forgotten to record in the diary. So I started adding in notes of everything I missed. It's amazing how much additional info came to me as I read. I mean, I'm talking a serious amount – it's like my memory is the razor-sharpest it's ever been. I think I'm putting that down to the fact I have far fewer distractions in life – less social life, social media, TV, games… everything. It just means more time spent actually concentrating on what I'm doing… and remembering all the details. I think I'm gonna re-write the whole thing when I get some time but that's a project for another day.

The other thing that stood out for me were the two encounters with the girls – back when I was a pre-comet stud! Those moments were so hot. Being touched, being intimate, having someone, I miss that.

****

Friday, May 9, 2014
11.30am: Fuel's been getting low in the generators for some time. I haven't worried about it too much because they run on standard petrol (with a bit of oil) and one of the blessings for me in the massive ash dump is no cars have moved since just after impact day. The street are literally littered with cars, half buried in ash, ready to lighten their load #easyenergywin.

I try to use the generators sparingly. I mean, they'd be on probably 14 hours a day, but I'll only have a couple of lights on for the bulk of that time. There's no fridge running anymore, which was a big power-drainer, and I'm not running any heating, despite how cold it gets in here. I've had a pretty good run with it and I've only just started using my last jerrycan this morning. I'm pretty happy with that as a pace, but it was definitely time to stock up.

It was a bit of a pain in the arse but I decided my best bet was to head to the car yard on Portrush Rd. For a start, there were plenty of cars there, and I didn't really want to steal from the neighbours if I didn't have to.

The initial plan was to take two jerrycans, but that was soon cut back to one as the extra weight was pushing me deeper into the ash and made walking difficult. That's not to mention how awkward it was struggling to keep balance with a jerrycan in each hand and a hose around my neck – I could only imagine what a struggle it would've been on the way back when the cans were full.

Anyways, the car yard turned out to be the perfect location to get fuel as it had a good dozen cars elevated above the ground. It might not seem like much, but those 30cm were like gold. The cars on the ground were up to their windows in ash and if I was to drain fuel from them I would've had to dig down just to access the fuel hole thingy. Then I would've had to dig down even further to position the jerrycan so gravity could do its work. So the cars on those 'show stands' (or whatever they're called) were a massive time-saver.

Siphoning fuel is a little trick I learned from Dad one day when we pulled over to help a car that had run out of petrol in the middle of nowhere. All you have to do is stick a hose in the tank, put your mouth over the other end of the hose and suck like hell. Once the fuel reaches the other end – and that end is lower to the ground than the end on the petrol tank – the fuel will keep on coming until it's empty.

I found a 4WD, smashed the driver's side window, flipped the fuel door, fed in the garden hose and went to work. I wasn't sure whether there'd be much fuel in a show car, but there was. So much so that I got a mouthful as the fuel ran down the hose quicker than I anticipated. Disgusting.

Oh yeah, that was a fine moment. There I was, laying on the ash, totally filthy, sucking on a hose pipe and then I got a mouth and faceful of fuel until I could jam the hose into the jerrycan. I'm not sure if it could've gotten any more humiliating for me... I'm just glad no dodgy pedo types were watching.

It was a big effort lugging the full jerrycan back to the house, so much so my plans for a three-round trip turned into a two-round trip, as I was exhausted. Still, a good morning's work and I think I'll have access to fuel as long as I need it. High-five!

*

2.40pm: Mr Nichols was looking very bad today. I took him some clean water and canned peaches and had to help him consume both. It was slow work and Mr Nichols had enough halfway through eating the peaches. I stayed around for a few minutes to offer small talk but he wasn't in the mood. Eventually I said my goodbyes and saw myself out. It's really difficult to know what the right thing to do is. Is it best to play bad cop and keep him alive a little longer or let him do what he wants to do – die? I think, for now, I'm just going to follow his wishes. I'm certainly not arrogant enough to think I know what's good for him more than he does.

*

6.15pm: Just got back from the school – Mia and Anthony were telling everyone about their trip to Norwood. They were – surprise, surprise – completely stonewalled. Everyone's pretty pissed about it and we're all meeting back at the school tomorrow to discuss what to do about it. Oh, and we're supposed to come 'prepared for action', as was stated by some of the more aggressive types. I hope this doesn't get too ugly – and I mean before we leave for Norwood.

*

9.30pm: I started rewriting the diary this evening. It's amazing how many bits and pieces I've managed to add in and how many things I think I've forgotten. Anyways, I'm pretty sure this little side project will keep me going for some time. I can see me getting obsessed over it too. I really think the lack of people to talk to somehow makes me want to do more with the diary. It's a form of communication after all, even if the person I'm communicating with is me.

I'm getting a little anxious about tomorrow now. I'm not sure I feel that safe with the group after today's meeting. Mia and Anthony both seem pretty trustworthy – and stable – but I really felt they were losing control of the group this afternoon. Who knows, maybe it was just talk and emotions running high, but if tomorrow morning starts with the same tone it could get out of control

****

Saturday, May 10, 2014

4.50pm: I had a feeling today was showdown day, both within the community and with the Norwood hub clan, but I didn't realise how goddamned crazy it would get or how quickly everything could unravel. It's not the first time I've written in this diary still shaking from things that just happened, but this is insane. I can barely write.

I headed to the school not really knowing whether I'd be going down to Norwood or not. I just wanted to get a vibe for the mentality of the community, really, then play it from there. Was the community after answers or blood? There were definitely people in the group who represented both sides; there was no shortage of weapons on display as we all gathered to talk game plan.

Just like the other day, it got heated – Mia did her best to calm things down but there was no stopping the armed majority. Wow, there were some brutal comments being bandied about and I definitely had to think long and hard about joining the crew to go down there.

In reflection, I didn't think long and hard enough. The atmosphere was clearly toxic and people were acting and speaking before thinking too hard about the outcomes. God, I could see all that plain as day, but I still went along. I guess I got caught up in the bravado of it all... and the action... the promise of something interesting happening... and maybe partly because I thought, despite the heat in the conversation, there could be something positive in terms of food for the community.

It was also the biggest crowd I've seen gathered at the school since the survivor register day. This guy called Brad Thompson seemed to be the voice of the shoot-first brigade. He definitely had the numbers on his side, too – people were almost getting fanatical and it was kinda scary. Again, Mia struggled to steer the plan to a more conservative one, but she was fighting a losing battle and I think she did well to at least not get overrun.

Brad managed to use the numbers to his advantage and get himself in a leadership position on the... mission (for lack of a better word). So it looks like he's now got the same clout around here as Mia or Anthony. Brad just screamed bad news to me. I didn't trust him in the slightest – what he wanted or what he was prepared to do to get it. Why everyone else there couldn't see he was bad news, I don't know. Maybe it was just me. Maybe with the safety of my food I was thinking more rationally. Maybe. Plus, he had a gun, some sort of pistol. Not sure what it was, but he was more than happy to display it in his belt. Part of me wished the thing would discharge itself and blow his knob off.

There was a bunch of posturing from all of them. Mia and Anthony used their 'credibility runs already on the board' to calm the masses down while Brad was the voice of kicking ass. It was scary watching everyone slowly degenerate into a bunch of bloodthirsty thugs, but as much as Mia, Anthony and a few others tried to call for reason, they were fighting a losing battle.

Brad had lathered the crowd into a frenzy preaching things like, taking what was rightfully theirs and survival of the fittest. It was all getting a little 'crazy cult' for my liking. But, again, it was one of those car crashes I couldn't turn away from. I'd pretty much decided to tag along to see what was gonna become of all this. But I also decided to hang at the very back – the very, very back.

So with Brad starting to call the shots the plan took on a more military approach. He had this idea in his head of splitting people into groups and targeting both exits of the Norwood shopping centre. The group at the rear entrance would stop people getting out and he and the rest of the group at the front entrance would force the officials into letting them in to take 'their share' of the food and water available.

The groups were split up according to strength and weaponry and then weighted 2-1 in favour of those heading to the front entrance. Mia was in charge of those covering the rear entrance while Brad, Anthony and another guy called Josh (a friend of Brad's) were in charge of 'negotiating' at the front entrance.

When they came to assigning me they ummed and ahhed for a while about whether I should even go on account of my age and physically lacking form. I think the fact I was carrying a rather large backpack to help carry supplies back was the reason I got asked to come – although I was ordered to Mia's team. Probably the safest result to be honest.

After a few pump-up chants and famous last words we were on our way.

The walk to Norwood was so different to last time. Gone was the sense of wonder and feeling of being part of some hobbit-like journey; all of that was replaced by anticipation and the fear of what was going to happen. It just felt like it was going to be big. But I don't think too many others shared that feeling. There was a lot of geeing each other up and singing. I started to wonder how well I knew these people after all!

It was interesting to note how many of our group had made their own pair of ash shoes. People were adapting to the conditions and it meant the walk was done in less than half the time as before. Instead of taking Portrush Rd all the way up to the Parade, this time we turned down Beulah Rd. I assume the thinking was the side streets would attract less attention. When we got to the laneway behind the shopping centre we peeled off to the back entrance while the larger group headed on to the Parade.

Mia had some kind of heavy duty CB radio she was using to keep in touch with the other group. We gathered around the bottom of the steps to the entrance and waited. The glass entrances were boarded up so we couldn't see what was happening inside, but there was enough of a gap to see some sort of light leaking out. They had power. It was a pretty eerie feeling, waiting there. It was cold and the wind was blowing. Ash was everywhere, but I'm not sure if it was falling from the sky or being picked up from the piles on the ground. Everyone was nervous. And the cold made us cling together like penguins. We all looked at Mia and her radio and waited for an update.

The wind and ash meant the signal on the two-way was scratchy at best and it also meant other noises were hard to pick up. That was good and bad – unless someone walked through the entrance door we could stay undetected, but if trouble started out the front and nobody got to the two-way radio we might not know.

We waited and waited.

Then the two-way burst into life and a bunch of inaudible pandemonium blasted through. No one was quite sure what to do or how to react. I looked at Mia for direction, but she was busy trying to get the other group back on the two-way. Seconds later the shopping centre doors burst open and a bunch of people ran for us. I can't remember how many but it was at least a match for our numbers. I remember hearing people screaming, seeing shots fired and watching one of their guys bury a shovel so far in the side of someone's neck he couldn't pull it out again. Then one of our guys hit the shovel guy with a cricket bat and he dropped to the floor.

It all happened within seconds. I was frozen to the spot just watching like it was a movie or something. What a dumbass. Then some object fizzed past my head at high speed and seconds later a splattering of someone else's blood flung across my chest – that helped me snap out of my imaginings.

I didn't know whether to run away or jump in and try to help. Then some old guy from our side (who's name I can't remember) pushed me back and yelled at me to get the hell out of there. I just looked at him, maybe still a bit stunned. He clearly thought I needed further instructions coz he told me to go back and prepare the school for the injured. So in the end I didn't have any choice to make at all… I left. Maybe the old guy knew that – knew I needed a reason. Either way, thank God I left.

When I was a safe distance away, I turned back to see what was happening. It was bloody and ugly and violent as hell – again I just stared at it all. Then another bunch of the Norwood crew burst through the door – maybe 20 or so more. I knew our guys were screwed. I kept watching but backed away as I did. Some skinny little prick who was hanging around the outskirts of the pack firing in bullets every now and then lifted his head up and noticed me. He lifted his gun in my direction and I turned and shuffled my sled shoes as fast as they could go. I heard three bullets whip through the air around my head but didn't get hit. I just charged my ass to the corner as fast as I could go and turned out of sight. Then I sprint-shuffled to Beulah Rd and kept the pace up until I reached Portrush Rd. It was only then I turned around to see if anyone was following me – luckily I was in the clear.

I felt so helpless and scared shitless. I'd witnessed total carnage... of people I knew. For all I knew I was the only one still alive. I just sat down on the ash and caught my breath while I figured out my next move. I wasn't sure whether to go back and see if I could help anyone, or stay and wait to see if anyone headed back or go back to Trinity Gardens. I decided to wait on the corner and see if anyone else came back. I thought about what I would do if I had to go back alone... and what I would say.

I waited for what must've been 20 minutes before it occurred to me if someone did come back this way they would be within metres of me before I could recognise them. If they were one of the Norwood crew, and armed, I'd be dead before I knew it.

I left.

I think I cried all the way back to the school. It was a mix of the high emotions, the things I've seen and the senseless waste. Why didn't I raise my voice at the idea of going down to Norwood guns blazing when I knew it was stupid? What would I tell the rest of the community? So many things. But most of all was the guilt that I'd just left them there to die.

Remembering what I said when I got back to the school is kinda fuzzy. I recall a bunch of people hoarding around me when I walked into the gym. I must've looked like death warmed up – crying, exhausted, shivering, blood-splattered and lost. They started firing question after question at me and I think I said something like, 'It was a massacre, I think I'm the only one who got out'.

There was screaming and anger and swearing. Someone – some lady – pulled me out of the craziness, took me aside and calmed me down for a while. She put a blanket over my shoulders, gave me a cup of warm soup and put her arm around me. I remember calming down a bit, catching my breath at first, collecting my thoughts and then trying to put into words what I saw and knew.

Thinking back now, I don't have the first clue what I told her. I think I'm gonna stop writing now. I can't add to the story and I can't get these thoughts out of my head. I hate this place.

****

Sunday, May 11, 2014

9.30am: I know I should go back to the school to see if there's any news on the others and perhaps give a more detailed account of what I saw, but I can't be bothered. Actually, it's not that I can't be bothered, more like, I really don't want to go anywhere near that place. I'm not in any hurry to relive the things I saw or the guilt I feel. So I'm just gonna hang here and do some healthy wallowing.

1.30pm: I tried just chilling out with some movies or a game or two, but nothing was doing it for me. It kind of feels like a puerile waste of time, which is really weird because I'm perfectly well aware it is (and has always been) a puerile waste of time, but that's never mattered before.

Reading wasn't cutting it either – and music was either too sombre or way, way too chirpy.

I ended up trawling through some of the stuff I had downloaded in the days leading up to impact day. I filed a mass of print-outs in folders and gave them labels. I now have folders for making stuff, survival stuff, food and water preservation/generation etc. A lot of print-outs weren't appropriate anymore so I set them aside to burn. While I was sorting through all that info I finally got back around to watching a few episodes of the *Doomsday Preppers* show I downloaded pre-rock. It was interesting viewing as you get to see a bunch of different American people/families preparing for one global disaster or another. I guess they could have appeared a little crazy to those watching the show a few weeks back... I know who'd be laughing now.

I didn't realise 'prepping' – preparing for an apocalyptic event – was such a popular pastime. It's hard to believe there was this massive sub-culture I'd never heard of. And these people didn't muck about either. They had food supplies, bug-out plans (often including a second form of accommodation to flee to), enough rations to last from several months to several years and guns... serious arsenals of guns!

It's funny how your perspective changes. When I first saw an episode pre-rock I just dismissed the whole idea of needing weapons as an American thing. I mean, don't they have just about one weapon per person in the entire country? Of course you're gonna wanna pack heat in a post-apocalyptic US. But I thought it would be different here. I never even considered weapons as being a necessary part of survival – not here, not in little ole Adelaide!

But sure enough, here we are. I'm in a house surrounded by properties where people have been murdered. I witnessed a shootout of Tarantino proportions not 2km from here and now I'm feeling totally exposed for underestimating one massive part of a survivalist's needs – protection.

I mean, I've got some things together. The bow and crossbow are good at medium range (but they're not the easiest things to carry around and they're certainly not concealable). I've also got a few knives but, at the end of the day, I don't have any competition for a gun. Maybe it was a mistake not to focus on finding a firearm pre-rock but, really, what could I do? I mean, I don't know the rules in Australia for getting a gun but I'm pretty sure it's tough (and impossible at 17). But I think I have to acknowledge the oversight – bad move me.

I guess it goes to show no matter the culture, when you start taking away people's ability to get basic food supplies, when they can't feed their families, then all bets are off. Welcome, me, to the sad but true reality of humanity.

A limited few preppers on the show decided they didn't need weapons either – I wonder if they're still alive?

It was also interesting to hear each of them had an imagined scenario for what was going to bring about the end of civilisation as we know it. Not one of them had asteroid/comet strike. In some cases it wouldn't have mattered. If they had time to get to their underground bunkers they'd be all fine and dandy now, apart from cabin fever. But most of them will be in strife, given what type of disaster they were planning for. Those preppers who imagined financial meltdown (of which there were a lot) and other non-environmental catastrophes were planning for the wrong event. Sure, they'd have a food source for some time and an arsenal of weapons to protect it, but in most instances their energy source was solar… not so helpful now.

It just makes me think back to those last reports from the US. The civil unrest then was already at breaking point. I wonder how much further it's degenerated. It would be very interesting to know. I mean, there's economic collapse, complete breakdown of food and utility supplies, and out-of-control social unrest, but they still have their cities intact and their hierarchy of government and military in place. How long can all that survive without the money or food to support it, given the shipload of privately owned weapons available? I think chaos will win. It has to. Maybe it already has.

One of the preppers talked about two kinds of people in the post-apocalyptic world – marauders and community types. The marauders would roam around, heavily-armed, seeking to take from the communities. And it would be a battle between the two as to who won. I'm not sure it's totally like that. I mean, there are the loners, who choose to reject either way of existence plus, in time, there won't be enough for the communities to survive on their own… then it comes down to community v community. That's where it gets nasty.

But I get his point, and it does make me think about my community again and how much I should be involved in it.

I think I should go back there but I know that day will take time.

*

4pm: I just dropped in on Mr Nichols again – he's really, really, really, really not looking good. He couldn't speak to me either. All he could muster the energy for was to gruntingly let me know he didn't want me around. I think he wanted to die in peace.

*

6.45pm: I just had a realisation. Today is one month since the comet hit the Earth. One month! Time seems so hard to plot these days. One month that in some ways seems like a day and in others seems like forever. I hate moments like this, when I've reached a milestone, because it makes me think back to the world before, which then makes me miss it and the people I used to share it with. Sure, there's the achievement of successfully surviving a month. That's great. That's something positive. But that's about the limit to my positives. The thing is, while I was successfully managing to exist I was systematically being robbed of all the things that made existence worthwhile. That's a completely depressing thought.

Is it wrong that I'm starting to think the already bleak outlook is going to be made a whole lot worse by the fact it's also been a month since I've gotten laid? And the prospects of that improving any time soon seem close to zero. I'm a monk filled with spunk. I've seen a few options down at the community but it's so cold down there and everyone is so covered up I'm only assuming half of them are girls. There's a mistake I wouldn't want to make. And I know I'm desperate and all, but no… just no!

So tonight I'm going directly to the top shelf of Dad's alcohol cabinet, I'm gonna reach right to the back and pull out something random. I'm gonna raise a glass to everyone I miss, all the girls I've hit, and I'm gonna get myself nicely plastered.

Happy freaking anniversary.

I would do anything for some company, though. Someone to spend time with away from the school would be priceless. I'd even settle for a pet. I've never been much of a pet person but it seems like a pretty tempting option right now.

****

Monday, May 12, 2014
8.30am: Why, why, why? Stupid, self-inflicted hangover is stupid.
*

10.10am: I just realised how quickly I am churning through my water stocks – 10% already. That gives me less than half of what I have left in food. Developing a strategy to produce/acquire/purify more water quickly jumped the charts to No. 1 priority. I'll sift through all the data I printed out pre-rock to see if any valid options for my circumstances appear. I mean, there is plenty of time to sort something out but I don't want to be stressing about it. Today I'm ripping though double the normal intake too (refer to last entry).
*

12.30pm: Vale Mr Nichols. Well, it had to happen and I'm glad it was a relatively quick end. I went around there just after 11am and knew something was up as soon as I entered the house. I can't explain it but there was just a vibe that let me know he was no longer with us. Creepy. I found him slumped over in his favourite armchair, blood and phlegm stains everywhere. I'm not sure it was the most dignified exit, but the end result is what he wanted.

So I followed his final wishes. I buried him in the backyard with a few personal possessions. I tidied the place up to make it look respectable. I left the notes to his family on the table and I left. I didn't take anything – even though Mr Nichols said I could help myself; it just didn't seem right. I think I'm gonna gather the rest of his food and head up to the community tomorrow. They could use the donation more than I can and it seems like the right thing to do.
*

7pm: Wow, this world has a funny way of working. Just when I thought the pattern of one day being bleaker than the one before would continue until the end, I had not one, but two pleasant surprises this afternoon. Both visitors :) Both female :)

APOCALYPSE: DIARY OF A SURVIVOR

The first was early afternoon. I'd just gotten over the worst of the hangoverness when there was a knock at the door. Once again I armed myself and prepared for invasion, but nothing could've prepared me for who was on the other side. Mia.

Yes Mia – I-thought-she-was-dead Mia. She looked terrible, her right eye was a shiny shade of purple and she had a bunch of cuts on her face. I must've had the most goofy, shocked expression on my face when I opened the door because she said 'Surprise' then laughed. I think she was laughing at me!

I couldn't help myself. I cried, then moved in and gave her the biggest squeeze I could muster. Then I realised it wasn't just her face that was damaged as she winced in pain. I apologised and invited her in.

She told me everything she knew from the failed raid on Norwood. Firstly they were more prepared and better armed than we had anticipated. She reckons they'd cleaned out the firearms shop on Magill Rd. Apparently Brad had gone in all cocksure and aggressive at the main entrance, demanding this and that. He ignored a couple of warnings thinking he was calling their bluff and before anyone knew what was happening a small army of Norwood hubbers burst through the front doors and unleashed on our lot. It was a massacre.

After I left, the fighting continued out the back entrance. We were already outnumbered and losing when I left, but not long after that more Norwood hubbers poured out from the front. We surrendered. They lined up the remaining survivors from our crew out the back (14 people) and Mia said at that moment she thought they were going to be executed.

Then the fat guy, Alex, who they reckon is the leader of the Norwood hub, walked out and ordered the survivors be let go. They had to leave all their weapons and also move the dead bodies from the back of the shopping centre to the other side of the car park. Mia was balling her eyes out when she told me this – it all made me shiver.

Once they were done they were taken to the front of the shops and made to help the other surviving members (18 survivors) do the same with the bodies out the front. Many of the survivors were injured and incapable of helping and Mia reckoned her and about 14 others did most of the work. It took hours. Only once it was completed were they allowed to head back to Trinity Gardens. All-in-all we lost 49 people, and have another eight or so with serious injuries. Mia's husband, Craig, was one of those killed.

It was a total disaster.

Mia and I embraced again – human touch, shared helplessness and loss – I can't explain that feeling. I cried again.

She asked me if I was alright and said she needed me back. I told her my experience from the day, how the old guy had told me to leave and my struggle with guilt and telling the community about what happened. She didn't seem disappointed in me at all. In fact, she told me I'd done the right thing. It was so good to hear those words.

I fixed her a drink of water and we chatted some more about what her plans were to make it up to the community. She reckoned the mood has shifted massively (only natural, I guess). Everyone is feeling low about what happened, our food stocks and the fact we are weaker than those around us. They now feel we should fly under the radar and forage for food in more obscure locations, avoiding the larger groups. Mia reckon stocks aren't gonna take us much further than a week. And more people are surfacing at the school to join the community, usually because they have run out of food and have nowhere to go. So the desperate situation is getting worse by the day.

I didn't have any electricity on when she came around, which spared a bunch of questions about my set-up. I did notice her having a good look around the place. Not in a suspicious way, but out of general curiosity. Maybe more in a mothering way really as she went on to ask me how I was doing. I told her I had enough to keep going for now and I went on to tell her about Mr Nichols and that I'd bring his leftover food into the school the next day.

We chatted for a while after that, mostly about things we were doing before the comet hit; small talk, but genuine small talk. It's interesting finding out about somebody's life in the pre-rock world. I like it, even though it brings up thoughts of how easy my life used to be. I really like Mia, too. Apart from being pretty hot she is very smart and sure of herself in a way that's not cocky but very confident. I trust her. And I think she likes me, too – I think I've impressed her with the independence I've shown. Plus I get that feeling with her. The one that tells me we are similar people from similar family backgrounds – just the things we talked about and what we put emphasis on as important. There's no rule for it, but when you feel it you know you can trust someone.

I think she's worried about her place in the whole community right now, at least that's just the vibe I get. I think it's from everything that happened in the lead-up to the Norwood raid. She lost control of the situation and people died. She's probably got more numbers on her side now, given what happened, but she needs everyone to be strong and stay united. In a way she was recruiting me. She was probably there for over an hour before she headed back to the school, or home; I'm not sure.

I just sat there reflecting on the conversation and all the new information I'd taken in. I felt good. I felt better than I had in days actually. Before I knew it there was another knock at the door. I could not believe my luck when I asked who was out there – Fiona J! With no boyfriend! I looked skyward and mouthed, 'Thank-you' before I let her in.

She looked in a terrible state, all skin and bone, dirty and shivering. When she saw me she just started crying and threw her arms around me. So many thoughts were going through my head. Why was she here? Was she planning to stay? As my partner? I knew in that instant I'd gladly turn two years of food for me into one year of food for me and a partner. For company. With everything that's been happening and changing so fast, and with all the emotions I've been struggling to control, I realised that's what I've been craving all along. Company.

Thank you, universe. You've been somewhat under-performing recently, but I wished for company last night and it arrived at my door today. You have slightly redeemed yourself. Don't think I haven't forgotten about the whole global catastrophe thing, though.

Fiona told me between tears her boyfriend started going psycho when the food ran low and she thought he was scary and dangerous. She left and didn't know where to go, just found herself drawn to my place.

God, that felt good. I'm still smiling as I write this several hours later.

She had a small backpack with a handful of clothes and a few other possessions, mostly beauty products and personal trinkets. I poured a water container into the bath, boiled the kettle a few times and managed to mix in enough to take the freezing edge off the water. It was a massive waste of resources from a strategic sense, but to help her feel clean and protected and safe; that was priceless.

She was gone for an age. I suggested she wash her clothes while there was water available and left her some warm clothes to put on while her's went through the drier. She emerged in one of my old tracksuits and gave me an embarrassed smile. She looked stunning.

I poured her a cup of tea and set out to make the least unappealing meal I could think of. It was cream of mushroom soup – with one of the long-life milks to give it some extra creaminess – and some of the bread I baked a couple of days ago. She was so thankful and it felt good to provide. Just the simple act of making a meal, using your resources to provide nutrients for someone and having such a heart-felt response, was heavenly. I felt wanted, needed, loved.

We talked well into the night about everything that'd happened since our last encounter, which felt like a lifetime ago. I told her most of my story, but kept my resource-rich position to myself. She told me that she and her douchebag boyfriend had pretty much holed up in his flat with his best mate until the food ran out. They then went around looting vacant houses in the area to keep the supplies up but that only lasted for the better part of a week until their options ran low. Clearly, others were doing the same, which killed off their supply.

I hadn't realised the hunt for food had gotten so desperate so soon.

They burnt their furniture for warmth, which only lasted a few days, then started raiding derelict houses for more to burn. She said they were so confident when everything first went down that they'd survive, but the descent into failure was a quick one. They were fighting constantly about food. There was tension everywhere. And the flat was in a totally exposed position with people walking past all the time.

Then it turned bad. They were desperate and angry and hungry. The two guys went out one day and came back with blood-stained clothes and a bunch of food. Fiona didn't ask but she knew what had happened. A few days later the same thing happened again. This time it got too much to tolerate and she called the boys out on it – asked them flat-out what happened. They lied and said everything was above board. She knew it was all lies and she'd had enough so she decided to leave. I gotta give her massive credit for that. She was rejecting the food because she didn't agree with the violence but she needed the food to survive. Instead, she just put on her warmest clothes, told them she was going for a walk to clear her head and didn't stop until she got to my place. That's a long, long walk from Campbelltown.

I shared a few stories too – the fight at Norwood, finding the bodies in the houses, finding Hardo's family. It's hard to know how much to share. Just telling your story to someone can make you feel better, but then you're giving them some of your burden. You're making things harder for them to deal with knowing the stories of pain don't end where they think they do. I decided not to mention the loneliness – that was one burden too far, at least for today. Maybe I didn't need to say anything about it anyway. I've got a feeling there was something in the way we talked to each other and what we talked about that we both knew it was there. Maybe now it's just a bitter reality that never needs to be said – maybe sharing that burden could push someone else over the edge. Maybe I'm just thinking too much. Maybe I'm too stubborn, or selfish or scared to share the load. Whatever the case, I'm just happy she's here and that for the first time since the night of the rock there will be someone else in the house I wake up in.

****

Tuesday, May 13, 2014
10.30am: Feel so good today after sharing my bed with Fiona. Nothing happened but we went to sleep in each other's arms and, for the first time in a long time, I woke up with a sense of future and purpose. You can't beat that feeling – it's like the fuel for survival.

I fixed us some breakfast and we ate and talked for a while.

Then I prepared for my trip to the school, via Mr Nichols' place. Fiona wanted to come but I thought her time would be better spent recovering. She still seemed fairly weak and there was no point pushing it too quickly.
*

4.45pm: As per usual I gave the key parts of the backyard a de-ashing before I left. That's getting harder and harder to do, partly because the ash piles are building up so high finding room to store it is a challenge and also because we're facing new levels of cold. Serious cold. Freezing cold. Literally. It was after 9am before I started and the temperature was still -2°C. The ash mounds had turned into disgusting grey/brown clumps of ice. I had to hack the pile outside the shed door with the side of a shovel for an age before I could open it and get the pick-axe out.

It's damn lucky I've been keeping the doorways by the house under control otherwise I could quite literally be iced-in right now. The back door is less of an issue because it's under the veranda, but the side sliding door requires constant attention.

After I'd gotten the tools I needed from the shed I decided to leave the rest of the manual labour until I got back from the school. I was already stuffed and still had a long morning ahead of me.

I got a few steps out the door to Mr Nichols' before I realised how the changing conditions affected everything. The ash had no give in it anymore. The hard surface was slippery as all hell. My sled shoes were of little use, except for giving more surface area to balance with. But underneath the hard surface there were mounds of softer non-frozen ash. Every now and then you'd hit a weak patch, break though the surface and sink into the goop underneath. The closest comparison I can make is say a soft serve ice-cream covered in that chocolate stuff that sets hard (IceMagic or something?) but then starts to melt underneath. This was similar but far less appetising. Once your foot broke the surface it took an age to get it back out.

Plus, what was a moderate problem when leaving home became a much bigger one when I had a backpack full of Mr Nichols' food. Even the 20-30 steps from the front of his house to the front of mine saw me get bogged three times. I decided to pit-stop back at my place to find a better transport method. The best I could come up with at short notice was a boogie board from the shed. I strapped the arms of the backpack around the board, attached the cross-strap, then covered the backpack-board combo in a large bag to stop the arm straps getting damaged. I basically dragged the thing behind me using the boogie board's wrist strap. It was slightly painful dragging across the undulating ground but better than it would've been carrying all that extra weight.

The conditions seem to change so often outside. Some days it stinks to high heaven, some days the ash is thick in the air and some days it's windy. When you get a few days of calm weather in a row a walking track almost forms on the footpath as people trudge about. Makes you wonder how many people are out and about. All it takes is one windy, ashy day, and any paths are covered over like they were never there.

The IceMagic surface would've been easier to handle if it was somewhat flat, but the undulations made dragging the boogie board only a slightly better option than lugging the whole lot on my back. Still, a win's a win, no matter how small.

The vibe at the school was very depressing. Obviously what happened at Norwood has taken its toll, but it was more than that. The ever present and ever diminishing food stocks in the corner were a silent reminder of what we faced. I added my stash and could feel eyes on me. When I looked around it was a pretty strange reaction – everyone was happy that it grew but, more than anything, disappointed I only had a backpack's worth to donate. Everyone knew that wouldn't get us far.

Mia came over to thank me as I was dumping the last of the cans on the pile. She told me about a strategy meeting happening just after lunch and asked if I could hang around. I thought it'd be a good chance to check out the group's thinking.

It's a pretty boring place to kill time though. I mean, don't get me wrong, it's really good to have people everywhere, but there's little in the way of small talk and I definitely feel like an outsider. Mia's too busy to spend much time with me so I spent most of my time looking at the giant map on the floor.

It is valuable time though – that map and I are closely acquainted now. I'm amazed how much I can remember when I sit and concentrate on it. I reckon I could almost draw half the suburb street-by-street and house-by-house. I'm like the real estate rain man! When I see all the different tokens on the properties marking their status (vacant, raided, empty etc), I see them like a giant pattern of colours that flows straight into the street map already planted in my mind. Then I become the rain man in the matrix – I can't explain it but I am 'one' with the data. It all comes together and I know when I get home I'll be able to update my map with all the new info.

Most of the properties had markers now meaning they were occupied or had been cleared of food. It was another reminder all of this would come to a head at some point soon. Food is scarce. I think it's that uncertainty that freaks everyone out. I mean the maths for survival just don't add up. Not anymore. Not for everyone. Not for most people.

The simple fact is unless another food source magically introduces itself then the population is still too big to sustain itself. I'm guessing, based on discussions the morning after strike-night, plus what I've heard here and there, that 150,000 Adelaidians (of a million and a bit) might have survived the rock. What has that reduced to now? What will it get to? What is the ultimate sustainable population for this area? My guess is with no real food source available, no sun to grow the trees and no clean water, then the ultimate sustainable population is zero, nada, ziltch, a big fat donut – nothin'!

That's why everyone is so grim. All the devastation, personal loss and tragedy aside, Adelaide is on a first-class ride to uninhabitable and we all have front row seats. That's the sad fact no one here is ready to admit.

I guess it was no surprise the meeting was a sombre affair. Mia was great, very positive given the circumstances, but it was in no way infectious. In fact it seemed a lot of people there expected her to have the answers. It was almost like they needed someone to blame and Mia, by the fact she'd put her hand up to take a leadership role, became the outlet for their frustrations. People are pathetic sometimes.

When you think about it, people aren't really trained to be responsible for their own lives. There are people to do this and that for them. There are systems in place to help people live their lives. They've got hoops to jump through every day, every week – hoops that keep them from actually having any control over their lives. I suppose the whole system, the system of life, is designed to offer just enough challenges and rewards to stop people going insane. But when you strip all that structure away people become lost, running around like headless chooks, as Grandad used to say.

But I digress. The meeting went for ages. Every angle of our plight was discussed. They were trying to come up with a plan to maximise the unclaimed food. The general consensus was that hitting the houses affected by the tsunami on the city side of Portrush Rd was the best bet. It took them forever to come up with that semi-consensus and I was very much torn when they did. It was good to hear them finally coming together in agreement, but I couldn't help but think they weren't thinking big enough. Eventually I got the courage to speak.

I'd been thinking about this for a while. We needed a big play to get ourselves back in the game. I thought sending an expedition to the city centre was a no-brainer. For a start, we were one of the closest surviving areas, apart from Norwood maybe, and they were busy protecting their stronghold. If we could get to the city in large numbers before anyone else did we would have the pick of the food that remained.

It could be a big fail as no one knows how much the tsunami damaged the city. It could prove too difficult to move around and I said as much to everyone, but, IF there were ways to get around safely, there were potentially more food sources than anywhere else – supermarkets, convenience stores, restaurants, vending machines, more food than we could dream of carrying back. I can't remember exactly the words I used but I do remember getting to the end of my spiel and looking out at a sea of blank faces. Well, they were blank at first, until some guy (I don't know his name but he's a constant negative pain in the arse) spoke. He said it was the best idea he'd heard since becoming part of the community. That seemed to give a few other people enough confidence to voice their approval and, before I knew what hit me, I was being peppered with questions about the logistics of it all. I couldn't believe it – suddenly I was some kind of expert. I remember trying to answer as many questions as possible. I had a few pretty good pieces of information others didn't, like my view over the city on rock night and my understanding of the topography, but I tried to stress multiple times I wasn't sure any of it was going to work. I remember feeling conflicted when I held centre stage – part of me was stoked to be in a situation where others were looking up to me (even though I know I should be keeping a low profile) but the other part felt pity that they had so little control over their destiny they latched on to my idea like it was the great white hope for survival. I also had this feeling they'd turn on me if it didn't reap the rewards they were hoping for.

At some point, Mia made her way to my side and started answering some of the logistical questions. She gave me a smile when she moved in next to me but I wasn't sure how to take it. I didn't know if it was a genuine smile or if she knew she had to sidle up to my idea to keep the group together. To be honest I think she tried to go about making my idea hers.

I don't really have a problem with that, as I certainly don't want to position myself as anything other than a fringe player in the community. But maybe it opened my eyes to how this whole thing works.

After an eternity of planning it was decided we would send out two scout teams tomorrow – one to check out the tsunami-affected houses and the other to the city. I've been asked to head to the city. I've got to admit I'm pretty excited about it. It will be the furthest I have travelled since the morning after the rock hit and just the idea of seeing a new area is exciting. Let alone what we could possibly find.

*

6.30pm: It was definitely nice to come home today. Home to company, home to Fiona – it makes all the difference. There's an energy that comes from it that I can't explain, but I like it.

I've given Fiona a run down on how all the things in the house work – the generator, where I keep all the food supplies and the location of weapons. I told her not to answer the door and, if she does, keep the lights off. I could tell she found it all a little overwhelming, but she wore a look that said she meant business and was going to run things as I did. It was very reassuring, because even though I trust her, I don't trust that douchebag ex-boyfriend of hers and there was a lingering part of me worried I was being set-up. But that would've happened by now if it was going to happen and I just can't see Fiona doing that. I guess there's a chance he might search for her here at some point, but I guess I'll just stay prepared rather than worry about it too much.

Besides, it makes no sense for her to go back. Purely from a survival point of view she'll last longer here than there. Even if she did backstab me she'd be dividing the same supplies between three people, so things would run out quicker. I don't even know why I think of these outcomes. I feel a connection with her that is just… right. That's all the proof I need. I guess this world does strange things to your mind sometimes. Paranoia.

Despite all that, I've still kept the existence of the cellar a secret. If the worst did happen and she was setting me up to take my supplies, I still reckon I've got at least six months' worth stashed away down there.

I do genuinely believe her though. I just have to cover all bases. I mean, she walked from their place in Campbelltown to get here. That must've taken hours – four or five at least! It makes no sense to set me up like that – from that distance, it's just not worth the physical resources for the food gains. Besides, they wouldn't be able to lug it back to their home.

But I'll stay alert, I always stay alert.

The other thing to consider is the fact Fi's ex-boyfriend (his name's Josh, by the way) may come after her. Part of him must think she's here, given what happened pre-rock. But geography works in our favour this time because it's a long, long haul to get here on what, for him, must only be a guess.

*

11.15pm: I've just spent the evening spooning on the couch with Fiona watching *This is Spinal Tap*. Such a funny film. In fact, I LOLed tonight… quite a few times. So did Fi. Afterwards we started talking about the last time we'd laughed. I couldn't even remember when that was. I'd watched a few comedies by myself since the rock, and I found them funny – I just can't remember laughing out loud at all. I think it's that the act of laughing hasn't seemed, well, right. With everything that's happened to the world and my family and friends and my city and my life, laughing at puerile stuff just didn't cut it. But tonight for the first time it did – and in a big way.

It's a sign I reckon. A sign that I'm beginning to rebuild. It's like that five stages of loss thing they always talk about. Maybe I'm finally starting to get to the acceptance stage. Whatever the case I think it's a good sign.

****

Wednesday, May 14, 2014
10pm: The freezing mornings aren't getting any easier to handle. My fingers felt like they would snap off if something touched them at the wrong angle.

We met at the school at 9am – there were more people around than I expected for that time in the a.m. I think there was a bit of a buzz about our trip – in a way today's expeditions represented the last hope. There were two groups of eight heading to each target destination. Joining me in the city group were Mia (she was still getting over her injuries but insisted on coming), a couple of people I'd met before (Steve K, Steve P, Kelly and John) and a couple I had not met before (Tania and Michael).

The two groups walked together for a couple of minutes until we reached Portrush Rd, then the tsunami house raiders disappeared into the side streets while we city raiders headed up to Magill Rd and the long journey to town. It's just under 4km to the city fringes – by far the longest journey any of us have undertaken since impact day.

I remember being totally pumped about the adventure as we turned on to Magill Rd, but by the time we reached the halfway point and we'd been on foot for over an hour I was over it. The realisation I had to make the return trip – probably carrying supplies – was pretty depressing at that point.

I also couldn't escape the feeling we were being watched, particularly in the early stages of the trip before we headed into tsunami territory. When a large group of people carrying torches walk by it's hard not to attract attention. Then my brain started working overtime, thinking some secret network would report our activities back to the Norwood hubbers. In my head that meant they'd send a crew after us… which didn't bode well for my life expectancy.

Magill Rd has a slight downhill slant that extends all the way into the city. Each step took us a little lower, a little further into the tsunami zone, a little further into the destruction and the stink of decay. It was eerie as all hell.

The pace slowed significantly. Above the tsunami line you would find paths created by others who had walked along the street. Sometimes they were fresh, sometimes they'd been partially filled by more ash, but either way they're easier to handle than slogging it step by step through uncharted roads. We took a break to put on our ash boots.

I remember not being sure whether it was a good sign or not there were little to no tracks heading into the city. It meant no one had swiped any food but it also meant nobody had dared make the journey. Surely someone else had thought about it? Did they consider it and decline thinking it was a hopeless idea?

Looking around as everyone focused on the slog ahead, I could tell others wondered the same. No one said anything but you get a certain vibe from a group of people and this vibe was saying, 'what the hell are we doing here?' and 'it's that stupid kid's fault'.

My faith in success was being tested too, especially as we neared the parklands that surrounded the city. It was hit and miss as to whether the buildings you were passing on the side of the road were there or not. It was a 50/50 hit rate, I reckon. I could see other people's torches shining off to the side, taking in the sheer devastation. Each empty block made me hunch a little lower, trying to hide my body from the group. I could tell they already hated me for wasting their time. It was the first time I managed to find a positive purpose for the lack of light – two even! Hiding me away from the group and hiding the level of destruction around us from others. I've got a feeling if we were able to take in the full scope of the broken buildings, or if we could see the city skyline, we would've turned back in a heartbeat.

As it was, we only had torch distance to go by, and the feeling of fail.

The ground was different. Even though it was still covered in the icy ash you could tell something was going on. Every now and then the ground would move underneath. I didn't say anything to the others but the only explanation I could think of was that the ash was piled up on top of a large layer of debris.

We were only halfway through the parklands when we hit a nugget of gold, which broke the tension. A vending machine had been lodged a few metres up the trunk of one of the massive Moreton Bay figs. Someone spotted it with the torch. I guess it did stand out, being in one of the only trees still standing! It was devoid of leaves and covered in all sorts of random muck, but gleaming through the brown and grey was the bright red of the vending machine. You could see all sorts of chocolate bars and chip packets still inside. We just needed to get the thing down.

That turned out to be easier than expected. The debris was piled all the way over the main branching point in the trunk. It was only a 2-3m climb from there. The two Steves wrestled the thing down in a couple of minutes. The glass smashed as it hit the ground and sweet goodies scattered everywhere. We swooped in like seagulls and started eating – I scored a Snickers, for the record.

I don't know who did it first but we started laughing. I can't even remember if anything was said to trigger it, maybe it was just the surreal situation. I just thought about how ridiculous it was to be the only people in the city of Adelaide getting a chocolate fix from a Moreton Bay fig tree.

We loaded up the chocolate bars in our backpacks and decided to leave the chips until we passed by on the way back – and maybe not at all. They take up too much space for the nutrition they provide, not surprising given the packets are half filled with air! Someone suggested leaving the chocolate until the way back, too, but no one else was prepared to part with it.

It was only when we reached the top of Rundle St that the scale of the destruction started to sink in. The Stag Hotel, which overlooked the parklands, was engulfed in junk up to the first floor balcony. The balcony itself was barely recognisable, having been ripped to shreds by the water passing through. The roof was destroyed, as were half of the walls. The only reason the rest of the structure appeared to have survived the pounding waters was the build-up of debris on the western side of the building. It seemed as if half of Rundle St was destroyed, only to be deposited at the base of the Stag, creating a protective barrier of sorts. Oh, and best of all, atop the pile was one of the Mall's Balls. That was a real indicator of the power unleashed here. That thing must weigh a shedload and had rolled (presumably) nearly a kilometre.

I wondered where the other ball was. A city shouldn't have its balls separated like that; it's just not right!

The next few blocks were gone – two and three-storey buildings no longer there. Our sense of the devastation was growing. The waves had lifted buildings up by the foundation and taken them along for the ride or pulverised them.

As I put all the pieces together I started to realise how potentially fruitless this trip was going to be. Not only was the damage far greater than I had imagined, some of the places I wanted to try first – food courts, grocery stores – were either on the ground or, worse still, lower-ground levels. Gaining access to any of these places would almost be impossible, let alone finding some hidden food treasure.

I kept my thoughts to myself and hoped there'd be more Easter egg moments like the vending machine tree.

The rest of Rundle St was a write-off. There was nothing to find food wise and not much more remained in terms of buildings either. I could sense the group's doubt starting to grow again. Despite knowing most of my major potential finds were probably going to end in a fail, I decided to head down Rundle Mall.

We crossed what used to be Pulteney St from Rundle St into Rundle Mall, which I had thought was going to be our best hunting ground. The first food court, the little one with the Maccas on the left, was gone. It just wasn't there; only rubble remained. A bit further down, right where the Mall's Balls used to be (the other one was gone too, no sign of it anywhere), Regent Arcade was impossible to get into. The entrance was buried under rubble too high to contemplate digging into. On the opposite side, Adelaide Central Plaza looked a little more inviting. The building looked to have held together pretty well and the multi-storey entrance meant we could walk over the rubble and in. The problem was the food court was on the lower ground level.

It looked like a lost cause at first, but Tania, who knew the layout well, was able to find a path down there. She led us up through level 1 and then down the middle set of escalators in the heart of the building. It was the only way in and out of the place as all the other paths were under a mountain of debris.

In the middle we discovered a bizarre oasis that was reasonably well preserved. Well, better than expected, at least. There was a layer of silt and debris on the ground about a metre deep and, in some areas, a build-up of sea water, but we had enough clearance to walk around. It did reek though, there was a stink of salt water, rotten food and who knows what else. Just general death and decay. And it was dark. I mean, everywhere is dark, but this was pitch black. The air also had a heaviness I couldn't explain, other than to say it wasn't as easy as normal to breathe. I'm guessing it was either because there was little ventilation and the oxygen was down or the dust particles in the air were up. Either way, it was uncomfortable. And being in a large enclosed space with your every movement echoing was more than a little creepy.

It was an oasis. Just a dark, cold, claustrophobic, stinking, freaky one!

We split up and swept the food stalls on a scavenger hunt. Most of the place was a write-off, but the David Jones Food hall proved the big provider. This was where they sold continental food – meats, nuts, oils, chocolates, deli foods etc. I'm surprised there was anything left after the panic buying pre-rock, but I guess it's true there were problems distributing all the food once the army took over. It was a win for us, doubly so since most of the food had a reasonable shelf life and provided some decent energy.

That said, it wasn't just loaded on the shelves for convenient scavenging. Oh no, not in our oasis! The food was strewn everywhere, buried in the filthy debris. We just had to get down on our hands and knees and dig. It was gross, and about 70% of the food we did find was in packets that had broken and been contaminated by water or debris. But the usable 30% we were able to find was enough to load our bags to the point we couldn't take any more. Some of it wasn't in the best condition, but we took anything that looked even remotely salvageable. I was beaming with every find and the mood of the group was unbelievable – everyone would yell out when they found something new and it seemed like someone yelled out every minute or so.

It must've looked funny to the flies on the wall (actually, are there any flies these days? I can't remember the last time one annoyed me). Here we were, covered in filthy muck, digging down into it, stinking, freezing, but at the same time celebrating like we'd won the lottery. But in a way, winning the lottery was exactly what we'd done. It was luck we persisted long enough to find a way into this place (two storeys below the new ground level) and dumb luck there was anything edible remaining.

We left for the long slog back knowing we had done something meaningful and life-changing for the community. What a great feeling. I'm sure we could get another load or two out of this place, plus we might even get lucky in one of the other food courts. Then there's the Central Markets still to explore – it's like money in the bank.

When we reached street level again I took a moment at the neutered Mall's Balls. It was a famous meeting place and something uniquely Adelaide. I mean, a pair of huge silver balls, really? But I got a bit superstitious today. Seeing one of the balls as we entered the city, finding food where they used to be located, to me it was a sign. The balls were looking after us.

We passed the vending machine on the way out and gave ourselves a rest break. Everyone sat down and scoffed the chips we'd left behind and told me what a genius I was. That was fine by me; they had no idea how sure I was this trip was going to be an epic fail right until the point we hit the mother lode. But that's how it works, I guess. People don't have the energy to spend an entire day exploring for no result. They are tough judges like that in today's world. I would've taken the hit if it hadn't worked knowing the rewards were potentially so much higher on the chance it did.

Today it worked. I win. I get to sit down and eat my Burger Rings like a boss because I kicked serious ass. Next time who knows.

It was nearly 8pm when we headed back to Trinity Gardens. That's a massive day in anyone's language. I got a little paranoid on the return trip and suggested we head up Payneham Rd instead of Magill Rd. It meant an extra few minutes walking, but even the most grumpy and tired members of the group realised it was worth it to avoid a run-in with the Norwood crew.

I'm home now. Tired, full of food, physically and emotionally drained – but I feel great. I did find a nice chocolate gift I stashed away for personal use and gave to Fi (once I'd spent 20 minutes trying to make it presentable). For my reward I got a huge kiss and a full body massage. I seriously could not feel better right now. Wednesday, May 15, thank you.

****

Thursday, May 15, 2014

11.30am: I spent the morning hanging out with Fi. We slept in, then lay in bed a bit more and talked, then did things, then talked some more, then did some other, more risqué, things. I finally got up about 11am to make us some breakfast (cereal – today seemed worthy of opening another long-life milk carton) and then we watched a couple of episodes of *Doomsday Preppers* for the lolz. It was just the perfect lazy morning. As much as yesterday felt like a turning point for me, this whole week has been a bit of the same for her. She's gotten her strength back over the last few days and is starting to be the Fi I used to know – assured, clever, funny.

I think I'm gonna take her with me down to the school today to meet the community.

*

4pm: The only negative to come out of today was my whole 'keep a low profile' plan is now officially shot. I've never had so much gratitude sent my way and I felt like I'd really made a difference. Between the adulation and introducing everyone to Fiona J, well, I'm pretty sure everyone now knows who I am. Was it worth it? Yes. Will I regret it when the going gets tough? Probably. But I'll worry about that when it happens.

The news from the other group wasn't bad either. They'd put together a reasonable bounty of food, but were quick to point out they'd covered a lot of ground for minimal reward and figured there would only be one more hunt of that magnitude possible before we would have to start exploring further afield for supplies.

Between the two groups we think we've gathered five days worth of food for the entire group.

Heading back to the city soon turned into a top priority and another group was heading out first thing in the morning, led by Steve P and Kelly, now city veterans :) Instead of eight people, they've got about 30 going along. They asked me if I'd like to come but I think I'll wait until the next trip, when we need to find a new place to explore. Besides, I was still coughing like a pack-a-day smoker after yesterday. It can't be good breathing in all that dust and muck. Even through the dust mask I'm sure stuff is getting through, and who knows what sort of carcinogenic, asbestos-laden particles are lurking in the air. Not that I think about my long-term health prospects too much these days, I doubt I'll live long enough for that to be an issue, but my lungs are still pleading with me to give them a rest, so I think I will.

Besides which, Fi and I were in the zone this morning and I want to enjoy as many moments like that as I can get.

Thoughts in the community are also turning to securing our premises and food supplies. Everyone is still on edge about recent events in Norwood, especially since there are other groups more equipped (weapons wise) than us. I'm definitely glad this is part of our future planning. We're going to start having a night shift so there are at least two people around the camp at all times. There was some talk of getting everyone to move into the school but there weren't many takers on the idea. The classrooms are ridiculously cold and it feels more like a prison than a home. I can see how it would be a good idea to have numbers there at all times but schools are such depressing places. I think I'd feel more like a prisoner than a resident if I lived there permanently.

*

11.30pm: I love the nights in with Fi. We try and make things as normal as possible. Something to eat while watching some downloaded TV shows and a movie. We just snuggle on the couch under a bunch of blankets. We don't say much really, beyond commenting on something funny or sad happening on the TV. I think it's because any other subject we bring up will have something to do with the rock or the havoc it's created, or the people we miss, so if we don't say anything we can exist those nights in pretend world, a place that isn't touched by the destruction, like it doesn't even exist. It's just me and my girlfriend having a cosy night in. I like that.

****

Friday, May 16, 2014
10.30am: One of the advantages of taking Fi to meet the community is I now have someone to bounce my thoughts off about the other people there. She remembered quite a few of the people she met for the first time yesterday and it's amazing how similarly she viewed them compared to me. It's good to get another read on those things, and hearing someone else thinks similarly means I'm feeling a little more confident with how I go about things.

The only real difference of opinion was Mia. Fi did not like her one bit, whereas Mia is one of my favourites. I'm gonna put this one down to being a girl thing though. Women!

*

4.15pm: I just got back from an afternoon date with Fiona. As much as our time in the house is fun, I thought it'd be nice to do something different for a change. I spent an hour or so in the kitchen making a loaf of bread and heating up some of the canned spaghetti bolognaise (which I then poured into a thermos). I then gathered together some wine, chocolate, candles, blankets, serviettes, knives, forks, glasses and plates – everything I'd need for the perfect date. I coaxed her into her outside gear, blindfolded her and lead her up to the Greek restaurant on Magill Rd (I hope I didn't offend the Greek gods by taking Italian food to their restaurant – but it was the closest option).

I thought I might have to break some glass to get in through the front door but the work was already done for me, despite the 'no food on premises' sign. I dusted down a seat for her then made her stay blindfolded while I prepared our meal. I put some music on my iPod, via the dock, to keep her company.

She kept abusing me for not telling her what I was doing (all in fun, of course) but I'm sure she had a fair idea. When everything was perfect I took off her blindfold and she stared at the table and the setting then cracked up laughing.

"Oh, you shouldn't have", she said to me, "this place is expensive."

We both laughed before I told her I'd been saving hard for this moment.

I quickly ran outside and wiped the window clean so we could at least see out. Then I came back in, took my outside gear off and poured us both a wine.

"To us", I toasted.

We were there for a couple of hours eating, drinking… just enjoying the crazy surroundings. Fiona's really started showing signs of her old self too, like she's putting recent events behind her. She's great company and I really got a taste of that today. She's funny, intelligent, perceptive and has a determination I like. It's a willpower of sorts, but she doesn't use it to overbear me or get her own way. It's like she wants to use it in parallel with me, work with me to make us stronger. I think she's seen how I've set myself up, has complete confidence I've got what it takes to survive, and has pushed her chips all-in beside me. Trust – that's what I get from her the most – and that's a pretty rare commodity these days.

I had such a great afternoon. I'm so glad I decided to do something a bit different like this to break up the day-to-day in the house.

We ended up pretending the restaurant was full and we could eavesdrop on other conversations and talk about other diners behind their backs. Like the group of middle-aged ladies being unnecessarily gregarious, or the family with the two grumpy teenagers celebrating their younger sister's birthday, or the older man and the younger woman having an affair. The maître d' was an arrogant man too – he copped his share – as did the waitress who kept giving me the eye.

Occasionally we'd look at the passers-by on Magill Rd, like the lady collecting cans in one of those blue-and-white bags, or the slightly overweight, lycra-clad cyclist stopping for a coffee across the road, posing way too much and showing way too many body contours, or the thirty something jogging by in that look-at-me kind of way.

We had a laugh at all our new imaginary friends – it was so much fun. Before we left we sneaked into the bathroom when no one was watching and did something the management definitely would not have approved of.

*

5pm: Everything seems to be coming together right now. I have a community I feel wants and needs me. I have someone great to share my time with. I have plenty of food supplies for now and there is potential for more to be discovered.

I decided to tell Fi everything. I told her I found out about the rock early and stockpiled food. I showed her the cellar as there was no point in hiding it anymore. She's shown me she's trustworthy but, more importantly than that, I want to tell her. I wanted her to know she was safe here and totally trusted.

Now she knows everything about this place – all the systems, all the secret stashes, all the protocols to make life safe and to survive.

I did an updated stocktake this afternoon, now that everything's out in the open. I think we have enough food to get us through until February, but that doesn't take into account any of the bonus food that will come our way from the community. Given there will be more hidden gems in the city I can see home supplies lasting a lot longer. Very happy.

The water is still an issue as I have nowhere near enough. I'm going to dedicate some time soon to working out a suitable purification process. I remember learning something about it in school once, when there was a project we had to decide what were the most important items to keep if you were lost in the outback. One of them was a plastic sheet as you could dig a hole in the sand, cover it with the sheet, pin it down at the edges and then put a rock in the middle. As the morning dew condensated on the plastic it would flow into the centre of the sheet, then drip into a container you put underneath. Now my circumstances are slightly different, but I think I could achieve something

similar if I boiled some of the dirty ice in a large pot. I could collect the steam somehow – pure water. That's the plan at least.
****

Saturday, May 17, 2014
8.15am: Feeling so motivated after the stocktake that I might top up on petrol for the generator after we get back from the community. If I can teach Fi how to do that she'll officially know everything to survive. She's keen to learn, too. I've got massive respect for how she goes about things. She doesn't use me for a free ride. Instead, she wants to show me she can be useful every step of the way.

I guess, from her point of view, she's in a far more vulnerable position than me. I mean, she needs me more than I need her to survive. But the truth is I need her too, in different ways, but just as much.
*

6pm: Oh my God. God no. Please, please no. It's happened again. This place has delivered me to hell, it's shown me how evil it can be, how evil people can be. Again I am left to pick up the pieces, for me and others.

As soon as we neared the school I knew something was horribly, horribly wrong. I could hear someone crying. The sort of bellow that tells of inner pain and curdles your blood with its pitch. When we got close enough to the gym to see what was going on there were three people huddled together, in tears. None of them I knew by name. One of the two middle-aged ladies saw us approach and ran over to tell us not to go in. She blurted out a bunch of words but the only ones I can remember were "they killed them all".

I knew what was inside that door was going to tear me apart but I didn't realise the extent of it all. It was a massacre. From the moment I stepped through the door I saw nothing but bodies, blood and bullet casings. Most of the bodies either lay around where the map used to be or where the food stocks used to be – both now gone. They'd just been herded into the corners and mown down.

There is no doubt it was the work of the Norwood hubbers. I hate them. A real hate that makes me want to dedicate my life to seeking revenge. How could they? We were already on the back foot. We had few weapons, no direct food supply, no decent headquarters – we weren't a threat. We were destined to die before them.

A wave of guilt hit me as I remembered back to my city raid, feeling a presence as we walked down Magill Rd. They were watching us then and they probably watched us return. Maybe the city raid idea put us back on their radar.

When the next crew went out they must've been ready. The spies passed the message back and they gathered in numbers to await the city raiders' return. They managed to get us when we had the greatest numbers to kill and the most food to take. It makes me sick they'd think like that. They killed people. For food. They didn't just kill them, they planned it for the perfect moment. It's psychotic.

Oh God, I put a chain of events in motion that lead to all this. It's my fault.

I said it out aloud. 'It's my fault'. But Fi tried to snap me out of it by protesting between her tears. We just embraced in the middle of it all. I can't remember how long we were there, but I just closed my eyes and braced for the job ahead. We needed to bury these people.

The other three no-names didn't look like they wanted to go anywhere near the gym again. There were two shovels in our supplies. I went out and handed them over, asking them to head to the oval and start digging holes, one for each person. They wailed at the idea but I told them we had to.

Fi and I went back inside and started the grim task of dragging them out one by one. Between the five of us we would identify each victim, before putting them in a grave. I would go back inside, mark their name on our records as deceased and move on to the next body. By no.3 I was numb to it all – the carnage, the disgusting smell, the heavy lifting, the way the faces contorted to make people I knew almost unrecognisable. It just became a job. Something that had to be done.

Just before lunch another few groups rocked up. Each time we'd have to relive the whole scene through fresh eyes. I'd become aware again, I'd hurt again, then I'd get back to business.

The numbers made my task a lot easier.

I saw Mia's body, Mark and Jemma, Steve K, Steve P, Kelly, John, Malcolm – everybody I had a reasonable connection with was gone. By about 2pm we had 83 graves lined up and 20 people to say a prayer for them.

The ones left weren't central players in the community – they were fringe people. They were the people who enjoyed the rewards without putting in the work. They were old or young or strange or injured or just plain odd. Some started asking me what we were going to do now. Like I was in charge.

I had too much running through my head to start leading a herd. I suggested they either bunker down in their houses or go to the Firle hub. I couldn't take responsibility for them and I believed they were the best options available.

Rebuilding was futile – the Norwood hubbers would be back. The others could offer nothing to help Fiona or me – any alliance will weaken us. At that moment, I didn't really care what happened to them. The community was gone. I wanted to go home to the way it was before the rock hit. I just wanted it all to go away.

Sitting back home now I'm still in a million places – angry, sad, lost, confused. I'm fearful of what the future holds and I feel vulnerable in this place. The Norwood hubbers will be back. How long until they start going house to house? Where do we go then?

I don't know what my next move is.

Today changed the game. It totally screwed everything. How can I stay here without the community around? Fi and I are sitting ducks, but we can't move, we have no way to transport the food stocks.

I need to come up with a strategy and fast.

First things first, I'm gonna seal the front door. There's no one I want coming into this house apart from Fi and I. I'm going to the shed to find three of the heftiest chunks of wood I can and some heavy duty nails, then make sure that door never opens again.

Next I need to figure out how to deter people from heading down the side of the house. I'm not sure what to do here and I'll need my own access at times, too.

Then I think it's best if Fi and I just hold tight inside for at least a week and not make any rash decisions. Maybe the Norwood crew will come back and start sweeping house to house for food. In fact, no maybes about it, they will. I think it'll be sooner rather than later, based on everything I've seen so far.

After a week we'll see what happens. We might need to do it all again and again. Who knows? I've got time.

I'll be getting bug-out bags ready to go next. Mine is collecting dust in the corner but I need to revisit what's in it based on the new circumstances. At the very least I'll definitely need to add some weapons. I also need to get one ready for Fiona. We'll need a bug-out plan too. Where to meet if we get separated? Where we will go? Do I set up some food in a second location, I think it's a good idea, but where? So many things to organise to stay ahead of the game.

Beyond holding the fort and bug-out plans, I really need to start thinking about our next move. The big move. The inevitable move – the move-away-from home move. It has to happen. Whether it's tomorrow, a month from now or when the food's running low early next year, we need to find another food source. Ideally it's a new home, a permanent home, with food resources and safety, with a small, welcoming community.

Not likely, I know. But a guy's gotta dream. I'd settle for the food supply right now.

The city has shown it can provide, for a period of time, but there's no way I can go back there now. The Norwood hubbers attacked us when they did because they followed our people back. That means they know what the city can offer. They'll be all over it like a rash. As much as I'm tempted, that place is now out of bounds.

In fact, I'm struggling to think of any place in Adelaide that will offer what I'm looking for. Even if there is some magical food supply lurking somewhere, chances are there's a trigger-happy horde holding on to it for dear life. I'm not totally upset with the idea of leaving Adelaide. Recent events make me feel it's the best thing.

*

10pm: I've just spent a couple of hours in the war room, looking at maps and trying to find a next move. It's more difficult than I thought. For a start, I'm not just deciding for me, the decision will also affect Fiona. And it's not like I can just drive somewhere for laughs and move on if I don't like it. On foot, a wrong decision could cost weeks, which will eat resources and cost lives.

Having a look at the map of South Australia is pretty depressing – every city or large town is on the coast. The only real exceptions are Mount Gambier (which must've been demolished in the Melbourne blast wave) or Murray Bridge (which wouldn't have fared much better). Gawler may have some potential. It's virtually an outer suburb of Adelaide these days, but it's still country. And there's potentially access to resources I could never get close to in the inner suburbs. Gawler also sits on that awkward topographic line where some of it would've been hit by the tsunami but some of the higher streets on the eastside would've survived. Most of the suburbs on Adelaide's northern fringe would be under the tsunami line, too, which may make it a natural oasis from the city. Even writing this down I'm starting to get excited.

The best bit about it is if it doesn't work it'll be heading us in the direction of the Riverland – Waikerie, Barmera, Berri, Loxton and Renmark – the only other large South Australian towns that could possibly be functioning right now. I reckon there are some likely looking conditions there, too (based on the map). And if nothing works out, we can just cross the border and hit every town from Mildura to Wagga Wagga. All rural, all on higher ground, all with potential. Beyond that is Canberra, the only Australian capital city to survive rock night intact. Who knows, maybe that's our Nirvana?

I'm starting to feel the seeds of a quality idea here. It feels right. Surely, if any community has survived in number and with resources, they are on this path somewhere? I mean, I can't be sure of anything. I've not seen or heard any news on these places for weeks, and I haven't visited since I was a kid (or not at all). They could be blown off the map, burned to the ground or a total warzone.

But I do know this – I rather die trying to get there than stay starving and scared on my patch here.

On the downside is the little fact Canberra is about 1200km away :S Hey, I never said it was a perfect plan, just a good one. I've got some logistics to think about regarding traveling and carrying food. Actually, there's a lot of work ahead before we set off, but that's not for me to work out today. I'm exhausted and I've distracted myself long enough from everything that happened today. I need to mourn. I need to hold my girlfriend and enjoy every moment with her – that's important.

But one day, not too far away, we're going on a road trip!

****

Sunday, May 18, 2014

8.45am: Last night was terrible. Not because of what I felt for everything that happened yesterday, but for what I didn't feel. I was expecting to be overwhelmed by grief and loss, but I wasn't. I felt violated, insecure, scared even. But for some reason the killings at the school have not hit me as hard as before.

Has something inside me changed? I'm starting to question myself as to why this doesn't hurt more, but no matter how hard I try to make it hurt, it doesn't. I didn't cry once yesterday. Maybe each time I have to deal with something like this a little part of my humanity dies. Maybe that's the way it has to be.

I sense Fiona feels the same. Even though she didn't know these people as well as I did, she wasn't struck to the core by yesterday.

Thinking back to what we did at the school, carrying all those bodies, burying them in the ash, well, the only way you could cope was by detaching a part of your mind. It's not a switch you can flick on and off at will. Maybe your mind automatically starts burying your emotions when there's too much to deal with, just like it cuts off your sense of pain when you're physically hurt beyond extreme.

*

4.40pm: The front door is now sealed. It has more wood attached to it than a Brazilian rainforest (assuming there are still Brazilian rainforests). Unless the hordes from some Middle-age-battlefield suddenly materialise in my front yard with a battering ram, I think I'm safe from attack. Plus, I always like to be doing something physical around the house; it makes me feel than I'm not wasting time. However, I'm not sure if I'll be able to conjure up enough jobs to keep that going while we ride this thing out.

*

6.30pm: I've been thinking about when's the best time to leave and it seems to me that, logically, the later the better. If we can survive here and stay safe – and that's a big if – then we are best to leave our run as late as possible. Two reasons. One, we have food supplies we can't possibly take with us and, two, the longer we wait, the more settled the new world will become. Supply and demand are gonna take their toll on a lot of people. I can't see anyone being generous with the food stocks now. But down the track when the bulk of people have been weeded out (starved/murdered) and people start working out how to produce food, then maybe things will change.

So, if riding things out here for a while is the best result – which it is – then we have to consider how to handle the Norwood hubbers. They'll be back and this time they'll have our map. They'll know I live at this address. What they won't know is if they've killed me or not. I see this as my only advantage. A very small one, but an advantage.

I've come up with a plan to survive and keep the majority of food intact. Part of me thinks I'm crazy for thinking this, but the other part knows it's the best way to stay alive and keep food stocks intact. They need to come in and raid the house. It's the only way. We need to leave out a minimal amount of food for them to take and feel like they've cleaned us out. Meanwhile, I need to move everything else down into the cellar. All the rest of the food and any other items we'll need for survival. Then we need to conceal the generator, which will be easy to hide with a tarp and some ash, I might do the same with the water – transfer it outside.

I'm thinking back to when I went from house to house with Mark and Jemma. We never checked outside. In fact, we'd poke out heads into every room but we really only had any interest in the kitchen/pantry. We had a number of places to cover and the work was tiring – it was the only way to be efficient. I need to put myself in their shoes when they come here. They won't be doing a thorough sweep, they'll just want to get in, get rewarded and move on. So if we give them an easy reward, hopefully they'll tick us off their book, take the 15 or so cans I leave out and go.

They won't be expecting me to have much food, as the community was sharing everything down at the school. It's a convincing food footprint to leave on the world.

Here's the tricky bit, though. For this to work, and to ensure they never come back, they have to think no one's alive. The safest way would be to leave the house for a while, but there'd be no way of knowing when they came or left. This could happen at any time. It could be tomorrow, it could be two weeks away. How would we know if we weren't here?

If we stay, we'll have to ride out the raid in the cellar or shed. I prefer the cellar. They'd never suspect it was there and, if we cover the entry door with a rug, they'd never detect us. If they did go down there, we'd be armed and ready. How many people would be raiding us? Two or three at the most is my guess. If they did manage to find the cellar and climb down, we'd have arrows in them before they knew what hit them.

It's risky, but if it works and we're not detected, we should be able to exist here undetected and undisturbed until we make our move for Gawler.

We will have to play things very carefully though; any hint of life and our cover could be blown in a second. That means no using the heater (which I don't use much anyway) and no eating inside – both dead giveaways. Even sitting on the couch for too long could leave a warm patch that could give us away. It also means I have to shut down Dad's laptop, which is connected to the courtyard security camera. Meanwhile, if we leave some food out to go bad and some dishes to gross up the sink we'll go a long way towards convincing any raiders this house is abandoned.

We'll have to practise our scramble to the cellar, time and time again, so we can pull it off quietly in a matter of seconds. We'll have to find a spot for the bug-out bags that is out of sight but ready to take if things go pear shaped. We'll also need to have a foolproof bug-out plan ready in the same circumstances.

Then we just have to wait.

****

Monday, May 19, 2014
11.30am: It's been a busy morning. I've found a spot for the bug-out bags in the side courtyard. It took an age to jimmy the BBQ out from the ice and ash, but I have managed to make enough room for the bags in the corner beside it. I've covered them in garbage bags to protect them from the ash and put a spare bit of tarp on top. I've used rope to link the bag handle to the tarp, so in theory I can heave everything out in one go, rip off the garbage bags and leave. At the moment the tarp is barely visible, and when the next ashfall comes it will disappear completely from prying eyes. I'll just have to keep an eye on it every couple of days to make sure it doesn't get frozen in.

It takes about six-seven minutes to put on our outside gear. We have bagged that up too, and hidden it under the laundry sink. If we are under the pump we can grab the gear, then grab our bug-out bags and head for the Greek restaurant. When we get there we can suit up and head off. At some point this week I'm going to take a few food supplies up to the restaurant too, just in case we have to leave in a hurry.

I'm yet to flesh out our full plan, but I think I want to make the Jamesons' our first port of call. I'm not sure if they're still around, but their house is about two hour's walk in heavy conditions – it's uphill, but very achievable and far enough away that no one will follow.

It would be nice to see a familiar face if they were still around but, even if they weren't, it would be interesting to see Adelaide from the same perspective as impact night.

*

2.15pm: I've used some of Dad's double-thick, double-sided tape to stick a foot rug to the cellar door. It makes opening it an issue, but once it's closed you'd have no idea it's there. Instead of keeping it closed I have wedged a piece of wood across the corner so it stays open a few centimetres.

We have done a couple of run-throughs of how long it would take to hole up in the cellar from the moment we hear a knock at the door. I'm on weapons duty, so I grab the crossbow, and the bow and arrows. Fi grabs any bowls, glasses or cutlery we've been using and takes them with her. If we've been sitting on the couch she turns the cushions over, just to be sure. Our best time was 48 seconds. That's plenty quick enough. It'll take anyone about that long to start trying to hammer down the door and another minute or two to realise they can't, before they try down the side of the house for another access point. We just need to stay quiet, have a bit of luck and we'll be fine... he says... somewhat confidently :S

The only real concern will come if we're at a weak moment. If I'm cleaning the ice away from the bug-out kits or, worse still, going to the toilet.

Going to the toilet has become a far more disgusting event than in the past. I'm not sure if it's frozen or has broken pipes or something else, but the flush mechanism hasn't worked for weeks. Since then I have been, well, pissing into a vase. When it's full enough or the smell is too overpowering I tip it out in the backyard. As for the more substantial of toilets breaks, that has been reduced to putting a large Tupperware container inside the actual toilet bowl, then emptying it out the back (or over the neighbour's fence). It's so gross I didn't want to mention it in the diary, but now it's become a factor in bigger issues.

The way I see it, we can't afford to get caught 'sitting down', so to speak. We definitely can't afford to get caught doing it inside – that would be a dead giveaway. That could cost us everything. So we've got to go outside from now until we're raided. It's a thoroughly depressing thought. It's cold and disgusting enough without adding this to it! Still, it's only temporary, and I'd rather do that than lose my food supplies or my life.

I've got to give Fi credit, because when I suggest some of these crazy ideas I can see the look in her eye – the 'that's disgusting' look. Despite this, she just accepts it as the gross reality of our situation. She may have also said, "You've got to be freakin' kidding me", too... but still, props to her.

So that's it. For now we wait in the dark and cold, without electricity, until someone comes visiting. Maybe I'm being over-paranoid here, but to my mind (and based on what the Norwood hubbers have already done), they'll definitely come back. They have the map that tells them which houses are occupied, or cleared, or were lived in by the Trinity Gardens community. They know everything; they have everything but the keys to my door.

Damn it! I've just remembered the notes I made about the deceased community members down at the school. I need my name in that book. I need them to think I am dead. I've got to go down there tonight and add it in. I'm not really up for reliving the scenes at the school anytime soon, but I have no choice. I figure I'll head off late – after 9pm. If there are Norwood hubbers in the area then surely they'll head home before that, given it takes a good hour to get there on foot.

****

Tuesday, May 20, 2014

6.45am: Last night went all to plan. There was no sign of anyone on the streets or at the school. I took a torch but barely used it. I was too worried someone would be watching. I took the crossbow with me and I'm not ashamed to admit I was sacred witless. I haven't felt like that ever. I hate that feeling, but I can't see it changing any time soon. Everything has changed. It's not my world anymore, I'm just a little fish wading through shark central.

I did manage to do some multitasking. When I was out, I took a bag full of food supplies (maybe a week's worth) up to the Greek restaurant – our bug-out meeting point. I've hidden it behind the cleaning products and I was able to find a removable shelf, which I've used to obscure my stash at the back. I feel like it's safe there.

That's it for me, no more outside until we get raided, except when nature calls.

*

1.45pm: This day has taken forever already. It's only early afternoon and I've long since run out of things to do. I've spent a bit of time working on the bug-out plan. I found a path from the Jamesons' out to Gawler that takes us mostly along streets and roads under the tsunami line. I have a feeling the less human interaction we have on the road the better off we will be.

As per the plan, if Gawler doesn't work out we'll make our way up to the Riverland. If we were taking a car we'd use the Sturt Highway but, given we're on foot, if we take the Murray St/Barossa Valley Way option (which is about the same distance), we'll hit a bunch more small towns along the way. Lock that into the plan.

*

7.30pm: I've been thinking about how fast we will move along the roads. It helps to then calculate how long the trip will take and, therefore, what provisions we'll need. My best guess says 2.5km/hr would be top speed, so I'm calculating for 2km/hr. Based on that I think it'll take 10-11 hours to get to Gawler. We could plan for 25km a day. That means it's probably five days to get from Gawler to Waikerie. If we don't have any luck there it would be another four days to make it to Renmark at the other side of the Riverland. Another five days to get to Mildura across the border in Victoria, which is about a third of the way to Canberra. The stretches a few days either side of Mildura seem the least likely to find anywhere to call home, but as we head into New South Wales and closer to Canberra the number of towns picks up again.

All up I think it would take about 45 days.

And therein lies the problem. Even on two meals a day, that's 180 meals for the two of us. Given that most of the food remaining is in cans, and it's about three cans to the kilogram, that's about 60kg. Fiona wouldn't weigh much more than 50kg! That's without factoring in water. This food thing is going to need some more research.

Besides, what else will we need to travel? I have my tent, which is light and packs tight, but we'll also need torches, can openers, knives, cutlery, weapons – so many things to consider, so much I feel I'm missing. This is a plan a long way from being ready.

Fortunately I've got nothing but time right now.

****

Wednesday, May 21, 2014
6.15pm: It was another nothing day of dark, cold and too little physical activity. It puts pressure on me to come up with some amazing solution on how to pack right for the road, but then I find it harder to make rational decisions.

It's also tough to think straight when you're constantly on high alert for Norwood hubbers. I think Fi senses I'm getting stressed. She's doing her best to take my mind off things but I keep finding a way to feel grumpy. Maybe it's just the hell of being cooped up in this stupid place the entire time.

My life feels like it's devolving. When you're a baby your world is your house. As you grow, it expands to be the street, the school, friends' places etc. Then, when you get your own wheels and free reign on the internet, your world – your awareness, your scope of understanding expands at a ridiculous rate.

But since rock day my world has closed in. It's devolved. No media, no valid mode of transport, less friends, my world is slowly shrinking back in knowledge and scope to the size of my house, as if I was a baby again.

That's the scary and depressing thought I can't escape today.

****

Thursday, May 22, 2014
7.30am: Feeling a little more positive today. Fi and I played some cards last night – euchre and cribbage mostly. Then we played a game of Monopoly (well, half a game). It's been years since I did that sort of thing.

We did have our first argument, over Monopoly of all things. She has some bizarre rule interpretations. When she got the 'Advance to go, collect

$200' card, she did so, but when she moved off go on her next shot she wanted ANOTHER $200! Erm… what? Not in this house! The other weird rule she had was if I landed on a property but chose not to buy it, she could. It's a total game-changer. She was adamant she'd read the rules and both were in there, but it just sounded ridiculous. I think I came across as arrogant with my argument because she got really annoyed with me, hence the half a game of Monopoly.

We soon found ourselves laughing at the stupidity of the whole situation. I mean, we're sitting in a cold, dark house waiting to be raided by armed killers for our supplies and we managed to have a fallout over the ownership rights of Old Kent Road. After we settled we had a couple of drinks to celebrate our first argument and retired early where Fi did an even better job of helping me take my mind off things. She's really good for me like that. Just knowing when to help me out (when I can't see it myself). It's made a big difference.

Monopoly aside, last night was what I needed and today is going to be a good day.

*

2pm: We just had the fright of our lives. There was a loud crashing sound outside – it must've been big to hear it over the gale that's blowing. Anyways, we immediately went into scramble to cellar mode. It took us about 1 minute 20 – much longer than our best practices. I guess we were caught off-guard and confused. There's a lesson in that.

My heart was beating out of my chest as we lay in wait in the cellar. I know that's a saying, 'heart beating out of my chest', but that's exactly what it felt like. I just couldn't control the adrenaline surging through me. Maybe it was adrenaline, maybe it was a panic attack – either way, I've got to control that.

After about five minutes we started to realise there was no one in the house. But I wasn't too keen to leave before I was sure. In the end we waited down there for 25 minutes. I was a mental wreck trying to convince myself it was safe to open the hatch to the cellar. I tried to ease it open gently but it's seen better days so it groaned and creaked loud enough to alert anyone within earshot. Thankfully, that was just Fi and I.

I remember saying something stupid like, 'Is anybody there?', but there was no answer. If there was I'm sure I would've known all about it. We did a sweep of the house and gave it the all clear.

Curiosity got the better of me and I went outside to investigate. Turns out the noise was the sound of one of the trees falling over on the street. I suppose a combination of high winds, zero sunlight in weeks and a heavy layer of ash and ice was its undoing.

****

Friday, May 23, 2014

10.45am: I am seriously bored. I've got things to do and plans but I can't bring myself to move. I'm frozen with boredom. Everything is on hold while I wait for the inevitable.

Is it inevitable? Surely it's the logical move for them to make? I mean, I assume they have the map. If they have the map, they have a house-by-house guide to the status of every property around here. Free resources for them to take. Why wouldn't they? They've done it before and the longer they leave it the more chance they give those remaining here to gather and use those resources. Tactically it would be a mistake to wait any longer than they have to. That's how it plays out in my mind – perfectly logical, strategic move.

The only thing missing is them. They haven't come. It's been days now… we're prime for attacking… why haven't they come? Maybe they don't have the map after all. But they have to have the map, who else would? Why aren't they coming? Why?

This is seriously doing my head in. Just raid me already, I'm waiting. Come at me bitches!

Random thought of the day.

So transport is all but impossible in this day and age. Roads are ruined and covered in ash, most coastlines and boats are destroyed and air travel is impossible. But there's one mode of transport that can't be stopped, even in these conditions – the hovercraft! Imagine if I could get my hands on one of those? That would be a game changer.

I mean, I know I'm dreaming – hovercrafts are something you use to cruise across the everglades in Florida, not in Adelaide. But life would be completely different if I could get my hands on one. I could cruise the city or beyond as I wished, zipping over the ash like it wasn't there. There's no shortage of petrol anywhere so the only limitation would be punctures. I want one!

My random thought of the day started as a loopy musing, turned into a slightly insane person's attempt at a joke and now I'm seriously thinking about it. I wouldn't know the first idea about how to make one or where to find one, but if I could somehow manage it I could own this world!

*

8.20pm: Just consulted the good old Yellow Pages and it was nothing but a tease. The only listing for hovercraft in the index pointed to the 'Tourist Attractions, Information and Services' section, but when I looked there I couldn't find any mention of a hovercraft. Swear word!

I really want one now. I'm starting to obsess. I'm going to build one*.

*He said, not knowing where to start.

*

9pm: I forgot to mention this earlier. Today the mercury reached the whopping height of 3°C. This is far worse than the more alarmist expert warnings pre-rock. It just goes to show we are dealing with events far beyond the scope of human understanding. We are breaking new ground in suffering! Great to be a ground-breaker some days :/

I shudder to think what the middle of July will bring. And I only hope we do actually come out of winter with something resembling warmth later this year.

****

Saturday, May 24, 2014
8.30am: Fi and I broke our own rules last night. I think the boredom got to us and we watched a movie – *Borat*. I love that film. I've seen it a dozen times, at least, but Fi never had the pleasure.

We used the laptop on battery supply and watched it in bed, under the quilt, so no light and little noise would get out. I haven't laughed like that in ages, partly at the movie but mostly at Fi's reaction to it. Especially the hotel scene... ewww!

*

9.15am: The house is really gross at the moment. It's through necessity, rather than laziness, but it doesn't make it any easier to live with. The smell of the mouldy food we left out a few days ago can only be described as overpowering. The scary thing is we've been living in the smell and, I assume, have built up a tolerance. When anyone comes to raid this place they are not going to want to hang around long, that's for sure.

I'm starting to worry about our battery situation, too – the torches are the only light we have at the moment and if we run out of batteries, well, that would not be nice! I've got a number of rechargeables but they're running out quickly and I won't be able top them up until we can run the generator again. All the heavy-duty batteries are already out of commission because we've really only got AA batteries left, which only go in the little torches. We're burning through those at a rate too. I've resorted to raiding every toy, remote control and electronic device I can think of to get us through. I might have to do a raid of Mr Nichols' place to see if I can stock-up.

*

10am: I'm still not letting the hovercraft thing go. I'm starting to think of ways to actually build one. I mean, if I could get my hands on a large fan, connect to a lawnmower engine, attach it all to a base, throw on a couple of seats and attach the whole thing to a bunch of inflated tyre tubes protected by some sort of sturdy material covering, well, I'd have a hovercraft.

There's only one problem with the last sentence – that's the word 'if', which has such big ramifications for the rest of the sentence. I've been shown how to build and weld, but it's not my strong suit. I'm not sure where I could source all the gear needed to do the job and I'd need to find a place to do it.

Dad's got some of the welding gear, but our shed is nowhere big enough, however I know Mr Nichols spent a lot of time in his shed, so I'm guessing he may have some additional equipment and some space to work.

As for the giant fan, well, Kennards hire is only around the corner. If there's going to be one anywhere, it'd be there. I know it's probably been looted to hell, but who in their right mind would take a fan? They may even have some motors I can nab, too. If not it shouldn't be hard to find a decent lawnmower engine.

Tyre tubes will be everywhere. I probably won't even need to jack a car up to take one, either. Just dig the tyre out of the ash, let the air out and take the whole wheel.

Most of the other bits and pieces will be around somewhere. I guess the main bit is coming up with a way to hook up a petrol motor to a large fan to create enough thrust to get the thing moving, the rest will…. Shit – they're here.

1.20pm: Raided. At last! And we survived, undetected. I'm still shaking.

I'm not sure how long we took to get down the cellar after we heard the knock at the door. I'm not even sure what they even knocked on the door with; it sounded metallic, maybe a crowbar. I was writing in the diary and Fi was reading a book. We didn't even look at each other, just jumped straight into scramble mode. Fi had already cleared the breakfast dishes up so all she had to do was flip the couch cushions and do a quick sweep of the rest of the living area. I crept to the entrance and grabbed the crossbow and other weaponry – I didn't make a sound. By the time I reached the cellar the door was already open and Fi was safe inside. I followed her in and we lowered the hatch down and waited.

It must've taken them 4-5 minutes to bust open the front door. We could hear the frame being ripped to shreds as they tried to bust past the defences I'd set up. Stupid raiders – they were supposed to give up on the front door and take the side entrance. It would've saved a lot of hassle.

Once they were in, our plans worked a treat. Judging by the voices there were only two of them, a man and a woman – she was obviously in charge. They were trying to talk but were on the verge of gagging with every breath. The woman ordered the man to raid the kitchen. He must've had a container or something because it sounded like he was sweeping handfuls of food in at a time. I don't know if they were in a hurry because of a schedule or because they were dying from the smell, but either way, it was perfect.

While he was crashing and banging away I could hear her footsteps go to the front bedrooms. This is when I was most concerned – had we concealed our presence well enough? About a minute later her footsteps came past again on the way to the back of the house. My heartbeat was going mental. It was so crazy my breathing started to get shallow. Fi grabbed my hand, which helped a little – we were in this together.

Then she came back to the kitchen and stood what must have been very close to the hatch. She asked the guy if he was done yet, he responded with a "Yep". Then she said, "Good, let's get out of this dump". Then the footsteps started again, this time marching more and more distant, and quiet, and never coming back.

We waited for a few minutes more. I didn't even realise Fi and I were in an embrace, not only holding hands but wrapped around each other's bodies, too.

Eventually we shared a little laugh down there – it had worked! Living without electricity, in a place degenerating into filth – it had sown the seeds we wanted. Now, according to the Norwood hubbers (and probably to the rest of the world for that matter) we were dead and this house was a deceased and raided estate. It now served no purpose to anyone. We held each other a while longer and kissed – it was a kiss less of passion, more pride and relief.

After we thought we'd given the thing long enough, and after waiting another 10 minutes after that, we pushed our way out of the cellar. The first thing I did was sneak to the entrance of the house to see if there was anyone outside. It looked clear to me – we were nearly home free.

I inspected the door while I was there. They did a fair job in butchering it. It's a major problem. That door is our security, from the weather and from others, so it needs fixing. I think we'll have to ride it out tonight as there's no way of knowing if the Norwood folk will still be on the street or not.

*

4.15pm: The wind has picked up this afternoon, and is doing its best to take the edge off my good mood. Worse still, I don't think it's a good idea to fire up the generator tonight. Just in case. Tonight we just have to rug up and embrace the cold, knowing things will be a whole lot better tomorrow.

After today I'm confident the Norwood hubbers won't be back any time soon. Here's my logic. One – they know the Trinity Gardens community raided every other house in the area, so the only houses they'll get any benefit from are those of community members. Two – they would've done this in one sweep. It doesn't make any sense to prolong getting their hands on the resources they needed. They would've sent everyone they could spare today to get the food and carry it back. It's the best use of their people resources. Three – they know the city has resources to offer. They'll view that as their best future prospecting area, and after that, the suburbs east and southeast of Norwood. I'm convinced we are seen as a dead zone now – no food or weapons to offer, no enemies to fear, we are nothing to them. And that's good news to me.

****

Sunday, May 25, 2014
8.10am: I put every quilt, blanket and sheet I could find on the bed last night, covered myself in two layers and wore gloves. It took all that to get comfortable. But I couldn't sleep; part of me was still on a high from the victory and part of me was spinning with ideas for the future. Today is a bright new day in devastated Adelaide, full of possibilities. I can breath in the sweet smell of opportunity… and rotting food… and ash.

It's hard to know if the door is salvageable. Most of the superficial damage is around the lock area, but the real impact was on the frame, which was shredded. I'm not sure what they used to make such a mess of it, but it clearly worked for them.

I'm not entirely sure on the best approach to fix it, as the lock itself is still functional, somehow, despite having a few chunks missing. Plan A is to see if I can use some of a doorframe from Mr Nichols' place. I'm really out of my comfort zone here, but if I can remove it in something close to one piece I might have a chance of replacing the whole side of my frame here. Then I just need to secure the lock back into place, cross fingers, and we'll be sweet. Plan B consists of just sealing the entire doorway so it never opens again. It's not a bad Plan B but I'd prefer to fix it properly.

*

3.30pm: Four hours to replace some wood – four hours! I tried to use the doorframe from the back door at Mr Nichols' place. I worked on the outer side panel of the door frame, the one the lock end was embedded in. I used a hacksaw to cut it top and bottom, then tried to lever it clear with a crowbar. I did manage to get it out but the piece of wood I was left with was too mutilated. I scavenged around and, between Dad's shed and Mr Nichols' shed, was able to find a couple of solid pieces of pine, some heavy glue, a saw, plane, hammer, screwdriver, drill, chisels and clamps. In the end I just started from scratch, removing the damaged frame and replacing it with a piece I shaped from the spare block of wood in Mr Nichols' shed. It took a number of attempts to get the fit just right, but it was worth it.

I've now just got to give the glue a chance to dry properly before I cut out a recess for the lock. Meanwhile, the door has to stay ajar while the clamps are attached, so the weather's still getting in, but not as bad as before. If all goes to plan we will have a fully functional door some time after dinner tonight.

Fi has done her fair share of hard work today, too. She's been on lookout duty while I've been doing my thing. I really doubted the Norwood crew was coming back any time soon, but if they did we would've been totally exposed. With today's visibility you could see torch light from about 50m away, so Fi would've had enough warning to grab me though, so we could scurry back down the cellar.

It's mid afternoon now so I seriously doubt we will be seeing anyone today.

*

6pm: Just had a chance to admire my own handiwork after taking off the clamps… gee I impress me. It's sitting pretty flush and the door action is smooth. I've now added the lock and everything lines up perfectly. I used to love helping Dad out in the shed, tinkering with bits and pieces, but I never took on anything like this before. It makes me believe I'm actually a silly chance to build a hovercraft. Sure, it's a whole world in advance of repairing a door frame, but I've got the tools at my disposal, I've got the idea and I've got plenty of time. Why not?

Tomorrow I'm going to varnish my handiwork on the doorframe, I want to finish the job off so you'd never know the door was damaged. #slightlyanal
*

9.15pm: It's Fi's birthday in a couple of weeks and I want to do something nice for her. To give her a day that takes her away from this place and all the thoughts that come with it. I feel for her; I mean, we're all doing it tough, but she's got less than me. She lived with her mum pre-rock, but they never really got along. Her dad has been in Western Australia working in the mines for years, so she hasn't seen him since she was 12. Her mum was her only Adelaide family, and she lived under the tsunami line, unfortunately. Fi was lucky she was at her boyfriend's that night – it saved her life. Maybe that was the only good thing he did for her.

I've got a feeling she's just one of those people who didn't grow up with close friends, was kinda rejected by her family and has developed a thick emotional skin as a consequence. It fits perfectly with the douchebag boyfriend thing. She just hitched up to the guy hoping he was the answer to her problems, but he wasn't. So now she has no family, no anything… the only thing she's got is me, my shelter and my supplies. I'm glad I was here for her when she needed me. I know, deep down, she must think about the fact she doesn't have anything apart from what I've given her.

I don't ask anything for it, her company is all the thanks I need. But she's forever going all-out to prove her worth. That's great in some ways. It means I have someone I can trust and, in this world, two is many multiples better than one. But I don't want her doing it just to show me she serves some purpose or value to keep her around. Love is better than that.

So the birthday gift I want to give her more than anything is the feeling of value in her own self. I want to find things that make this place feel as much like her place as it does mine.

The one thing she talks about missing the most is her guitar. She's mentioned it a few times when we've talked. So that's my mission. I'm going shopping at some point. I'll just hit all the abandoned houses in the area as I'm sure guitars would be reasonably common. While I'm there I might see if I can find a few of the movies mentioned as favourites on DVD, some jewellery and maybe a nice outfit to wear. Then I just need to think of something nice for dinner and maybe somewhere different to have it and I think that's starting to sound like a good 18th birthday.

****

Monday, May 26, 2014
3.45pm: Lazy day today. It's been a long time coming. The only thing I did that resembled work was varnish the doorframe. It's not a perfect match with the other wood, but it's close enough to be passable. I gave it two hours to dry then, once I was able to shut it, I repaired the light block-out and marched straight to the generator. For the first time in a week we have light. I'm even running one of the heaters for a while. It'll burn through the fuel but it's totally worth a trip to resupply just to feel normal again.

The trick is to not get the place too hot, just a little something to take the edge off is all you need. It sounds crazy, but we're both getting used to the cold. I don't want to lose that because I've got a feeling it's here to stay. But taking the bite out of it helps. It's currently 10°C in here and that's about right in terms of a balance between comfortable and maintainable.

*

5.30pm: Fi's playing some *Guitar Hero* games on the old Xbox360 at the moment (she's better at it than me already). It's not a real guitar but a little something to make her happy, I suppose. I've been fighting the need to plan my next step today. Part of me has this need to constantly plan for the future, whether it's the Canberra trip or the hovercraft or the bug-out plan – I think it's some sort of genetic or instinctual survival mechanism kicking in. But some days I've just got to say 'no'. I mean, I don't want life to be all about survival. I don't want to live in a world where that is the only thing driving me. Just existing – I want more than that. Maybe it's unrealistic but I just want to have those days where nothing happens. I like nothing. Just slobbing and doing things I choose to do because I like them – and for no other reason. So I'm just going to chill and read some *Game of Thrones* then I'm going to flick back through the diary again, see if I can add anything else in.

At some point I'm going to re-type the diary out on the computer as I wouldn't mind a digital copy. It has been a reasonably interesting 10 or 11 weeks, after all!

****

Tuesday, May 27, 2014
12.15pm: I've just spent the morning reconfiguring the war room. I've taken down the world poster as I doubt I'll get more global news anytime soon, and replaced it with a map of the path I intend to take to Canberra.

I've started to put together a list of what we'll need to survive the trip – and it's scary long! I think the best strategy is to start two lists. One would be the dream list of what I could take if I could build a functional hovercraft to carry us and the other would be the bare bones, what-we-can-carry-on-foot list.

The second list was a very depressing one to put together. In fact, I'm really struggling to see how it can work at all. There is just no way to get to Canberra if we have to set off with everything we need to survive. I think I'd be forced to construct some sort of sleigh I could tow behind me; it's the only way. It shouldn't be too hard to put together, but I don't want to spend any time thinking about it until I've explored every possibility with the hovercraft.

Speaking of which, I've started to draw up some loose plans for the hovercraft (HC). I can break the construction down into four areas – mechanics, chassis, base and engine. The last one is the most important. If I can get a functioning engine working then I can fudge the rest together, I'm sure.

I'm going on a road trip tomorrow. I'm looking for a guitar for Fi's birthday but I also want to nosey around Kennards Hire to see if they've got any industrial fans. That's the key. I need a way to generate enough thrust to drive the HC forward – if I don't have that the rest is meaningless.

While I'm on the road I might also have a look through Mark and Jemma's place. I assume they got raided at the same time we did a couple of days ago but I wonder if they found their stash. Mark and Jem kept two thirds of the big haul we found going house-to-house and it was their idea not to share it with the community. My guess is they may well have hidden the food in a secret location on their property that might not have been discovered by the Norwood hubbers. The extra food would be very handy, particularly the pasta and noodles (I remember them taking the bulk of that) – that stuff would be so much lighter and easier to haul long distance.

Gotta go, the smell of fresh bread is in the air… yum!

*

8pm: I've just spent the last couple of hours running Fi through the Canberra plan. I'd given her a heads-up on the idea before, but today I went though all the pros and cons on making the move. I found it really hard. As I was saying the words out loud to someone else it started to dawn on me this place won't be a part of my life forever. I could tell Fi was also affected by this. She agreed with all the logical points I made, but her eyes told me she didn't want to leave. The security of having a home does have a value, doubly so considering what we've gone through to keep it. But, in the end, the numbers don't lie – we cannot survive here long term. Fi agreed with this assessment and the general plan to head in the direction of Canberra.

Fiona had her reservations about Canberra as a final destination, given their population might now be suffering from the same food supply drain as anywhere else, and I agreed. I don't see Canberra as the destination, I see it as the direction we are heading in with any number of towns and cities between here and there our potential new home. Other than that she liked my way of thinking, although I suspect her belief I can build a HC is somewhat less than mine. Strangely, I'm not offended; maybe I'm deluding myself it can be done.

****

Wednesday, May 28, 2014
4.50pm: Massively successful day today. It's amazing what little gifts this world has to offer when you look hard enough.

My first stop was Kennards Hire and I think I found something just about perfect within minutes. It's a cooling fan that is seriously industrial strength. It's about a metre in diameter and says it spins at 850rpm. I don't know how to do the calculations but that seems like it's going to be perfect. It runs on 240v electricity, so all I need to do is rig up the second generator on the HC, plug in the fan and I'm away. They had three of them in stock so I thought my best bet was to take all of them. I'm not entirely sure if my HC will work better with one or two fans. Come to think of it, two fans might be better in case one breaks down in the middle of nowhere.

I was going to leave hauling them back to the house for last, but it was too good a find to wait. I dragged them back one at a time. They were heavy, very heavy, but on wheels. This helped for most of the trip back, but every now and then they'd break through the ash surface and take all my energy to pull out. Talk about hard work. Talk about totally worth it.

After I dropped the third one back home I stopped in for some food and drink to re-energise then headed back out on a high.

I had a delicate shopping request from Fi (erm... feminine hygiene products and the pill) and headed in the direction of the chemist on Magill Rd. Along the way I stopped in at every house I knew was abandoned and went shopping for Fi's birthday. I visited most of the same houses I had with Mark and Jemma, but this time I didn't bother with the kitchens. Instead I headed for the lounge rooms and bedrooms. I found so much cool stuff. I found a kickass mink coat (I think it's mink, whatever a mink is), plenty of DVDs I know she likes (*Mighty Boosh* box set, *Easy A*, *Juno*, and about six movies starring

Johnny Depp), a pair of his and hers matching watches, a nice necklace and a holy-crap-huge diamond ring!

I might keep the ring for a little while down the track.

When I arrived at the chemist it had predictably been looted. Almost everything of any use had been taken, including feminine hygiene and birth control products. That was not good news. I had a feeling if I arrived home without said products no amount of holy-crap-huge diamond rings would've atoned. There was still a quality selection of hair dye and heel balm, but they were useless.

Looters had got to most of the good stuff behind the counter. Most of the stuff on the shelves had been taken or landed on the floor and been buried in ash. All of the heavy duty painkillers had been swiped, but I did find some generic brand versions after sifting through the ground ash. I actually kept any painkillers I got my hands on – probably not something you think you'd need until it's too late to get them I figured. There were also a few containers that looked like antibiotic tablets of different varieties which I took as well, just in case. I ended up with about a dozen packets of things that were all in pretty bad shape – not the most successful trip it must be said.

On the way home I took the next street across and went into all the abandoned houses, this time visiting bathrooms instead of bedrooms and lounge rooms. The mission soon turned from boyfriend fail to success as I found an ample quantity of the missing items. Not only that, there were more painkillers, a couple of first aid kits and other 'could be handy one day' items.

I also found a pretty sweet-looking acoustic guitar in the third house I visited. It's got its own hard case with spare strings, picks and some other guitary looking stuff, too.

By the end my backpack was nearly full. I carried a guitar in one hand and dragged the coat behind in a couple of garbage bags (for protection) in the other. A good few hours' work.

As a final stop I dropped into Mark and Jemma's place. I had a pretty thorough sweep of the house before checking the garage and shed, but there was no sign of the food. Based on my conversations with them I knew they would've kept it somewhere hidden. I'd probably spent a good 20 minutes there when I had the idea to check the manhole. They had a ladder in the laundry, which gave me the idea (who keeps a ladder in the laundry?). Talk about pay dirt – there was not only food from the big find but a bunch of other boxes, all neatly marked and itemised. I didn't have a chance to check through it all but I took all the pasta I could cram into the backpack, filled another box with food and vowed to come back again in the next couple of days.

So, from today's little expedition, I have the crucial item to make my HC a reality, I've stocked up on medical supplies, got Fi's birthday covered plus I've found another stash of food and other goodies. High five, me.

I managed to sneak all of Fi's birthday gifts into the shed without her knowing. I'm still debating what the best thing to do with the HC fans is. I think my best bet is to move two of them over to Mr Nichols' shed. I'll probably end up building it there as he has way more room. I'll leave one fan here to tinker with in the meantime, to see if I can actually get the generator and fan working. The other thing that needs solving is steering. This should be pretty simple. From what I remember of hovercraft I've seen, they have a series of vertical rudders positioned behind the fan. When the rudder angles to the right, directing the air that way, the HC moves right and vice versa. Shouldn't be too hard to figure something out.

So, engine and steering development at my place, build at Mr Nichols'.
*

9.30pm: I've been thinking about the base. The tyre tubes could do the trick nicely but, if I could find the right material (resilient and malleable enough) I could make a more 'legitimate' HC base. I could keep it fed with an air compressor as there were plenty at Kennards I could borrow. I'm so pumped (pardon the pun) about this. I really think I can build one.

****

Thursday, May 29, 2014
10.15am: Finding the food stash at Mark and Jemma's has been a real bonus. I'm going to save all of the pasta and noodles for the road trip, which is going to save a hell of a lot in weight to carry. The flip side is I'll need to bring equipment to light a fire with me. Dad has a little camping BBQ somewhere in the shed I can use. The biggest weight issue there is the hotplate. I'll also need to carry a bottle of gas and a pot with me. We would have to use the gas sparingly so wherever there's the option to burn wood instead we would need to take it. Access to fresh water is also a massive issue I'm struggling to resolve. We'll need it for drinking and boiling pasta. I think I need to test my water purifying theory soon to see if it works.

Speaking of testing – this afternoon I'm going to try to rig the second generator up to one of the fans to see what sort of thrust it will generate.

If this works and I can build a HC, one of the side benefits is we'll have a petrol-powered generator travelling with us, so we can take any other electrical appliance we think we'll need. In theory we could find a place to camp down each night, pitch a tent over the HC and run lighting and heating within. We'd be a mobile house.

The more I crunch the numbers of travelling by foot the more I realise I need the HC to become a reality.

*

2pm: Mission very successful. I connected the generator to the fan unit and turned it on. The power that thing generated was quite impressive. I then put the generator/fan combo on a piece of wood balanced on a couple of old skateboards. It was a bit of a rickety set-up, but I barely had to ease the fan past 2 on the meter before it began moving forward. It worked! Now I have to take into account that the skateboard wheels on the concrete floor gave some pretty generous friction, but it's a success, nonetheless.

Weight is already becoming an issue. With the generator and one fan coming in at about 70kg, a second fan would make it close to 100kg. That's before people, food, water and other requirements. I think two fans is the way to go; it will give a better power-to-weight ratio and will mean if one fan goes down we still have some power. I think I'm going to push my focus to the base now. I need to come up with a solution for the best way to keep the base light, air-filled and resilient. Once I have something that meets the brief I need to put the engine parts on and run a test. It will either move forward or it won't – I'll either have a winner or go back to the drawing board.

I'm struggling to think of a solution that works. With real hovercraft, I know they have a compartmentalised base, which means one puncture won't stop the whole thing working. That's why I was initially leaning towards the tyre tubes, but I'm concerned I won't get the stability I'm looking for. Maybe I could use two larger truck tubes with car tubes supporting them on the inside (in case there's a puncture in one of the truck tyres). I then need a skin to protect the tubes – maybe a combination of bubble-wrap (if I can find some) and towel material for cushioning, then something water resistant and smooth for an outer layer. I think it's a case of see what I can scavenge and work backwards from there.

There's a Tyrepower on Magill Rd and a SuperCheap Auto on Glynburn Rd. I can smell another expedition tomorrow.

While I was tinkering out the back we apparently had a visitor. Some older guy (at least that's what Fi thought by the sound of his voice) knocked a few times and kept calling out my name. Eventually he left, without trying to break in or anything. I'm trying to think who this could have been but I'm drawing a blank. It all seems harmless enough, but at the same time it's a scary thought – we were totally unprepared. I think Fi and I will sit down tonight and work out a scramble plan for random strangers. We should come up with reasonable actions for all circumstances – whether the visitors are friend or foe.

****

Friday, May 30, 2014
8.45am: It's funny (or maybe sad) that someone visiting your place is a major talking point for the evening, but that's what happened last night. I literally could not think of one person it could've been knocking at the door and calling out my name… which means I also have no idea why they were doing it!

The best thing to come from the whole incident is Fi and I have now got a series of action plans in place for when someone knocks on the door. First priority is not to let anyone in. Unless someone we know drops over completely out of the blue, there's no one left in this immediate area I want in the house. There may be a few remnants of the Trinity Gardens community still around (I think last night's door knocker is probably one of those) but anyone I had any relationship with is no longer with us. So, if someone like that comes again, we will just see what they have to say and try to avoid engaging them any longer than necessary. If there are visitors with less benign intentions, we can assess the threat while they're on the other side of the door. We can either hold our ground and fight or, if the numbers and weapons are against us, flee to the cellar or enact the bug-out plan.

We talked long and hard about what sort of threat constituted us abandoning the place and I think we are in agreement that with any sign of a gun, or if we're outnumbered by more than 2-3, then we run and never come back.

I think we're both glad we've had the conversation now, but I'm a little annoyed and embarrassed it took a random visitor to spark it.

Well, must sign off for now as a busy day awaits. I'm heading to Kennards Hire to grab an air-compressor, drop it home then head out to Tyrepower and SuperCheap Auto to see what I can borrow for the hovercraft. Should be fun;

I might even take a few things just to pimp it up too :D. Fi wants to contribute a bit more to the planning of the Canberra trip, so while I'm out she's going to investigate a way to distill water from the ash ice.

*

5.30pm: Another busy afternoon. It only took about 30-40 minutes to get to Kennards Hire and back with a couple of air compressors and a leaf blower for good measure, but that was the easy part. TyrePower proved less successful than I'd hoped. There were tyre tubes in the workshop, but the largest ones I could get my hands on were for 4WD cars when I was hoping for a couple of large truck tyres to make the core of the base. But maybe six 4WD tyre tubes isn't a bad result, after all – it does mean one puncture is not going to be a complete fail on the HC. If I can find something smaller to fill with air between the tyres, connect them in a strong structure and make sure the covering is as sturdy as possible, I might still be on a winner.

Supercheap Auto, on the other hand, was an absolute bonanza. It was a reasonable hike to get there, but completely worth it when I walked in. The only limit I had was what I could physically drag back to the house. Every aisle I went down had something I could potentially use. I decided to limit myself to only the absolute necessities for now, but vowed to return when I was closer to completion for some optional extras.

I ended up with a couple of sweet, lightweight bucket seats, storage containers large and small, lights, tape, every material I could get my hands on... so many goodies!

By the time I finished dragging all my new toys back to the house – probably nearly 2km – I was exhausted! It was too much to carry by hand so I found a couple of pieces of plastic I could flip upside down and use like a sleigh, connected some rope and dragged it around my shoulders. I was happy with the plan as I probably transferred 3-4 times the amount of gear I could've carried alone, but that was at the expense of my shoulders, legs, back and arms. Actually, I could name every body part I have right now – everything hurts.

I didn't even have the energy to take the gear out to the shed. I basically dumped it all down the back of the lounge room, sat on the couch and didn't move. That's a lie, I did try to move about 45 minutes ago but my body said, 'I don't think so'. Actually, it probably swore at me, too.

But I have to force myself to get somewhat mobile in a minute – nature calls. Plus, Fi is very excited about the water purification system she's come up with and can't wait to show me. I can't wait to see it, but the thing is I could wait, happily, on this couch, until tomorrow... but it is the right thing and she sounds like she's come up with something very useful.

OK body... on the count of three – one, two, three...

*

6pm: Just got back to the couch, AKA my new home. Fi's demo was pretty sweet. She filled the kettle with ice-ash sludge and brought it to the boil. She'd place the kettle in a large stew pot and put a small pot on top of it as it boiled. The steam condensed into water and dripped into the large pot. By the end, the water in the large pot was slightly murky, but far better than before. The remains in the kettle were a sludgy mess. It had to be cleaned and the process repeated again on the murky water. After the second run you were left with something close to water. There was still a slightly funny taste to it, but it was nearly clear and infinitely cleaner than what she started with.

I suggested we could think of a way to filter the water before we started the process. Fi thought the best way was to cut the top off one of the water cooler containers and fill it with iceash. As it melts we're hoping it settles, with the sediment going to the bottom and the water to the top. If we could separate the water from the sediment we might be able to start the process at the second phase, saving time and keeping the kettle cleaner. We are going to run a test on that tomorrow.

So some pretty positive progress on the water front.

*

6.30pm: Finally, I've hit a wall. My body is still complaining I asked too much of it earlier. I'm back on the couch again, looking at a huge pile of car parts on the ground and getting thoroughly depressed I've bitten off more than I can chew with the hovercraft. How the hell am I really going to make that? I must be delusional. And if I don't make it, what the hell are we going to do next? Travel on foot to Canberra – no thanks!

I've gotta control these thoughts and stay positive but I can't help myself sometimes. Now I'm thinking about my parents. Mum and Dad would be perfect to have around right now. Mum would get way too pampering about my sore body and probably make me something nice and warm to eat, while Dad would push me to come up with ideas for the hovercraft in a way that would force me to think positively about it again. I miss them.

I miss Jason, too. I miss him every day, but I just got hit by a wave of it, all at once. Not in the way that's just a thought but in the way it physically hits you, like your heart expands to fill your entire chest cavity and breathing is difficult.

God, I can feel my heart pumping in an uncomfortable way. I don't like this at all.

*

7pm: Feeling a little more settled now. Fiona helped me calm down. She reckons I was having a panic attack, which sounds like something middle-aged businessmen have, not teenagers. Anyways, she just helped me with my breathing for a few minutes and gave me a drink of water. Once I'd settled down we watched another episode of *Doomsday Preppers*. My feelings towards some of the subjects on the show ranged from impressed to pitying. I wonder how many actually survived the doomsday they were preparing for.

*

7.45pm: OK that was too close for comfort. We had another knock on the door– the same guy Fi heard yesterday. I didn't recognise his voice. He knocked three times over about a minute. We didn't answer but prepared at the door with our weapons. Next we could hear a number of voices outside discussing something we couldn't make out. Before we knew what was happening there was a massive bash at the door then another. They were trying to break in.

I yelled out, 'stop' several times before they heard me and ceased ruining my beautifully repaired door. Then we had a conversation that went something like this:

Me: Go away.

Guy: Who is this?

Me: None of your business.

Guy: Is this your place?

Me: Yes. Go away.

Guy: What's your name then?

Me: None of your business.

Guy: If you don't tell me your name we will be forced to break in.

Me: Why?

Guy: This house belongs to someone who died. You are taking their food, which belongs to the community and to us.

Me: I am not dead. I am here in my house with my food.

Guy: Prove it.

Me: Why?

Guy: Otherwise we will think you're lying and we will break in to claim what is ours.

Me: Are you armed?

Guy: Yes.

Me: Me too. How many of you are there?

Guy: Four.

It was so tense. I didn't really know what to do next. Through the peephole I could see they were older (in their 40s or 50s) and didn't look too physically daunting – I can't say I recognised any of them. The weapons they claimed to have amounted to a couple of knives and a cricket bat. I decided to open the door (with chain attached) to try and disarm the situation. I made sure the first view they had was the tip of the arrow in the crossbow. That got their attention. In fact it totally changed the game. The tone went from aggressive to apologetic, then to pleading as they begged for food.

Pfft… amateurs!

I got a better look at them and I definitely did not recognise any of them. My guess is they found the register at the community with my address and my existence status listed as 'deceased' and decided they might score a lucky free feed.

I was really torn about how to handle the situation. Part of me wanted to help, but the other part didn't want to set a precedent for helping scavengers. Who knows where that could lead. They might come back, they might bring more with them. I know it sounds tough, but I decided I couldn't give them anything. I told them I was nearly out of food myself and their best bet was the Firle hub. I also told them to scavenge through houses in the area as there was surely food around if you looked hard enough.

Honestly, and I know it sounds cruel, but surely the four of them could've figured out some of this stuff for themselves. Some people, when they're in a group, grow extra strength. These people did the total opposite – they were unsure, panicky and meek. Their 'leader' was clearly selected because he was the least useless of the lot of them, but that's all.

They didn't say much as they picked up their weapons and prepared to leave, defeated. But I couldn't help myself, I gave them Mark and Jemma's address and said I was pretty sure they might find something there. I pointed them to the second biggest stash of food I knew about – just handed it to them on a platter. The thing is, I was 100% confident they wouldn't find it. I replaced the manhole cover last time I was there and I just didn't see them having the wherewithal to look in the roof. If they did, well good luck to them, they were learning. If not, they got no sympathy from me.

Wow, I just read back that last paragraph and it seems somewhat heartless. But where do you draw the line with your heart and your own survival? At some point you have draw it somewhere.

*

9pm: What a day. Fi and I are going to sit down with a cup of tea (using our recycled water) and watch a movie. I'm probably going to half watch the movie and half sketch out a design for the hovercraft. I may as well start doing something with the pile of crap on the carpet.

****

Saturday, May 31, 2014

10.30am: Finished my initial hovercraft designs this morning. The base will be a rectangle of steel with two diagonal pieces crossing in the middle for strength. I'll build the deck separately and screw it on to the base when ready. I'm going to raise the deck 30cm high. This will leave lots of secret hollows to store important resources out of view. I'll put the steering column with the generator in the middle of the deck, with the two fans at the back. I'll have to adjust the fan speed using the knobs attached to the fans, unless I can learn how to run the wires up to the steering console.

I'll raise the edge on the sides of the deck so we can use that space as storage too. Back to feeling positive again. Time to go and play.

*

4pm: Busy afternoon in Mr Nichols' shed. I put the base together and attached the tyre tubes. Luckily I brought a few spare tubes, because when I laid six out (two rows of three) it didn't look big enough. I added an extra one in the middle of the front two. The seventh tube allows the front to taper in. It'll look like the front of a boat when completed (in theory), and hopefully the taper will mean the HC passes over the ash easier. The structure seems pretty strong.

The tubes are protected from the frame by a cover and the entire section is shielded in a duel layer of tarpaulin and silver car cover material, joined together and connected to the frame. The cover is in two parts, which meet vertically down the middle. This wasn't by design, I just couldn't find a large enough sheet of tarp to do it in one piece. I'll have to secure the two separate sections straight down the underbelly with velcro (and maybe attach it to the frame in a couple of places). The happy accident of all this is if I get a flat tyre I'll have easy access to the underside. I'll just need to dig a hole in the ash and jump in, get Fi to drive the HC over the hole and I can then rip the velcro apart and replace the flat tube. It's a great result given I was thinking the only option would be to remove the top section from the base, which would have taken half a day!

I also shaped the wood for the bottom side of the chassis from a few sheets of chip board. Once I drill it to the frame it should be strong, yet light enough for my needs. I look forward to getting back out there tomorrow, when I can finish the tube cover, attach the chassis base and start configuring the main part of the HC. I've got a few storage options from SuperCheap Auto, which have given me a few ideas for the set-up. I might revisit the design tonight. I'm very conscious of the fact I want a number of hidden storage areas. If we're ever attacked, or the HC is raided, I don't want the thieves to steal my most important assets.

*

5.45pm: There was something about the air this afternoon. It looked lighter and I swear I could make out the glow of the sun out west. Maybe it was my eyes playing tricks on me as they'd gotten so used to the dark, but maybe, just maybe, it was the first sign conditions are changing. I got Fi out to have a look and she reckoned she could see it, too. We just stood, arms around each other, watching the darkest, ugliest, least-impressive sunset we'd ever seen. It felt great.

*

6.30pm: Another random door-knocker this evening. He knocked, waited a few seconds and knocked again then started asking if anyone was home. I told him there was and to go away and not try the neighbours' places either. He was very apologetic, just said he was looking for food and would move on.

It's weird. When I'm inside it's easy to forget there's anything going on outside at all, but the fact is there are probably people sneaking up and down the street quite often. I'm guessing they're becoming more and more desperate. Norwood hubbers aside though, there seems to be a code of 'if somebody's home, move on to another place'. I like that code.

*

9pm: There's only seven days until Fi's birthday. Eighteen – adulthood, the right to vote, the legal drinking age – so many things that make the 18th so big just don't seem to matter anymore. But I want to make this moment nice for her. I want her to have a memorable 18th. I've got the presents sorted but I want to make a nice meal, and even bake a cake if I can. But I want this all to be a total surprise. I think my best bet is to sneak up to Mark and Jemma's; they would have all the things I need to make a cake, assuming the newbs didn't actually find the stash.

Tonight I'm gonna give Fi a couple of wines and secretly probe her about her favourite foods. Hopefully there's something on the list I can make for next Saturday.

****

Sunday, June 1, 2014

7.15am: I had a dream last night. Maybe not a dream, but my dying thoughts before I drifted off. I think it was last night's sunset… got me fired up that change is coming and we can get through this. I started thinking about the fact I'm building a hovercraft that doesn't hover. Sure, the tubes are a reasonable solution, but I think the whole thing will actually work better if it hovers. In truth I think I've been avoiding it because it feels like a much greater challenge than strapping some tubes together. But I want to do this right. I was thinking back to my design and how I could configure what I already had to make it happen. I don't think it'll be too hard.

I think my best bet is to use the leaf blower, drill a hole in the base I've already designed and point the blower in. As for the base, I've got to make sure that's as airtight as possible. I can line the underside of the wooden base with something like a shower curtain, staple the edges flat to the wood then gaffer tape the whole thing down and cover the edges and holes. With the material I'm using for the air-cushion, I'll need to line that too, with more shower curtains I suppose. Either way, two layers have got to be better than one. I still need to make the air-cushion in two parts, given the length of material I have, but if I use two rows of the thick velcro and gaffer tape it, I should be fine. Finally, I'll need to add some holes to the underside, which will release the pressure and direct a layer of air under the HC, to help it hover. I just need to reinforce the holes, probably with more gaffer tape, to make sure they're strong enough not to rip open.

I'm going to keep the tubes in position inside the air cushion though; they'll serve as a back-up if it doesn't work or if something goes wrong. But if I can get this thing to hover properly it'll be a good day.

Oh, and Fi says her favourite dessert is sticky date pudding and her favourite cuisine is Mexican – anything Mexican. I need to do some recipe research then see if I can acquire enough ingredients (or substitutes) to make it possible.

*

3pm: Oh. My. God. Fi just told me she was pregnant! I must've stood there like a stunned mullet for about two minutes while I tried to process the news. I mean, not that, not now. It changes everything... the supplies, the trip, the HC – everything. I tried to put on a brave and supportive face but I don't think she was buying it...

Right until she cracked up laughing and told me she was messing with me. Bitch! Naturally, I chased her around the house 'til I caught her, then tickled her mercilessly.

She'll get hers. Maybe not today, maybe not tomorrow, but someday soon I will have my revenge!

*

5.30pm: The word genius gets bandied about quite a bit, but sometimes, like now, it may be warranted. After I went back to Kennards for a leaf blower, I visited a few vacant houses and took eight shower curtains. Then I stapled, double-sided taped and gaffer taped everything together. For good measure, I also cut some garden hose down one side then wrapped it around the rim of the base then hammered it into position. Not only did it act as a backup to ensure the air cushion was airtight, it also created a bumper to protect the HC. I sawed the nozzle off the air blower, cut a hole in the base wood and fitted the blower stump tight in the hole. I then gaffered around the blower/hole and hit the on button. Within seconds the air-cushion filled and my HC was hovering. I don't think words can express what a good feeling that was – from idea to functioning hover within a day. I seriously cannot wait to attach the fans and generator and see if this thing will move.

I've already got a head start on tomorrow's work, too. I've secured the two seats in position, just in front of the fans. They are high enough off the deck to give us leg room and far enough from the back to allow room for the fans. With these in place I can build up to deck level using every inch of space I can get for visible storage and hidden storage.

*

7.30pm: I've been sneaking a look through a few cookbooks whenever Fi's been pottering away from the kitchen and I'm having ingredients issues. I have no idea where I'll find cream or eggs for the sticky date pudding. As for the Mexican dish, well, I'm not even close to anything there, I'll hit Mark and Jemma's stocks tomorrow to see if that inspires something.

Our little hint of sun didn't materialise again today. Hopefully we see him back again soon.

****

Monday, June 2, 2014

11am: Hit the motherlode at Mark and Jemma's today – a container of condiments! I'm talking sauces, mayo, dressings, dips and mustards and everything in between. Not only did I thank their memories, I admired their forethought. It is survival genius, pure and simple. One of the most depressing things about living off long-life food is the lack of flavour and variety. Depressing is not quite the word for eating similar foods day after day, but it's in the ballpark. It's just a constant reminder you are eating to live and not to enjoy. But a healthy and diverse array of condiments, spices and sauces changes everything, and what Mark and Jemma had was top-shelf. To think I gave the newbs this address – thank god they didn't find this stuff.

I literally stared drooling as I looked at all the new flavours I'd soon be eating. Best of all, there were a few shakers of parmesan cheese (a personal favourite), some guacamole dip and salsa sauce. In another box I found a stack of biscuits and chips, including corn chips. So I reckon I can whip up some nachos for Fi on her birthday. If only I could find some sour cream it'd be perfect. I have the feeling my dreams of cream, sour cream and eggs will be unfulfilled, and I might have to think of what I'm going to do in their absence but, assuming I don't totally stuff things up, this birthday dinner is going to be seriously not bad (ish).

*

3pm: Mr Sun returned today. There's no doubt – I could make him out over the hills to the east this morning. When I say 'make him out' it was just a blur through the haze, but it was a lot lighter than the rest of the haze. Twice in three days makes me very excited. When you're cocooned in the middle it's hard to know how much dust is in the atmosphere, what it's made of or how high it goes. I know I couldn't walk a toffee apple down the street without it turning brown from the ash that would cling to it (I would never do this as I hate toffee apples), and when you multiply that by every part of the Earth's surface and then by the fact it must go right into the upper atmosphere, well, it must be unthinkable tonnes. All of which still has to make its way to the surface. There's no way of knowing how deep the ash will get, or how long the process will take but, seeing evidence of change is huge. It means this 'new normal' existence might just be a phase after all. It means one day the sun will return. It means hope.

*

6pm: The HC is getting super interesting now. I'm building everything up from the base, and around the seats, which are already in place. The seats are at the back of a 'cockpit' section, separated in the middle by a bench, under which is storage for core stuff like tent and torches. We'll be able to sit back there and control steering and thrust or move forward to the bench to gain access to the generator or leaf blower. Along each side I've built a toolbox and a smaller storage container in the wall, for all the bits and pieces we may need along the way. Each side also has two hidden storage spots for food and water. I have the generator sitting on deck level and I have built up around it – I've allowed about 15cm each side as I don't want it to overheat. I'm going to use a couple of the sturdy looking black plastic containers to shape covers for both the generator and leaf blower as I don't want them exposed to too much dust.

I'm still in the process of shaping the front of the HC. I initially wanted to angle everything together smoothly, like the front of a boat, but I think that's beyond my skill level. Instead, I may just make a couple of angular lines so it's easier to finish. The back is raised slightly higher than the rest of the deck so the fans are sitting above the top of the back of the seats. There are many spaces both front and back to secretly store food and other vital supplies. I mean, if this baby could take the weight, we could seriously carry 2-3 months' worth of food. That would be enough to get to Canberra and back if this thing has any speed at all.

*

7.15pm: My mum was a freak; her cookbook collection is truly world class on the obsession scale. I knew the cupboard above the microwave had some cookbooks, and there were some in the bottom of the pantry, but what I didn't realise was she'd also hoarded two boxes of older cookbooks on the top shelf of her walk-in robe. I was snooping around because I remember having a particular recipe book with a heap of Mexican dishes in it. I couldn't find it anywhere in the obvious spots and I knew she wouldn't throw something like that out. It took about 20 minutes of searching to find her stash!

Side note: I hope it used to take my family members longer than 20 minutes to find any stash of publications I may or may not have had.

This is where it gets a little ironic. Mum used to be into a bit of self-sufficient cooking and food production – ya know, like, growing and making your own stuff. I remember those days all too clearly, with the amount of home-made jam and chutney I had to eat. Especially in the old house, I had to suffer through an endless supply of apricot jam each spring – enough was produced to last three years and Mum couldn't give the stuff away as fast as she could make it. Meanwhile, every week shopping I'd ask for a different flavour when we'd pass the jam aisle – strawberry, blackberry, fig, anything – but would be told there was no need to buy jam when we had so much at home! All those beautiful flavours staring at me, teasing me, and I was stuck with apricot. Again.

When will adults ever learn that kids are allergic to homemade products? Toys, clothes, food – everything! It's like Dad's homemade pizza – why can't you make it so it tastes like the ones from the delivery place? It if wasn't mass-produced, in a nice new packet, smothered in MSG or preservatives, or it didn't have a loud TV commercial with a super-cool jingle, then it wasn't gonna taste good, look good or make you feel good. Everyone knows that's Principle#1 of the Elements of Kids Logic 101.

Funny how that view has changed now. I admire self-sufficiency – in fact, my moments of greatest pride since rock night have been when I thought up a solution, or made something from scratch that helped me in some way. That's true success and achievement these days. So I retrospectively dip my hat to my folks – it's a little too late to tell them, but I have a new appreciation for what they were trying to do.

Which takes me back to the cream. One of Mum's crazy self-sufficiency books had a recipe to make cream from processed milk! Now, first things first, the picture of the final product looked less like soft floating clouds of whipped yumminess and more like paper glue or a sample you'd freeze on an IVF program; but supposedly it tasted pretty good. And for my needs, it's going to be used in the caramel sauce, and never seen in its natural state.

The same book also says you can mix cream and lemon juice to make sour cream AND that in cooking you can use apple puree as an egg substitute! That's all a bit exciting – I've got a good vibe about the sticky date pudding now, the sour cream for the nachos maybe not so much. But they'll be better than nothing (hopefully)!

****

Tuesday, June 3, 2014
2.30pm: Productive day again on the HC. I positioned the generator and finished the decking at the bow and stern where I positioned the fans on top. There are now five hidden storage spots within the HC – two in the cabin part on each side, another one each side at the front and the huge one at the rear of the craft, under the fans. The only sign any of the spots hide something is

the odd hinge, which I'll obscure from visibility before she's ready. 'Bow'... 'stern'... referring to the HC as a 'she', all a sudden I think I'm Captain Jack Sparrow!

Everything is set for me to do a launch test tomorrow. I just need to secure the fans, connect them to the generator, cross my fingers and turn everything on.

Hopefully all goes according to plan and I have myself a working hovercraft. If that's the case I just need to do a bit of fine tuning and finishing. I still need to add a couple of the storage containers as ash covers for the generator and leaf blower. Plus, I need to find a windshield of some sort (it could get pretty intense if we build up any speed on an ashy day without one). Come to think of it, we might need helmets and maybe some riding leathers.

I also want to paint the HC black – Jack Sparrow would've wanted it that way. For a start it will look super cool in black, and it will also hide some of my shoddier craftsmanship. Besides which, it makes practical sense. There's no point making a song and dance to other people about it. The harder it is to see the better. That may not make a difference when it's running (as it'll make quite a bit of noise) but when it's sitting idle, then the harder to see the better.

I also need to find the best headlights I can as visibility will definitely be a factor in the driver's seat.

Fi's run another test on the water purifying. She used one of the water containers to let the ash sediment settle to the bottom, then I helped siphon out the water layer before she went through the old boiling process. The result was so much better than last time. In fact, you could almost drink it! Well, you could if you were desperate, but there's still a metallic taste in there.

She also found some of the water purification documents I printed out pre-rock. She's gonna try another method where she fills one of the empty water containers with layers of rock, sand, leaves and pebbles. As the water runs through the layers most of the random nasties will be removed – then we can use the boiling process and we're done. We'll see which gives us a better result, but this new option sounds far less fiddly.

Fi is also busy putting together a list of what we need to take. She knows how much storage we have and is working backwards from there. Not only food but cooking equipment, weapons, survival equipment, camping gear, clothes – everything we think we'll need. It's all getting put in a pile in the back family room and, even without food, it's looking dauntingly large. It's a

bit hard to know exactly what we can pack until we start loading up the HC...
oh, and testing to see if it can actually handle that much weight.

While Fi was working on her jobs I managed to collect a bunch of
ingredients to make the cream. I can't believe Mum had gelatin – I didn't
even know what it was, yet she had some. Score! I'm going to disappear next
door and give it a try.

*

5.15pm: ...well, that was harder than expected. I was supposed to heat
the milk but I got a little carried away and burnt it. Take two worked out much
better. I had a sample and it's not too bad. I've got to let it cool for a couple of
hours before I whip it into cream shape, so I might do a bit of house-to-house
action to see if I can find any riding leathers.

Cream whipped and bike leather procured. The leathers look sweet.
Admittedly both sets are slightly big, but they're black and leather and that's
the main thing. Honestly, when the HC is a black mean machine we are going
to look like something from another world as we zip across the ash.

*

7.30pm: I saw five people out on the streets this evening. Not in a group,
but individuals like me, doing some house-to-house shopping. Like I said,
things are getting desperate out there. Just out of habit I try to use the torch at
a minimum on the streets. I'm so familiar with walking in the conditions I see
no point in drawing more attention to myself than I have to. I see these people
long before they see me, so they're easy to avoid. But it's a gentle reminder
I've relaxed after the Norwood hubbers left – maybe too much. They are not
the only threat in this world and, even though I have a secure property and
move far more stealthily through the streets when I'm out, it doesn't mean
I'm safe. It just takes a run in with the wrong person at the wrong time and
it's game over. I think tonight and the little visit a few days ago are a gentle
reminder to not get too cocky.

When I did have my close encounters I laid low and just watched for a
while. There's a look they all shared in the way then carried themselves. It was
aimless, hopeless even, as they stumbled through the ash looking for food. I
couldn't escape the thought they reminded me of zombies.

...and today's 'reminder' wasn't all gentle. At one point I saw two of
them fighting each other over something. Not sure what it was. One of them

clubbed the other guy and laid him out cold. That was a scary moment – glad I kept my distance. Fight zombies – that's something new. Wow!

****

Wednesday, June 4, 2014

6.30am: I could hardly sleep last night – I was obsessing about the hovercraft and this morning's test. I haven't looked at myself in the mirror this morning but I think it's safe to assume I'm looking more zombie-like than any of the street walkers I saw last night. Anyways, slamming down breakfast now so I can get on with it.

*

11.30am: Repeat 500 times: I am awesome. It worked. I can't believe it. Well, I can believe it, but I can't believe it! It took me about three hours to rig everything up, then I asked Fi to witness the glorious event. I fired up the leaf blower and the HC rose into the air – it's a nice feeling being on board as it floats on the cushion of air. Then I cranked up the generator and turned on the left fan. I turned it to speed 1 – nothing, speed 2 – nothing (but I could feel it was getting ready) then speed 3 – we had movement. It eased across the yard in a few seconds, on one fan at very low power. Fi leapt into the cabin and gave me the biggest kiss. That was the moment we both realised this was no mad teenager's pipe dream, this was our ticket to anywhere! We kissed some more… and more… and then we did more (which would've been more comfortable with the car seat covers on).

*

3.30pm: We've just toasted the successful test of the HC with a mid-afternoon wine. I was tempted to get Fi to smash some champagne across the bow but there was a fair chance the bottle would've taken half the bow with it #shoddyworkmanship! I'm not sure what to do next. Part of me is tempted just to push the HC out on the street, fire up both fans and see what she's got, but the boring half of me knows I still have so many things to do to finish it off. Stupid boring jobs! But the bigger test run can't wait too long. I'm going to sort the steering out this afternoon so I can take it for a spin ASAP.

*

7pm: Steering mechanism connected. I used a lever positioned between the two seats. It's a pretty simple set-up that moves the rudder left and right accordingly. There are three rudders for each fan. I piloted another test and it worked a treat. God, I really want to take this thing for a spin, but I'm trying to resist the urge until I've finished her off. I might aim for Saturday morning and take her out to the school oval – it'll be a good way to start Fi's birthday.

****

Thursday, June 5, 2014

10.15am: We had another little visitor this morning. They knocked a few times before attempting to make their way into the house. I quickly shut the guy down by telling him where to go and how to get there – he moved on quick enough. I'm getting shorter on patience and far less pleasant with each encounter!

Street walkers are definitely a growing concern, though. I'm not sure it's a coincidence that they are showing up in greater numbers now the Norwood hubbers threat seems to have died down. It's either that or we're reaching critical food mass time. Even the most loaded pantry and fridge pre-rock will be starting to run very low; it's just inevitable people will get more brazen as they get more desperate. In a crazy way I preferred the Norwood hubbers situation better – a large, organised threat, acting as a group, is far easier to predict than a bunch of free-roaming radicals. Sure, we have more freedom and we can use power if we're careful, but there's an unpredictability at the moment that makes me very uneasy.

*

1.45pm: I painted the HC black. It looks so kickass – the paint totally hides all of my dodgy work. I sat in her for a while after the paint dried and imagined myself cruising the ash cross country. But something didn't feel right. I've had this sense I've been missing something and I've decided it's the comfort factor. We're going to be spending a lot of time in this thing, so I'll have to consider what impact that'd have. I guess all the boat references I've been making recently led me to think of what boat design brings. They're very similar to the HC in a way, far less designed than a car, just a floating device with a couple of engines on the back. But when I've been fishing before the one thing I've noticed is the strength of the wind as you cruise to your destination – you don't even have to be at high speed to get annoyed as it buffets your face. The best spots are under the canopy. That's what I've decided this design needs – a canopy as well as a windshield. My best bet is to get one from someone's boat. There are a couple of houses in the neighbourhood that I know have them. That'll be my task for tomorrow.

*

6pm: I couldn't help myself – I just ripped the interior carpet from Dad's car and lined the base of the cabin. I can't believe I did it either – Dad was so protective of that thing. I can't imagine what he'd be thinking if he was looking down on me. I justified the move as keeping a little bit of Dad's car alive. Surely he would approve of that? Maybe? A little bit?

Whatever the case, the floor of the cabin looks a whole lot cooler than it did at lunchtime. Not just cooler, but more inviting.

*

6.45pm: Revenge is sweet. I just told Fi the generator had crapped itself and the HC would be out of action until I could find a new one, which could take months. I was awesome with the acting skills – not bad for someone who struggles to keep a straight face when lying. She totally bought it, too. She was on the verge of tears as I told her it would be next to impossible to find another one. I felt somewhat bad when I saw her hopes fade. I kept it up for about five minutes until I felt I'd toyed with her long enough. She punched me when I told her it was a joke – on the borderline between playful and violent. It hurt, but it was worth it for the sweet taste of revenge!

*

10.30pm: Had a pretty chilled-out evening with Fi (after she started talking to me again). We watched a few episodes of *The Walking Dead*, our street walkers look pretty similar to *The Walking Dead's* walkers (question: why don't they call them zombies?). After that we started working on a mission: give the HC a name. Surely something that's going to be such an important part of our lives deserves a name? We came up with a list of about 60 ideas but the only ones I really like at this stage are…

Ashram (it rams itself through the ash – but in a religious way)

Adelaide (named after the city that is no more)

Phoenix (because it was built from the ashes of the disaster)

Wilbur (just because it's cute, according to Fi)

We'll need some more time to mull it over. They are all good options (except Wilbur). Maybe one name will just feel right when we take her for a spin on Saturday.

****

Friday, June 6, 2014

11am: Well, everything's set for tomorrow food and present wise. I'm going to earn enough boyfriend brownie points to last through to Christmas! The last piece of the puzzle is sorting out the windscreen for the HC. The two boats I'm sure are stored in backyards in the area are only a short walk – unfortunately, in different directions. I'm gonna scoff something down and go shopping!

*

6pm: So boat no.1 had a pretty good canopy. I was tempted just to save time checking out option no.2 and remove it on the spot, but something (probably my perfectionist side) made me check out the other boat. And I'm glad I did. Boat no.2 was slightly bigger than the first but the canopy was infinitely more encompassing. The only downside was the hull beneath the windscreen angled upwards in the middle, which would require some tinkering on my HC to make it fit. But the upsides were so much more. For starters, it was a mix of a glass windscreen (about a foot high), see-through material siding and a kickass black roof. It was just made for the HC.

It took about an hour to remove the screen from the boat. The solid windscreen was screwed into position so I removed the entire attachment panel from the hull. The see-through material was attached further down the hull with a series of click studs. I had to remove the stud panels from the hull too, which was fiddly and annoying work.

It took a good half hour to haul the thing back to Mr Nichols' garage. I was exhausted by the time I got there but just had to finish in readiness for tomorrow's test run.

In the end I didn't quite get there but I reshaped the bow end of the HC so the windscreen sat snugly on top. I also attached the screen – it felt strong. What I failed to get to was the soft canopy section, which I'll tackle in the morning (I'm gonna set the alarm for early). Oh, and the additional section of the bow hasn't been painted black. Just cannot take the test drive without the mean black exterior all over.

*

8pm: Just had a nice massage from Fi. Mmmmmmm... feels so much better. I was just a ball of ache since this afternoon's exploits.

I've also baked a loaf of bread this evening... figured toast for breakfast will be a good way to start Fi's birthday.

Anyways, now I'm off to help Fi celebrate her last few hours of non-adulthood with a few drinks, some stupid movie and some reminiscing.

****

Saturday, June 7, 2014

11am: I've been a busy boy this morning. I was up at six and headed straight out to the HC to tidy up loose ends. It took longer than expected, which I can predominantly put down to the hangover. Anyways, it's all locked and loaded now and looks sa-weeeeet!

I'm slightly jealous Fi's still asleep, but her laziness has allowed me to get everything as close to perfect as it's going to be. Time to wake her up with toast and presents.

*

2pm: What a perfect couple of hours. Fi absolutely loved her presents, so much so she cried when I gave her the guitar. Said it was the best present anyone had ever given her. She gave me a hug so big it took my breath away. I couldn't help it and may have shed a slight tear myself (although I would deny it if anyone asked). I have never felt so loved before.

It took her a few minutes to tune the guitar, then she played me a song she'd written a few months before the rock. It was a cute little love song, and she sang it with an Aussie twang – far more noticeable than her speaking accent. It was beautiful and I told her as much before she led me to the bedroom.

When we'd recovered from that workout, I blindfolded Fi and took her to the back of Mr Nichols' place where the HC was ready to go. She hadn't seen the canopy, didn't even know I was attaching one, so laughed when she saw the final result. She looked at me and shook her head, like, it was typical of obsessive, perfectionist me to go into that much detail. I knew what the look meant but just replied with a defensive, 'what?'

The canopy did present some problems. The HC was now so tall it barely squeezed between the built-up ash in Mr Nichols' backyard and the top of the garage, but with a bit of fiddling we got there. We pushed it with the base inflated and the fans on level 1 so it was actually very little effort to manoeuvre. Once we were out the front though, that's when it became, well, magic.

We hopped in and cranked up the fans. Slowly at first – level 3 – but it was enough to get us moving. I turned her on to the street and we travelled up the middle where the ash is most even. God it felt unbelievable! I let out a big, whoooo-hoooooo!, and Fi joined in. We looked at each other and laughed. This was the game-changer. We were moving – far faster than we could ever walk.

I travelled up the street and around the corner to the oval. Pre-rock there was a metre high fence around it, but that was lost now under the ash so I could just drive straight from the middle of the street onto the oval. A big, wide open hovercraft play space. I turned the fans up – slowly through 4 and 5 speeds, eventually up to 7. We took turns steering and getting to know how she handles. I don't think I can ever truly express how liberating that ride was. We just laughed the entire time. The weather was clearer again today with a slight hint of light and, between that and the lights on the front of the HC, I reckon we could see a good 50m+ ahead of us.

I had intended to stay out for about 20 minutes, but I think I got a bit carried away. I saw a couple of human silhouettes in the distance, then a couple more. Our joyride had attracted some attention. I looked at my watch and realised it'd been over 40 minutes since we'd left – definitely time to call it a day.

I certainly didn't like the idea of a bunch of walkers seeing what we were doing. It was way too much attention for my liking and, although I was annoyed at myself for getting carried away, I was not going to let that feeling overwhelm how damn good I felt.

We had the HC around the corner, up the street and out of sight before anyone knew what had hit them. I also turned the headlights off to avoid being followed.

When I shut the garage door Fi gave me another big kiss and announced she thought we should call the HC Phoenix. Considering that was my favourite name from the list, I was hardly going to argue.

Phoenix was born.

*

6pm: Still on a high from the successful road test. My mind is absolutely buzzing with the possibilities that present themselves now we have this new travelling capability, chiefly, the potential to source food and other stuff from far and wide. Maybe we wouldn't have to hit the road to Canberra as soon as I thought. I mean, why hastily leave a quality fortress for the unknown? Sure, there will always be randoms walking the street, and there's the high probability the Norwood hubbers will be back some day, but they're known threats we have a plan to deal with. Am I being crazy to trade them in for the unknown?

But I guess by even having Phoenix we are drawing attention to ourselves – as today's test run shows. I'm sure there are people out there who would go to great lengths to get their hands on the sort of technology we were showing off. I'm sure there are those out there who would kill for it. As much fun as today was I don't think I'll be letting Phoenix strut about out in the open again unless there is good reason.

Still, they're all thoughts for another day. Today I'm just going to enjoy the accomplishment, celebrate Fi's birthday and get my cooking on, because as far as days post-rock go, this is a high point.

*

8pm: Wow! I'm on fire today. Dinner could definitely be described as above average, for a post-rock meal, that translates as 5-star. I'm pretty sure Fi agreed as I had a second round of bedroom appreciation after we were done.

I'm just popping the top off a second bottle of wine and Fi and I are going to watch a movie and maybe a few more eps of The Walking Dead. Then I might...

****

Monday, June 9, 2014

1pm: There are no words to describe how I feel right now. Fi is gone. Everything is lost.

Fi and I were just settling down for her birthday evening. We had full tummies and a couple of drinks. I was also hitting the wall after burning the candle at both ends trying to get Phoenix ready. We were at a weak moment. It was the worst time for a knock at the door.

God, I hate this world. We'd played everything so well and so carefully, but it couldn't even let us enjoy one damn day.

Fi was at the door before me and told those knocking there were people home and they should move on. That was when a voice came back and we knew we were in trouble. It was Fi's ex, Josh, and his mate Duncan. I could see the blood drain from Fi's face as Josh called out to her. She didn't respond and I just yelled out and asked them to move on. There was a short pause as they talked out of earshot outside the door, then there was a thumping sound.

They were attacking the door with something, trying to knock it down. We stood back, armed with the bow and crossbow, yelling at them to stop. At one point I opened the door to the latch so I could try to find out what they wanted. I didn't know what else to do but it was a bad, bad move. Josh started calling Fi all sorts of names and threatening to kill her. I told him to back off. He told me to shut up. Fi started screaming at Josh and the door kept getting pounded. It was pandemonium.

I shoved the nose of the crossbow through the gap in the door and yelled out that if they didn't stop I'd shoot. Before I knew it, there were three loud bangs and my hand exploded in pain. I looked down and my little finger on my left hand was mangled. I'd been shot. There was a scream outside and as I retracted the crossbow and shut the door, I noticed the arrow was gone. I'd fired it in all the chaos and hit one of them. Josh swore so loudly I figured it was him.

There was a lull for a few seconds then I heard footsteps out the front. I knew one of them was headed to the side door. Fi was saying "stop" over and over again. I went over, grabbed her and said, "We need to go now!"

The house was a mess. Everything we had set up was in chaos because we were packing for the Canberra trip. It slowed us down just enough. There was a moment of confusion as we realised the only thing we could afford to take with us was us – no time for bug-out bags, no time for anything. All I could do was reload the crossbow and think of the best way to get out of there.

As I opened the sliding door by the courtyard I could hear one of them negotiating the side fence. I took a couple of steps outside to see if I could get a gauge on whether we had time to make a run for next door. I heard another bang as a bullet fizzed past me. I turned and hauled ass inside. Maybe, thinking back on it now, we could've come back in and headed out again via the back patio while we had the chance. We definitely could've made a run for it in the confusion. But we didn't. It was my fault, it was my call. I yelled out to Fi to head to the cellar.

I locked the sliding door behind me, but we hadn't even reached the cellar before I heard the shatter – I assume they put a bullet through it. They would've been entering the house as I lifted the rug and opened the cellar door. I kept the door open with my injured hand while Fi climbed in. My other hand was on the crossbow, ready to fire should anyone come into sight before we got in.

Fi got down and I moved into position to follow her. I threw myself on my stomach under the door and stuck my bum up so it could take the door's weight. I remember my feet searching for a rung on the ladder just as Duncan entered the room. I fired an arrow at his head but it hit him in the collarbone. I heard the arrow lodge and his shriek of pain before I tumbled backwards into the cellar.

Maybe it was a dumb move. Maybe I could've slipped into the cellar before he noticed. Maybe if I did we could've hidden unnoticed. They could've taken what they wanted and left. But I didn't and now they knew where we were.

I reloaded the crossbow and we just sat at the back of the cellar, as quiet as we could. My heart was going crazy and my hand started to throb with pain. I looked at Fi. She was a wreck, tears streamed down her face and she mouthed 'I'm sorry'.

Above us Duncan swore in pain and then thumped his feet across to the front door where he let Josh in. We sat and listened as the footsteps made their way to right over us. Duncan said 'they're down there' before asking Josh what they should do.

I'll never forget Josh's response. 'They shot us, we'll kill them'.

They argued about it for some time. They were both clearly hurt, Duncan with his shoulder and Josh with his leg. Both wanted different outcomes. Duncan just wanted to get some food and get out of there, but for Josh, it was personal. I'm not sure if it was personal with me for shooting him, Fiona for leaving him, or the hour we spent together pre-rock, or all of it – and in the end it didn't really matter.

Fi and I moved as far back in the cellar as we could. I moved myself in front of her and positioned the torch between my legs so it was shining on the door to blind them when they opened it. Behind me, Fi leaned out and had her bow and arrow cocked and ready to go. I held her with my sore hand and aimed my crossbow with my good one.

I whispered to Fi that we had the advantage. They didn't know the layout of the cellar or where to fire and they would be blinded by the light. We, on the other hand, knew exactly where to aim. I wasn't sure if I totally believed what I was saying. I mean, they had guns and we had arrows, but I figured it was a thought worth hanging on to.

We just waited. Listened and waited. Duncan was stalling; he clearly didn't want to go after us, for whatever reason, and started trying to draw Josh's attention to the food and supplies he'd seen at the rear of the house. He also complained about the pain in his shoulder. Josh was drawn away for a moment, but soon returned his focus to the cellar and us.

We could hear every word as they planned how to attack us. They were going to open the door and shoot like crazy. Fi said 'I'm sorry' again. I told her I loved her and I kissed her. Then I moved the torch from my lap to a pile of cans to my left. I wedged it so it was aimed at the door... my thought was they would see the light and aim for it and I didn't want them shooting at my groin. Then I lined up my spare arrows on the floor between my legs.

I was shaking and I could feel Fi doing the same. She kept saying sorry over and over again. Then we heard them doing a countdown above – three, two, one...

177

The door creaked open about a third of the way and a pistol filled the gap and fired straight down. The sound was overwhelming. The shots echoed through my ears and they crushed under the weight of the noise. You could hear the bullets ricocheting around the cellar. The door slammed shut again. Neither Fi nor I had fired.

Above us we could hear them arguing about whether they'd hit us or not. Duncan kept asking what happened and Josh was screaming that he didn't know. Duncan said he was going to leave before Josh told him they were going to finish us off now.

Josh counted down again. This time he partly opened the door, fired a couple of shots then opened the door further to look in and aim. I fired my crossbow, Fi fired hers, both arrows connected – mine with his face and Fi's with his neck. Josh reeled back from the impact and screamed in pain. The door shut once more. Josh's swearing echoed through the house. I could hear footsteps leading to the door – just one set. Duncan had left. Josh called him a pussy and screamed again in frustration.

We took our chance to reload. While I was at it I repositioned the torch to my right; I hoped it'd throw him when he opened the door again.

I could hear him above, screaming and swearing. He stood up and paced around for a while. I could hear his mind ticking over. He hadn't expected this. Hadn't contemplated losing – getting injured. And now he was alone and in a world of hurt. The scream was sickening. It was the scream of someone in total meltdown. A dangerous scream – confused, angry, helpless, out of control.

I heard him start to cry and breath in and out like a madman. Then I heard him release the clip on his pistol and load another one. I knew that was the moment. He didn't care anymore. He didn't care if he died as long as he hurt us.

Fi kept saying "I'm sorry". I told her to wait until you could see his face and shoot straight at it. Seconds later the door opened fractionally again, two or three bullets were pumped in. My ears screamed again. Worse still, the torch became dislodged and landed on the ground, facing us.

I slid forward to try to kick it away just as the door opened further. I saw him and, for the first time, he saw me. He fired, I fired, Fi fired. I felt a pain in my shoulder – I'd been shot. Then I felt another pain as Josh's body fell face first on to the cellar floor, and on to my legs. His gun dislodged from his hands and slid across the floor towards me. I picked it up, turned it on him and pulled the trigger until it wouldn't fire anymore. I was in pain and deaf. It was only when I turned to Fi that I realised she'd been hit.

She was bleeding from the chest on her left side. It was bad.

I grabbed the torch, turned to face her, looked her in the eyes and screamed 'are you OK?'

I couldn't even hear myself talk. I looked in her eyes and she was conscious. I picked her up, putting her over my shoulder – somehow – and stepped over Josh's body towards the ladder.

I managed to get three rungs up. From there I put her bum on the floor above and pushed her back as gently as possible. I don't think it was a graceful landing, but she didn't scream. I pushed her legs far enough out of the hole that I was able to climb out. She was bleeding from the chest and the mouth.

I ripped her jacket off and then her two tops so I could inspect the wound. It didn't look good. I asked if she was OK, but she didn't respond. Her eyelids started to droop. I screamed at her to stay awake. I just yelled it over and over again while I tried to clear my head as to what to do next.

I ran and grabbed the first aid kit. I took out some gauze and dabbed the wound. Fi winced in pain. I pulled the gauze away and it was red. I sprayed some antiseptic then applied some fresh gauze then wrapped some white medical cloth around her chest four or five times, using sports tape to keep it all in position.

Fi started drifting off again. I slapped her face and yelled at her to stay awake. She started coughing and spluttering and I knew I was losing her. I struggled to work out what to do… this was beyond my limits. The only thing I could think of was the Firle hub – maybe there was a doctor there. It was a remote chance but it was all I could think of. If I could drag her to Phoenix I could get there in 10-15 minutes. I ran to the bedroom and pulled the quilt off the bed. It was the only thing I could think of to use as a stretcher at short notice.

But when I got back her eyes were closed and she was making this strange gurgling sound. I checked her pulse on her wrist – there was nothing. I tried again on her neck with the same result. I remember trying to give her CPR. I'm not sure if I was doing it for one minute or 10, but when I stopped, I knew it was over.

I screamed.

I started going crazy. I remember thinking if I could get her to the Firle hub there might still be a chance someone could save her. I rolled her on to the quilt and started dragging it towards the back door, towards Phoenix. I knew it was useless but through the shock and the pain and the deafness and the haze it was all I could of think to do.

Then the quilt got snagged on something. I tried to wrench it free by giving it a couple of big tugs. I turned back to Fi only to realise I was smashing her head against the doorframe.

I stopped. I moved back and apologised. Then I laid down next to her, cuddled her and cried some more. That's when it all became too much – the pain in my shoulder and hand, the pain in my heart. I just closed my eyes and shut down.

I woke up at some point… I don't know how long I was out for. I just lay there for a while with Fi's body in my arms. I cried.

I've lost my best friend. I've lost my only friend. I've lost my lover and my reason for even surviving in this bastard world. I cried and cried.

****

Wednesday, June 11, 2014
I buried Fi yesterday. Nothing I ever do in this world again will be as hard. I buried her with all her possessions and all my love. I told her life story, at least what I knew of it, to the ash and dust and to the absent friends.

I buried her with my hope.

I'm crippled now. Emotionally spent, physically exhausted. I've got nothing left to give. Everything is meaningless. Everything.

I don't know what to do or where to turn. Signing off.

****

Sunday, June 15, 2014
Today I leave you behind, diary. I leave you behind to collect dust with the rest of my past world. There's nothing left for me here now. I am going to finish this post, wrap you in plastic and leave you on the table to guard the house.

Who knows, some day someone might discover you. The looters will ignore you, as you have nothing for them, but years later, centuries later maybe, when the world has repaired itself, someone may come to free you, to bring you to life again.

Maybe Adelaide will be buried by then, just a few building shells poking out of the top of a sea of ash like giant tombstones to the life and humanity that perished here.

I leave here wondering what will become of life, partly my life, but at the moment I can see that doesn't count for much. I'm surviving, but I just need to find a reason to do so. It's more about the BIG life, the life of humans. When this all ends – and who knows when that will be – months, years, centuries – are we destined to die out? Starving, suffocating on ash and killing each other for the final traces of food?

We could survive, but what will we become? A scattering of tribes, armed and dangerous future cavemen, maybe? Is that any better than dying out altogether? If we lose the things that made us human, then maybe we are no longer human at all.

And what of the centuries of knowledge and art and technical advances – will that survive? Will future mankind blow away all the ash and start again? Or will it be like apes staring at the monolith at the start of *2001: A Space Odyssey* – a puzzled bewilderment at an ancient, glorious and misunderstood halcyon day.

That would make me sick to the stomach, knowing we had it all, we had endless possibilities and we squandered them. I try not to let the thought come to my head too often, but the truth is, we knew something like this could happen one day, probably the only thing that could kill us off, but we threw some coins at a few scientists and assumed it would go away. Risk management they'd probably call it. Human risk management. Meanwhile, the amount we spent on our military budget was a crime. We chose war and killing over our future and we got caught out by an unlucky roll of the dice that cost us everything.

Maybe I'm talking rubbish. Maybe I'm just looking for someone to blame for all this. I have spent so much time trying to survive I couldn't afford to think too much about blame. But it was always there in the background and now it's raging through me. Surely this is someone's fault?

Maybe it's God. Maybe it was the biblical apocalypse. Maybe the second coming came and went and I didn't get a ticket to heaven. I probably didn't deserve one to be honest. Maybe I'm destined to walk this hell on Earth for all eternity.

Maybe it was just super random, bad luck on a galactic scale. It happened to the dinosaurs and now it's happened to us. Maybe that's life's ultimate joke, just an epic highlighter pen marking the pointlessness of it all.

Just ignore me, diary, I'm not in a good place. Sorry we have to leave on such awkward terms.

Positive thoughts, positive thoughts...

My hope is that one day, when survivors emerge from the ash into the sunshine again, they'll keep the lessons of the past. They'll rebuild the cities, restart the servers, revive the sense of community. They'll build again and always remember why they are where they are. We are all at the whim of Mother Nature, or her cosmic cousin, and if we are truly going anywhere as a species we can never forget that.

In reality we are all small twigs on large family trees, intertwined in a global forest started by the same acorn. Funny how quickly we forgot that. Maybe I'm partly to blame for keeping my resources to myself, for not sharing with my community when it was in need. I didn't kill anyone for food, but maybe I was a small step down that slippery slope. Not a day goes by where I don't think about the community and what happened. Not a day goes by I don't feel guilty.

That will haunt me forever as will the memories of everyone I've lost – family, friends, Fi. Especially Fi. So, too, the sky will haunt me always – a dark, cold daily reminder this is my life; the days of light and colour are gone. I was there once, with my friends and family and first-world problems. Now it's just a distant dream.

And my brother, I miss my brother. I have no idea if he's alive or dead and the reality is I never will. He is lost to me, like those who have died. There's nothing I can do or say that fill the void.

That's why I can't stay here any more. There is nothing left but painful reminders of what cannot be again. Whatever lies for me out there over the hills and to the east is a new start for a new day. It's the only way I'll be able to function. The only reason I can give myself purpose without being weighed down by guilt and pain. The only way to put one foot in front of the other and walk again.

I've decided to take Fi's guitar with me. I'm going to learn how to play. It's going to be my physical reminder of her. She only played it once. One song.

Goodbye diary. I hope your lay in wait is not forever. I will miss you as you have been the only constant friend I have had since this all began. But this is where our time together ends. I hope you understand.

Goodbye diary, goodbye Adelaide.
Jack J Baldwin

####

Alms for an author
Your reviews matter big-time to this indie author.
If you can post your thoughts on Amazon.com or Goodreads.com
it would be greatly appreciated.

Review on
Amazon

Review on
Goodreads

****

Jack's story continues:
Apocalypse: Diary of a Survivor 2

Start the Norwood story here:
The Parade: Apocalypse Survivors Norwood

Author Q&A:

Where did the idea from the book originate?

I was largely inspired by my great grandfather's WWI war diary, where he shared his personal journey through a harrowing global event. He was shot, gassed, hit by shrapnel and survived a bomb exploding under the horse he was riding (yes, that actually happened) – all told in a daily matter-of-fact journal. One day he wrote of epic events, the next he complained about eating bully beef and biscuits again. It was such a riveting and personal read and I wanted to transpose that style into a modern, end-of-the-world tale.

How long did it take you to write and research?

Research was a huge part of this book. It started well before I put pen to paper (OK fingertips to keyboard) and continued right through the editing phase. It was pretty far-reaching too, as I had to consider the comet strike itself, the level of damage it would create immediately after impact, and then the change in environment in the ensuing days/months. There was some really interesting information available online about asteroids/comets, their frequency, their TBC - everything. I also found a fantastic internet tool which lets you enter the size of a comet, it's speed, angle of impact and what it's made from and then tells you how much damage it would cause, depending on your distance from the impact site. Apart from that I also spent a great deal of time watching documentaries, webisodes, movies and reality TV shows on related topics such as the demise of the dinosaurs and apocalypse prepping. I got some great information from these sources (and some not so great), but my inner geek was happy I could justify it all as research.

The weather is a major character in the book, and not often for good reasons. How did you get into that?

The change in weather post-impact also required a lot of research. This was mostly based on what scientists believe happened to the dinosaurs 65 million years ago in terms of atmospheric changes, food shortages etc. Some of this has been proven, but a lot is educational guesswork. It was such a great tool for writing because it really was such an important character. It dictated what our character could do, his mood and how he interfaced with the world around him. It was a moving feast from start to end and played a key role in my writing. I wrote chronologically and the weather changes were a big inspiration for how the story shifted, society evolved (devolved) and how Jack's day-to-day life worked.

Speaking of characters, how real is the dark comet that is the 'villain' of the piece?

The notion of the dark comet has been mentioned by a number of readers, and they do exist in theory - just one of the many hidden gems in our universe. The dark comet in this story allowed for a very late detection on Earth, which was critical to the plot. In truth, most objects (regular comets/asteroids) of this size would be discovered months in advance. However, our detection systems are far from perfect, and there have been many cases of smaller objects (but still very deadly) not being discovered until they were days away from Earth. As for the large objects, experts believe they have discovered 90% of the asteroids in our solar system over 1km in diameter. Comets, on the other hand, are a much more unpredictable beast. Still, I'm sure the stats would say you're more likely to meet your maker crossing the road than you are being hit by a comet, so don't lose any sleep over it.

Was Jack inspired by anyone you know?

I guess he represents the type of person I would like to be if such an event transpired. On the whole he makes good decisions, is very resourceful, good with his hands, creative and thinks on his feet. He shares the surname Baldwin with my great grandfather.

Who would play him in the movie?

Hmmm… tough one. Help me out casting agents.

How did Fiona come about?

Well, pre-rock, I guess she was a representation of how crazy the world would become if everyone knew there were just days remaining. When she comes back into his life, I saw that as part of the natural need for people to gravitate to others. People need people – doubly so in extreme situations such as the book presents. I think the crazier the world is spinning around you, the more heightened your desire becomes to find normality. A home, a partner, food – the simple things can make all the difference.

In the book, Fi and Jack are pretty tight, but one of their few differences of opinion is on whether Mia should be trusted. However, we never find out who was right. Can you tell us?

I think Mia was a trustworthy person. Sure, she had agendas, but most of those were concerned with steering the Trinity Gardens community in the right direction. The way I see it, Mia and Jack could've ended up together if Fi hadn't entered the scene, despite the age gap (people need people). I think Fi sensed that and was protecting her territory as much as anything else. It's also a conscious part of this book that not everything resolves in nice, neat packages. Life rarely works like that on good days, let alone during the apocalypse, where utilities and communications are very limited.

Authors have really struck a chord in the last few years with books that put teens in peril, fighting for their life. Why do you think this sort of situation resonates so strongly with young and old readers?

Who doesn't want to read stories where the stakes are life and death? When I read them, I have a tendency to put myself in the story and see if I would do what the main characters are doing. Would I be resourceful enough to survive? Would I make the right moves? I think our lives (in affluent countries) are so removed from high-stakes struggles and basic survival needs – which conflicts with integral parts of our genetic makeup – that we are drawn to stories like that.

You finish the book on an open end. Are you planning a sequel?

Yes, I am currently revisiting this world. I really wanted to see what happens to Jack, society, the ash cloud, communications, everything. I realised if I want to know what happens, I had to write it. The first draft is complete. Exciting times.

AND NOW FOR THE BIG ONE. SPOILER ALERT … and we're not even slightly joking…

What made you decide to kill off Fiona?

Don't hate me! I seriously mulled over that decision for a long time. I know it wasn't the ride into the sunset you'd expect, but to me it was a far more fitting finale to what the world had become. It was random and dangerous and, ultimately, sad.

OK, one final question, what's next up for you?

As I said earlier, the first draft of *Kings of the World: The sequel, or maybe book two in the trilogy, which never ends well for the good guys* (working title) is in full swing. The boys are back and this time the galaxy is at war. The world's leaders can't stand them, which isn't surprising, since the boys can't really stand each other. They are back at their cringe-worthy, inappropriate, embarrassing best.

****

FAST FIVE WITH MATT

In an apocalypse I would save …

No idea – it's too hard to choose between something practical and something to keep me sane. And that's not even mentioning condiments ;)

If I could choose the only other person to survive, it would be…

That is a really unfair question for someone with three kids. Does that mean I get to save the one most well behaved at the point of disaster? That can be arranged, bwahahaha.

My favourite canned food is …

The thing about canned food is… it's not great (see condiments rant earlier). Cream of mushroom soup – there, I said it.

Reality TV shows are …

Hit and miss.

The best thing I learned while researching this book was …

It's lead me to become a bit more DIY. In fact, I'm working on a project at home upcycling (as they call it) a number of old wooden pallets into outdoor furniture, including couches, a table and a bar!

\#\#\#\#

About the author:

Like the legendary R M Williams, Matt was born in Jamestown in rural South Australia. But that's where the remarkable similarities between these two end. While Reginald went from bushman to world renowned millionaire outback clothing designer, Matt is a complete dag who was lured by the city lights of Adelaide. Kindergarten in the big smoke was a culture shock, but it is here he first discovered his love of storytelling.

In high school that love found an outlet in a series of completely unflattering cartoons about fellow students and teachers alike. He survived long enough to further his art into a successful career in multimedia design but, like a zombified leech, the lure of the written word gnawed at him, forcing him to pen his first novel, the award-winning sci-fi comedy epic, Kings of the World. It was followed the next year by Amazon Australia dystopian sci-fi best-seller Apocalypse: Diary of a Survivor. He has now published eleven books and won several international awards for his works.

Matt donates part-proceeds of each book sold to find a cure for Rett Syndrome, a neurological condition the youngest of his three children, Abby, has. As a gorgeous Rett angel, Abby cannot walk, talk or use her hands in a meaningful way. So, not only is each of your book purchases a ticket to fantastically rounded, character driven, hilarious and poignant sci-fi awesomeness, it wraps you in a warm feeling that you've made a difference to people who deserve your help the most. Like the zombified leech it's a no-brainer.

****

More ways to connect:

Facebook.com/
MattJPikeAuthor

Instagram.com/
matt_j_pike/

Subscribe to Matt's
mailing list

####

Made in the USA
Middletown, DE
11 December 2024

66698101R00113